A Wishful Eye

A Novel

D. L. McIntyre

NEW YORK

LONDON • NASHVILLE • MELBOURNE • VANCOUVER

A Wishful Eye

A Novel

Published in New York, New York, by Morgan James Publishing. Morgan James is a trademark of Morgan James, LLC. www.MorganJamesPublishing.com

Proudly distributed by Publishers Group West®'

Publisher's Note: This is a work of historical fiction. The story was inspired by true events and the places are real, but only the following names were actual people who lived and operated during that time frame and in those places: William Anderson, Chapman Harris, and John Tibbets in Jefferson County, Indiana; Richard Daly in Trimble County, Kentucky; and Lewis Robards, in Fayette County, Kentucky. The remaining characters, and events are fictitious and any resemblance to a person living or dead is purely coincidental.

All Bible verses used are the King James Version, public domain.

Come Ye Disconsolate, public domain
I Am Bound for the Promised Land, public domain
Oh Susannah, public domain

Morgan James BOGO™

A **FREE** ebook edition is available for you or a friend with the purchase of this print book.

CLEARLY SIGN YOUR NAME ABOVE

Instructions to claim your free ebook edition:
1. Visit MorganJamesBOGO.com
2. Sign your name CLEARLY in the space above
3. Complete the form and submit a photo of this entire page
4. You or your friend can download the ebook to your preferred device

ISBN 9781636985282 paperback
ISBN 9781636985299 ebook
Library of Congress Control Number: 2024940571

Cover & Interior Design by:
Christopher Kirk
www.GFSstudio.com

Author Photo by:
Jenny McIntyre

Map design by:
Grace Bowman

Morgan James PUBLISHING Builds with... Habitat for Humanity Peninsula and Greater Williamsburg

Morgan James is a proud partner of Habitat for Humanity Peninsula and Greater Williamsburg. Partners in building since 2006.

Get involved today! Visit: www.morgan-james-publishing.com/giving-back

*In honor of my parents, Lovell and Virginia (Adams) Monroe,
and all the generations of men and women before them
who have passed on their faith in our merciful God and Savior.*

Acknowledgments

A book is not written by one person alone, not if any author is being honest. First of all, the book would not even be possible if not for the actual people who inspired the story, Daniel and Sarah "Sally" (Judd) Adams. They were my great-great grandparents on the paternal side of my maternal grandfather. See the Historical Note at the end of the book for more information.

I'm deeply grateful for the encouragement and guidance afforded to me, a rookie in novel writing, by members of my team at Morgan James Publishing. These are Terry Whalen, who believed in my book from the start and convinced MJP to offer a novice a contract; Bethany Marshall and Gayle West, who helped me through the next steps; to designer Christopher Kirk for creating such an attractive cover; and to founder and CEO, David L. Handcock, whose enthusiasm for my book and Christian faith came through so clearly during my planning meeting.

Next I want to thank the following people who pre-purchased my book, helping me greatly with financial needs early in the process: Tamara Aguilar, Kathy Allen, Darla Anderson, Nancy Becker, Georgia Bowers, Joni Bradley, Dawn Brinson, Carol Brooks, Jo Brosius, Franzeya Choate, Vivienne Collins, Tony Crachiolo, Neryssa Crisp, Connie DeBurger, Cindy Ellington, Liberty Fragua, Regina Giltner, Marianne Hudson, Kate Jester-Brod, Timothy Jordan, Emma Judd, Kelly Korb, Diann Marksberry, Randy Marksberry, Beth Mathes, Cynthia Monroe, Sherry Myers, Susannah Prather, Krista and Zach Rhodus, Peggy Roberts, Jane Rogers, Christine Rosiere, Connie Shiflet, Melissa Faith

Singletary, Denise Spear, Deb Vantreese, Kent Wagner, Karen Walters, Crystal Welch, Laurene M.K. Whittmer, Sandra "Missy" Wright, Jennifer Yeazel, and last, but not least, my friend since my preschool years, Yvonne Yocum.

I want to sincerely thank my beta readers for their kind words and critique: Naomi Elliott, Barbara Woods Henderson, Lois Hoover, and especially my sister-in-law, Cindy Monroe. Through email, Cindy read many scenes as soon as I wrote them. Her prompt feedback and enthusiasm pushed me to muscle through the times when my motivation ebbed. Thanks also to the talented Grace Bowman for the beautifully designed map.

I wish to thank my close friends, Marianne Hudson and Beth Ringled; siblings, Darlene Ogata, Diann Marksberry, and David Monroe; my children, Chris, John, and Megan McIntyre, and other extended family members and friends for their encouragement and support.

Lastly, I wish to give my husband of 43 years, Cleon McIntyre, all my love and gratitude for his belief in me and my calling, and for encouraging me to finish what I started many years ago in answering the Holy Spirit's prompting to "Tell their story."

*"On Jordan's stormy banks I stand and cast a wishful eye,
to Canaan's fair and happy land where my possessions lie."*
--Verse one, *The Promised Land*, by Samuel Stennett, published 1787.

INDIANA
OHIO
NAPOLEON
FLATROCK
VERSAILLES
CINCINNATI
OHIO RIVER
LANCASTER
MADISON
CAROLLTON
KENTUCKY RIVER
FRANKFORT
KENTUCKY
LOUISVILLE
LEXINGTON

Introduction

The greater part of Indiana in the years before the Civil War was still a wilderness. A large majority of the population lived within 75 miles of the Ohio River. This great river was the highway by which most settlers arrived in the first decades after Congress established the Northwest Territory in 1787. Settlers were lured there by cheap land prices and endorsements that promised them acreage that was "intersected and bounded by navigable rivers or lakes, enjoying a temperate climate, and an immense variety of soils."*

Indeed between 1830 and 1840, the state's population rose 180 percent, according to the U.S. Census. Into this land of promise came rugged pioneering people—people like the settlers of Ripley County, which lies in the southeastern region of rolling hills, just one county north of the Ohio River. It was organized in 1816; the same year Indiana became a state. By 1849, the Flat Rock community, where this story begins, was buried deeply in the chiefly uncleared northwestern section of the county and was comprised of a few families who settled near the small creek that has a bed so flat and relatively shallow it was used as a transportation route for several generations.

*Information taken from a dissertation by Roger H. Van Bolt, "The Indiana Scene in the 1840s," published at the University of Chicago 1950.

Part One

Ripley County, Indiana

Chapter 1

*I*n one of those cabins on a mid-July morning, Jane Cowper, 41, was attacking a cabbage. Her nimble hands flew as she chopped away at the head with the large knife her husband had just honed for her. She wiped perspiration from her forehead with the back of her hand and pushed a stray strand of graying wheat-colored hair behind her ear. Across the table her 16-year-old daughter, Lydia, was tucking cornbread cakes into a wicker basket. The hustle was unusual for a Saturday morning, but church members were picnicking in a clearing downstream at noon and Jane was racing the clock.

"Chores are done," shouted 12-year-old Frank, skipping in from his father's work room.

"There's no need to raise your voice," rebuked Jane distractedly as she continued to attack the hard vegetable with vigor.

"Yes, we have more than enough noise in here already, added Lydia, placing forks in the basket and glancing to the corner where 3-year-old Alice was bouncing on their bed and repeating "pic-NIC, pic-NIC pic-NIC" at the top of her voice, her sunny pigtails flying.

"Sorry. I guess I'm just excited about the pic-NIC," Frank shrugged, shouting the last word in unison with his little sister.

"Mother, she's jumping on our bed again!"Lydia said, brows knitted. Aren't you going to *do* anything?"

Jane pursed her lips at Lydia's accusation and then shouted over the din, "Alice, you come down off of there!"

The bouncing continued.

"Quit jumping!"Lydia shouted but got no response either.

"Just let her go, Lydia. At least she's not under our feet."

"You're knocking cabbage on the floor, Mother,"Lydia remarked, jaw clenched.

Before Jane could respond, Lydia leaned over and picked up the pieces, quickly tossing them in the fireplace. Jane caught her eye and received a glare in return. Lydia then strode over and grabbed Alice's plump arms, forcing her to stand still.

"Stop it, Allie!"

Jane opened her mouth to admonish Lydia when she caught Frank sneaking a cake out of the basket. She smacked his hand, and he pulled it back, turning red. The back door then creaked open, and she breathed a sigh of relief when her husband Seth strode in, looking handsome in his best shirt and straw hat.

"I got the wagon hitched and ready," he said, snatching his pocket watch from the mantle.

"Hooray!"yelped Alice. Jane saw her jerk out of Lydia's arms and leap off the bed catching her foot in the blanket. She pitched face forward on the pine floor. Shrieking commenced.

Jane quickly set down the knife and rushed over to pick up the squalling figure from Lydia, who moved aside. Brushing her stray locks aside, she checked Alice's forehead and found a red bump.

"Is she hurt?"Seth said, hurrying beside her

"She's got a bump raising up."

Lydia hurried toward her father holding out a damp cloth.

"Here, Papa,"she said, shaking her head."I knew this would happen. She was jumping on the bed again."

"There, there," said Jane soothingly, taking the cloth from Seth and sitting on the edge of the bed. She gently placed the cool cloth on Alice's forehead and spoke softly to her, calming her cries. Her baby's tears wrenched her heart. She felt remorseful about allowing the horseplay, but the joyful abandonment of childhood was so brief, and Alice was quickly losing all remnants of her baby ways.

"Will she be alright?"asked Frank, eyeing the basket of food.

"She's fine," said Lydia."Mama, let's go or we'll be late."

Jane whispered to Alice, then put her down, wiping the rest of her face with the cloth and quickly walked back to the table, keeping an eye on her while she finished preparing the cabbage salad.

Alice sniffed and then reached out for her father's legs. "Dance, Papa, dance,"she demanded.

Jane smiled to see Seth's face break out into a grin at the frequent request.

He looked down at Alice. "Are you ready?"

She looked down and firmly placed a foot on each of Seth's and looked up and nodded. He took each of her hands in his and began a slow waltz around the room, humming tunelessly.

"Eeeeeek! Faster, Papa, faster!" The pair swirled round the sleeping area of the cabin, Alice's shrieks of delight growing increasingly louder. Suddenly the back of Seth's knee hit the bedstead, and he pitched backward, causing his feet to fly up and Alice to land giggling in his lap on the bed.

Jane joined in the laughter as she was tying on her sunbonnet. "We're ready, Seth."

Seth looked up at her from his sprawled position on the bed and winked at her. "Jane, you look so nice in that yellow bonnet the bees will think you're a flower."

"Let's *go*! We'll be late!" said Lydia, followed by a heavy sigh.

Jane grabbed the basket and handed it to Frank. "Everyone please carry something to the wagon. It's all on the table."

Quickly they had the wagon packed including Alice, her fall forgotten, who sat between Jane and Seth chanting "picNIC" once more. Jane placed her hand gently over her mouth and turned back to check on her other children. Lydia was sitting in a corner then looked down and quickly untied her stained pinafore, wadded it up and stashed it behind her back. Frank was cross legged behind the springboard grinning from ear to ear. Jane knew he was thinking of pie and fried chicken as he had talked about little else all week. She nodded at Seth, and he gave the reins a shake.

* * *

The following Wednesday afternoon Lydia quickened her steps as she rounded the last turn in the path before home. Perspiration dripped from her forehead and into her eyes, stinging. Despite the shady trees, the summer heat was stifling, the windless air filled with the humming of insects. She paused to pass the pail of blackberries into her other hand then pulled a handkerchief from her pinafore pocket and wiped her face, pursing her lips at a glimpse of her stained and scratched hands. She hurried on, anticipating the feel of cool water down her throat and splashed over her face and hands.

Suddenly something caught her foot and knocked her off balance, pitching her forward. She shrieked and flung out her hands. The pail hit the hard footpath with a thump. She glanced around, hoping no one had witnessed her clumsiness, and she quickly pushed herself up and brushed off the dirt. No harm done.

Then Lydia saw the bucket. It was on its side a few feet away and at least half of the berries were scattered in the dust. When she began gathering them, she found that many were bruised and crushed, their sweet juices oozing out and mixing with the dirt. She let out a groan and kicked the head off a tall dandelion, spilling its downy seeds as it flew.

She quickly picked up what berries she could salvage, dropped them in the pail, then stomped to the house, jerked the door open, and threw her loosened bonnet across the room as she strode in. Out of the corner of her eye she saw blurred movement coming from a corner of the cabin. Allie was scrambling backwards from beneath their bed, her chubby dirt-caked feet leading the way.

"Alice Elizabeth Cowper! Are you getting into my box *again*?" She put the pail on the table and roughly shoved the three-year-old aside and knelt to look. The wooden box Papa crafted for her keepsakes was askew and the lid was not latched. She rose quickly and grabbed Alice, who was hiding her face in the bed quilt, stood her up and shook her.

"How many times have I told you to leave my things alone?" she spewed, releasing her with a swat to her behind. "Get out of my sight!"

Instead of obeying, Alice took a few steps back and hung her head so low her hair made a curtain around her face. Lydia watched her, narrowing her eyes at Alice who seemed to stare at her own grubby feet. "But I just…" Alice began.

"I don't want to hear your excuses. Don't you ever let me catch you or I'll spank you again. You are so spoiled," said Lydia who found herself shaking her finger with her hand on her hip, just like her grandmother.

Keeping her head down, Alice pivoted and flew to the back door and into her father's lean-to workshop. Fortunately, for both sisters, their father was away. But just as the workshop door closed and Lydia started to pour water into a basin, the front door opened.

"What was all that shouting I heard just now?" asked Jane, coming in with her arms full of beans she had been gathering.

Lydia turned around, her face dripping and grabbed a cloth to pat it dry. Her mother silently waited where she had stopped just inside the door.

"She was getting in my box again! Can't I have anything without her messing with it?"

Jane walked slowly over to the table and dropped her armload, then turned around to face Lydia. Her light brown eyes were snapping as she faced her daughter. Lydia's eyebrows rose at the sight, and she took a step back.

"Yes, she must learn to leave your things alone. I'll talk to her about it later. But that is no reason for you to shout at her. Why I heard you way over in the clearing!"

Lydia opened her mouth to answer, her brown eyes wide with outrage, her brow furrowed.

"Don't you say a word in your defense, Lydia," broke in Jane. "You *must* learn to control your temper and to speak softly and with respect to others – even with your little sister," she said, brushing dirt from her hands. "Now I want you to get the Bible and read Proverbs chapters fourteen and fifteen three times before you speak another word to anyone." With that she turned and walked to the fireplace, grabbed the poker, and began probing the embers to bring them back to life.

Lydia bit her tongue. She knew the discussion was over. Her mother might be mild mannered in many respects, but when it came to her beliefs, one of which was the obedience of her children, there was no compromise.

Still fuming internally, she quickly grabbed the thick book from beside her parent's bed and knocked the chair over when she jerked it out from the table. *Mama hadn't even asked about the berries! She didn't care about the briars and the heat and all the work she'd put in that bucket of fruit. All she cared about was Alice's feelings.* She flipped through to the pages until she found the right spot and began to read.

Her pulse slowed with every word. After a few minutes, she stopped and closed her eyes. Her cheeks were burning, and her chin dropped to her chest

"He that is slow to wrath is of great understanding: but he that is hasty of spirit exalteth folly. .... A soft answer turneth away wrath: but grievous words stir up anger."

Behind her closed eyelids Lydia could clearly see the part in Alice's hair when she'd hung her head, afraid to meet her eye. She could hear the stifled whimpers that rose up when she'd fled the room. Lydia's throat swelled. She opened her eyes and swiftly wiped away a tear, wrinkling her nose at her still-purple fingers. Lydia pulled her handkerchief out and blew her nose. Why was she such a mess? Why couldn't she remain calm and dignified when something went wrong? She had acted more like a child than Allie.

She forced herself to read the chapters again slowly, absorbing the ageless advice. To be wise a person needed to fear the Lord. That meant to respect him, she knew, and to be honored, something she truly longed for, she needed to be humble. Lydia heaved a big sigh and prayed silently.

Father, forgive me for letting my anger get the better of me. Help me to be obedient and respectful, even to Alice. And help me be soft in speech and slow in anger. Amen

She rose from the table and quietly put the Bible back. Wiping fresh tears from her cheeks and fighting the lump in her throat she approached Jane who was setting a pot of water on the hook over the fire.

"Mama, I'm going to go tell Alice I'm sorry. Then I'll be right back to help you with supper. I brought back some berries, although I did spill some of them."

"Thank you, Lydia and thank you for the berries. About Alice, remember she has a soft heart and she still so young. You may not know it, but she looks up to you so much. I'm sure she's hoping you'll come looking for her."

* * *

Lydia opened the creaking door into her father's workshop, a small smile breaking over her face as the familiar odor of freshly cut timber hit her nostrils. The golden curls lay ankle deep, piled on the floor from the careful strokes of his plane. The brilliant afternoon sunlight light poured in from the big window, the heat magnifying the scent of pine.

"Alice?" She looked behind the door, under the work bench and in the corner where her sister liked to play with discarded blocks of wood. The door leading outside was ajar. Lydia went through it, took a few steps and then halted. Muffled sobs were coming from the outhouse down the hill.

"Alice? I'm coming!" She ran to the outhouse and found the door locked.

"Open the door, Allie."

"No!" her voice was weak but determined. "I want Mama!"

"She's getting supper. What's wrong?"

A frightful wailing began. "I messed myself and my belly hurts."

"It's okay, sweetheart. Maybe you're sick. Open up and let me carry you back in the house."

After a moment's silence, the door opened a crack and Lydia peeked into the dim space. Alice sat bare bottomed on the rough board. She was shaking like a leaf, big tears rolled down her dirty cheeks. She looked up at Lydia, eyes full of fright. Lydia felt a weight drop in her stomach, making her catch her breath.

"Oh, Allie. I'm so, so sorry I yelled at you. Poor baby. Let's clean you up and put you to bed."

* * *

Jane had just finished dressing a rabbit and was washing her hands when she heard Lydia's shout from behind the house.

"Mama! Allie's sick." Jane looked up to see Lydia rush through the workroom door carrying a whimpering Alice, her face wet with tears. "I think it's summer complaint." Before Jane could react, Lydia laid Alice on their bed and

9

walked briskly to the wash basin, threw the dirty water out the front door and poured hot water from the kettle in.

Jane Lightly grabbed Lydia's elbow. "What are you doing? I was heating that water for coffee for Seth."

Lydia shook off Jane's hand and carefully carried the wash basin to the bed. "Grab a cleaning rag, Mama. She's messed herself. It's run like water all down her legs. I've got to clean her up."

Jane's stomach slid to the floor, and she fought off the resulting lightheadedness and put on a teasing tone. "Oh, Alice, honey, have you been eating green apples again? Mama told you not to," she said walking over and sitting on the edge of the bed.

"No. I promise. Mama. Ooooo! My belly hurts bad." She burst into a loud wail and writhed on the sheet.

Jane grabbed her hand as it flailed wildly and held it tightly. Her throat constricted as she watched Lydia gently wash Alice's lower body. "Where does it hurt, Baby?"

"Ever'where," Alice turned her head to the wall and vomited all over the sheet. Jane reached quickly to help her sit up so she wouldn't choke. When she was done, she helped Alice lay her head down, alarmed at how weak she seemed.

Jane stood up. "I'll fetch a clean sheet and a nightgown and some blankets. Lydia, when you're finished, get the rest of her clothes off," she said as she hurried to a storage chest.

"I gotta go again, Liddy!" whimpered Alice as Jane began searching for a sheet.

"You'd better fetch the chamber pot. It's under our bed." Jane directed, her pulse racing.

* * *

The sunfish was the biggest one Frank had seen that summer. The 12-year-old gave a whoop when he pulled it in, splashing and full of fight, with his cane pole. He grabbed the line with his spare hand, holding it up close to admire the shimmering scales.

"Just enough for breakfast tomorra mornin'," he said with a nod as he threaded the stringer through the gaping gill. "Reckin' I'll quit. 'Bout chore time."

Always cheerful with a crooked front tooth and serene grey eyes, Frank had developed the habit of narrating aloud when he explored the world outside his cabin. He'd started talking to ants and toads as a toddler and advanced to Bessie, the tan hound dog that rarely left his side. In the absence of an animal, he'd just talk to himself or to God, whose presence he felt keenly when in the woods.

"Bessie! Here, girl," he shouted, cupping his soiled hands around his mouth, and turning in the last direction he had seen her trot off, her sensitive nose to the ground.

"Ahhoooo," came the answer from a hollow of cedars.

While he waited for Bessie, Frank waded up stream to where the water was clear and rinsed off. He brought a handful of the cool water to his face and splashed the refreshing liquid over it. He then waded to the bank where a spring fed the creek bed. He bent down and stuck his entire head, light brown hair wet with sweat, in the outflow, sucking up the cold refreshment. He spluttered and stood upright, shaking his head to rid his hair of the excess. "I betcha that's the best water in Indiana," he said, leaning over for another drink.

"Ahhoooo," Frank jumped, startled by Bessie's presence on the bank, panting right in front of him as he raised his dripping head.

"Good girl. Let's get home."

Frank splashed back downstream and grabbed his pole and the dripping stringer. He lifted it up to admire the shiny bodies, still twitching with life: two sunfish, three bluegill, a small bass, and a large minnow, just right for Allie because she couldn't choke on its tiny bones.

He grinned imagining her running out of the front door to meet him.

"Did you cotch me a fwish, Fwank?!" she would ask him in the high-pitched tone she used when excited. His smile widened, thinking about how she loved to watch him scale and gut his catch, hiding her face in her hands then peeking through tiny fingers. He loved to teach her where to find the heart and tiny air sacs, and to look for the scores of yellow eggs in the mama fish.

He looked up as he climbed the rock-strewn bank, checking to see the position of the sun.

"It must be nigh 5 o'clock. "I'll be late for milkin'." Swinging the long pole off his back, he gathered it and the string of dripping fish in his fist and shot off toward the pine woods and home.

* * *

"What'll ya take for the lot?" Seth Cowper asked, his deep-set gray eyes squinting in the bright afternoon sunshine as he looked up at Peter Perry.

Perry was the storekeeper, lumber mill operator, and postmaster at Perry's Corner. The three houses that clustered around his business were the nearest the Flat Rock community had to a town. Instead of answering, the businessman ran his hand over the fresh cut end of one of the large logs that were stacked neatly in Seth's wagon. It was good white pine and straight as an arrow; perfect for building and easy to cut. He remained silent.

Seth didn't even blink. He knew a good bargainer waited to avoid making the first offer.

"Would you take store credit?" Perry asked, raising his eyebrows and glancing at Seth's threadbare shirt.

"No sir. It's summer. We won't be needing anything for quite some time, and I don't believe in credit. It just gives the old devil an avenue for temptation," he said, stopping to remove his hat and fan himself.

"Well, I'm cash poor like everyone else, Mr. Cowper," but I think I could sell some cut lumber right now. I'll tell you what. How about I fill your next lumber order at no charge – enough to fill your wagon."

Seth sighed but didn't hesitate long. "That sounds like a fair bargain to me, Perry." He extended his calloused hand, which the older man took, sealing the deal.

With the help of Perry's son, Will, the three men had the heavy logs moved to the mill's storage shed within 20 minutes. Seth stepped into the darkness of the store to see if there was any mail. Eliza Perry, Peter's wife, looked up from the back corner of the crowded mercantile.

"Oh, it's you, Mr. Cowper. Hot one, isn't it?" she said, setting her broom against a wall of canned goods and hurrying to the counter while wiping her hands on her apron.

"Yes, Ma'am, it sure is. I thought I'd stop in and see if we had any mail. I'm expecting some hardware too."

"Just one letter for you today," she said, reaching down for the Cowper's slot on the post office wall. "All the way from New York."

"That must be from my wife's aunt in Albany. Jane will be pleased. We haven't had any news from our New York family in a long spell," Seth said, reaching for the fat envelope and sticking it in his shirt pocket.

"Say hello to Jane for me, will you?"

"I'll be glad to, Miz Perry."

"How old is that baby of yours now?

Seth looked at his hands and counted his fingers with his thumb.

"Turned three four months ago. She's not a baby anymore."

"Well, they do grow up fast. Our Will is nearly 19. Seems like he'll never stop growin'. Taller than his daddy now." The screen door creaked as tall, muscular Will stepped in, wiping his wet brow with his shirt sleeve. "Now Will, you'll get your shirt filthy doin' that. I've told you that's what your handkerchief's for!" scolded Eliza.

"Ah, Ma. I don't…" Will stopped short when he saw Seth standing there.

Seth grinned up at him. The young man blushed and looked at the floor and pivoted to walk away. Seth reached out and patted his arm.

"Now Will, don't mind your ma. Mothers never get over wantin' to mother. My ma was still telling me what to do until the day she passed," he chuckled.

Ten minutes later Seth sat behind his mare, Ruby, headed toward home. It was nearing chore time, but the sun was still high in the sky as he turned the horse onto the creek. Flat Rock Creek was just that – chiefly solid flat rock that channeled a small stream. In the summer it often became no more than a string of big puddles when rain was scarce. Today the flow was continuous, if no more than four inches in most places. Ruby seemed eager to plod through it, splashing the cool spring-fed water over her hooves.

Seth looked with delight at the horse, nearly prancing in the harness ahead of him. When she stopped to drink, he didn't even urge her on, but sat admiring the daisies, goldenrod, and other flowers growing along the bank.

Putting the reins aside, he climbed down and began picking a bouquet for Jane. In no time he had a variety of blooms he was sure she could arrange prettily in a jar for the table. Seth pictured them sitting on the white tablecloth with a supper of stewed rabbit and dumplings. His stomach growled in anticipation, and he climbed back in the wagon to hurry Ruby home.

* * *

The following morning Frank stealthily crept down the loft ladder to do the barn chores. The early summer sun was escaping through the edges of the closed shutters. Bird songs filled the air outside, but the cabin was silent after a night filled with Alice's whining and wails. The putrid odor from the unemptied chamber pot near her was a testament to her travail. She had begged for water, but no matter what they had given her to eat or drink, her body had rejected it, accompanied by painful cramps.

"Make it stop! Make it stop!" she had begged each of them, her face draining of color and her voice turning into rasping whispers. It had been a relief when she had drifted into sleep not long before sunrise. Frank had dozed, but the rooster jerked him awake soon after.

He tiptoed to the workroom door and soon was outside, deeply breathing in the fresh air. He saw his string of fish where he had left them, forgotten in his fear for Allie and the ensuing frenetic activity. A family of coons or other critters had made short work of them. He burst into tears at the sight that recalled his carefree dash home just yesterday to show off his catch to his little sister.

Fearful his cries would wake the family, he dashed into the barn where Bessie greeted him with a wagging tail. He knelt and put his arms around her and sobbed, lost to all but his fear of what might lie ahead.

"Oh Bessie! Allie's so sick. I don't think we can stand it if something happens to her!"

He felt a hand on his shoulder and looked up to see the red-rimmed eyes of his father.

"Son, I don't think old Bessie can help Alice, but we both know someone who can. Will you pray with me?"

Frank nodded and before he could stand up, Seth knelt beside him and grasped his hand.

"Heavenly Father, we thank you for the joy that little Alice brings to our family. We fervently ask that you heal her from this sudden sickness. Restore her to health and keep the rest of our family safe from this contagion. Above all we ask as always that your will be done. We thank you for your son and our salvation and the hope of Heaven. Amen."

Chapter 2

The following morning Seth paused to wipe sawdust from the white oak plank he was smoothing. He leaned over until his beard brushed the worktable, then blew away the remnants. His fingers caressed the wood. Still too rough. He picked up his plane and began another swipe down the grain.

The fine powder filled the hot lean-to with atoms of dust that filtered through the late morning light. His chest tightened and he grabbed his handkerchief from his trouser pocket and coughed. Seth paused as he crammed it back in his pants, listening.

Silence. The heartrending sobs emitting from Jane were no longer audible. He turned his focus back to his task. Another coffin. He'd gotten quite skilled at crafting the bleak boxes over the years. Unfortunately, too many held infants and children who should have lived to see the dawn of the next century. Like Alice.

Images of the blue-eyed tot with her wheat-colored braids flying as he tossed her into the rafters slammed into him like buckshot. His throat tightened in a grip that threatened to block off his air. Seth screwed his eyes shut and forced himself to take a deep breath. Grief hung over the cabin like a literal shroud. Keeping himself busy was the only way he could cope.

"God, help us," he mouthed. He blinked, sighed, and stood up straight, trying once again to swallow past the lump. Soon he was running the plane over the wood once more, the fresh shavings spilling over onto his boots when the hinges on the door creaked slowly. He glanced up and saw Lydia's brown eyes peering at him through the cracked-open door.

"Can I come in, Papa?" she whispered, the door opening further to reveal her red, tear-stained cheeks.

"Of course, daughter," he said attempting a smile.

Lydia held his gaze as she quietly closed the door behind her back. Her focus then shifted to the cut boards, barely a yard long, on the workbench. She swallowed and returned her eyes to his.

"Mama's lying down. I helped her get Alice washed and dressed and ready for..." Her voice trailed away as she reached out and put a trembling hand on the pile of oak.

Seth's heart swelled with love and admiration for her willingness to help Jane with such an agonizing task. "Thank you, Lydia. I know that must have been hard," He reached out and wiped a tear rolling down her cheek. Suddenly his thoughts went to the tender-hearted Frank, Alice's playmate.

"Where's your brother?"

"He left with the rifle right after you came in here," answered Lydia. "Said he was going to get some squirrel for supper. I tried to stop him, but he wouldn't listen."

"It's just as well. He needs to be alone. The loss of Alice is quite a blow to him — to all of us."

Lydia bowed her head and bit her lip. Just as Seth was about to gather her in his arms for comfort she spoke.

"Papa, I've got to do something or I'll ..." Lydia's red-rimmed eyes bore into his. "Can I make you some dinner?"

Seth shook his head. Food held no appeal. Then he remembered a task that needed to be done. Was Lydia up to it?

"Well..." his voice trailed off.

"What?! Please, Papa, tell me."

"Someone needs to go break the news to Grandma. Your mama needs her here and word needs to reach the rest of the church."

"I'll do it," she said decisively, heading for the door. "I'll leave now."

"Wait!" Seth grabbed her arm and pulled her close, nestling the top of her head in his neck giving her a squeeze. "Don't forget. God is still God, Lydia."

She pulled back, holding herself an arm's length away from him. Her lips pressed together, and she looked at him, brown eyes wide. Slowly she shook her head.

Seth felt a weight land in his stomach as she quickly turned the knob and left. He turned around just in time to see her fly past the window heading for the creek. He picked up the plane again and set it down on the board and sighed heavily. "Why, God?!," he hissed at the ceiling, clenching his fist.

Lydia's faith had ever been mercurial, changing with every perceived high and low she encountered. For months now she'd matured emotionally and spiritually, helping the family without complaint, enthusiastically attending church meetings, and reading the Bible, even discussing theology.

Now Alice's death. How could he help her understand that God continues to love even when he seems to hate?

* * *

Jane rose from the bed as she caught sight of Lydia dashing past the window. Her heart yearned to follow her and offer comfort, but she wouldn't leave Alice alone. Amid her initial uncontrollable sobs and wails, Frank had fled for the woods and Seth excused himself to start on a coffin. Heedless of the unstoppable tears, she had then washed and dressed the wasted body of her little Alice. Lydia had lent her usual able assistance, but remained silent through the whole process, nodding numbly and then obeying Jane's instructions.

With the muffled sounds of Seth's saw, Jane reached for the Bible and sought comfort from the Psalms in her rocking chair. David's anguished words while voicing his constant faith in God's goodness was always reassuring. Totally absorbed, she only paused when Seth entered quietly from the workshop. His eyes sought out Alice. Jane rose and clasped his hand and led him to the bed. Alice lay on top of the coverlet in her pink summer dress, a spray of daisies in her chubby hands. Her sunny rippled hair splayed over her shoulders. A beam of sunshine bathed her gray-hued face in a rosy light.

Seth and Jane looked down on their daughter. Jane's chest grew uncomfortably tight in the stillness. Then choking sobs burst from Seth and he released her hand and fell to his knees, burying his head on the bed. She watched him put out a fumbling hand and wrap a lock of Alice's hair in his rough fingers. The sight of him, usually so strong and supportive, did her in and she sank beside him on the floor. At her gentle touch on his hair, he reached for her, and they cried in each other's arms.

* * *

Lydia winced and stopped short in her flight. She put one hand against a tree and lifted her foot to examine it. Yes, she'd stepped on a hickory nutshell in her haste. Those things were wicked – hiding unseen beneath last year's soft carpet of leaves.

She plucked the sharp bit out of the ball of her foot with a yelp. Blood oozed out. She jammed her free hand into her pocket for her hankie and dabbed at the wound, nearly losing her balance as she jerked with the pain.

"Blasted nut!" she said through gritted teeth.

Despite her resolve to remain strong, she choked on a sob that rose out of her throat. For years she had longed for a sister and now she was gone. For two nights she had lain next to Lydia in bed, whimpering at first and then growing quieter and paler as the sickness drained her of life. Just hours ago, her own screams had woken the family when she'd discovered Alice cold and lifeless beside her.

The world was a horrible place: pain and sickness and death. Why hadn't God answered her prayers? Last night she knelt beside her bed for what seemed like hours begging and pleading for him to save little Allie. Another cry rose in her throat, and she sat down at the foot of the tree and gave herself to the tears. Here she could let go and not worry her parents or brother with her grief.

Moments later her shoulders still shook, but the storm had passed. She wiped her cheeks and blew her nose. Wadding up the wet linen, she put it back in her pinafore pocket and stood up, shakily. "I'll look a mess for Grandma; bleeding foot, red eyes and nose, leaves and burs stuck in my skirt," Lydia mumbled as she swiped at her rear with her hands.

Her mind raced ahead as she began limping to the creek. How was she going to break the news to Grandma? Her mother's mother lived about two miles downstream. The church met in her home.

Lucinda "Cinda" Breeden, who once taught school in New York state as a young woman, was always neat and clean and proper. That and her perfect posture made it seem as if she reigned in her log cabin as a queen in her castle. She would be sure to give Lydia that certain disapproving look when she saw her all disarrayed. Lydia shuddered to think what she would say if she knew she'd said "blasted."

Suddenly she wasn't in such a hurry to complete her errand. Just telling the sad news was sure to get her crying again and she didn't want to do it in front of Grandma, who always kept a stiff upper lip, or Rev. Johnston, her border, who always seemed to be seeking her gaze and paying her special attention.

Still, she had volunteered to go. She couldn't bear the thought of going back now to that empty house with her heartsick father, weeping mother, and that cold little body lying in her gingham dress on the bed. A dose of Grandma's fortitude might be just what she needed.

* * *

The next morning Will Perry was keeping his eyes on his father's shoes, a yard or so ahead of him as they climbed the burying hill. Clutching his best hat, he was the last of the crowd following the tiny casket to its spot next to other graying markers on the west side of the clearing.

As they neared the freshly dug grave, Will glanced quickly up at Lydia, hoping she wouldn't notice. There she stood by her mother wearing a mourning dress with a black sunbonnet shielding her face from the glaring sun and his gawking. The Rev. Edward "Ned" Johnston was pulling a little black book from his pocket and calling upon everyone to pray.

Obediently Will closed his eyes and lowered his head, but no prayers would come. Instead, he saw Lydia's eyes sparkling at him and heard the echo of her voice when he'd last seen her in his father's store a few weeks ago. A yellow dress had set off her brown eyes and hair and he had teased her about the sprig of Queen Anne's lace sticking out from behind her ear.

"I think it's pretty and I don't care how ridiculous you think it looks, Mr. Perry," she'd said, pink flaming her cheeks.

Lydia had come with her father and brother, as she often did when he had lumber to cut. They would buy very little, but always asked for mail. The siblings would comb through the store, looking for anything new to admire and discuss. Since Will had been minding the shop while his father was at the sawmill, he'd taken his time admiring her while he perched behind the counter.

"Come, ye disconsolate, wherever ye languish…"

Will lifted his head with a jerk. His father's gravelly bass was joining the other attendees in the familiar hymn. Apparently, he had foolishly stood there daydreaming with his eyes tightly closed during the entire service.

"Earth has no sorrow Heav'n cannot heal," he joined in the last line. It was one of the few hymns he knew and that was chiefly because it always seemed to be sung at funerals, a fairly frequent occurrence even in sparsely populated Otter Creek Township.

Will slowly shook his head and grimaced, not bothering to sing the remaining verses. "What kind of God allows babies to die and children to lose their mothers when they're so young?" He glanced around and saw his father's eye seek his as the crowd began the last verse. An understanding passed between them. Neither one believed in a higher power.

Peter Perry had been raised a Presbyterian in Kentucky, but after his first wife, Will's mother, had died he had ceased to follow the tenants of his faith. Will knew the only reason his father attended the occasional community religious gathering was because it was good for business. Every person in the gathered crowd traded in his store and his absence would be noticed and discussed.

People were now filing past the family and Will and Peter began inching forward in line to speak to them. Mrs. Breeden stood next to her daughter, who

19

clutched her arm. She and Seth flanked Jane, who struggled to keep back her tears. Then there was Lydia who had her arm around the gangly-legged Frank, who was nearing her height. The boy's eyes had a vacant look that was disturbing to see.

"Sorry for your loss," Will mumbled to each one in turn, squeezing each hand while keeping his eyes downcast. Before he was ready, he was face to face with Lydia. His mouth opened to repeat the practiced words, but Lydia's eyes met his.

"Thank you for coming, Will," she said, returning his squeeze and holding his gaze so long his eyes darted to Frank, seeking an escape.

"Sure. I am glad to be here." He hurried past Frank after a quick handshake, stumbling down the hill after his father and shaking his head.

"Glad to be here!?" Will heard himself saying it. It echoed in his head. "At a funeral? What a foolish thing to say!"

* * *

Seth crouched down and viewed the casket one last time. At his request Frank had led Jane and the rest of the family to Lucinda's where a meal was waiting. His friend, Matthew Martin, stood back a few yards respectfully, holding two shovels.

A sudden breeze ruffled the petals of the white cabbage roses Jane had placed there. He grabbed at them to keep them from sliding off. Seth had spent a long time on the lid last night, carving "Alice" on it along with a crude etching. Hidden from the public under the flowers was the likeness of a mouse.

Alice had emitted a high-pitch sound whenever her emotions rose. In laughter or in tears, she squeaked. And he had called her his mouse. He would play cat to her mouse, chasing her around and around the cabin. Frank would laugh heartily, and the resulting tumult caused Jane and Lydia to cover their ears. The smoothed coffin with his carvings would last but a few years, unseen by all but God, but he knew they were there and that was all that mattered. Alice had loved and been loved. Period.

Seth blinked, releasing two tears that began making their way to his whiskers. He stood up, grabbed his handkerchief, and wiped his face. Then he turned to Matthew and nodded. It was time.

* * *

In the tidy cabin Lydia sat watching her grandmother's hands flying as she cleared the table. Then when the tea kettle began whistling, Grandma grabbed a dish towel and picked it up, steam threatening to scald her wrist, and quickly poured the hot water into the wash basin.

One hand on her cheek, observing the room, Lydia tried to motivate herself to get up and help. Mama sat in the cushioned chair by the window talking. Rebekah Martin next to her, was patting her hand, and Lorna Hillman stood over them, her baby balanced on her hip. A few others were hidden from sight. Frank was standing with his arms crossed near Rev. Johnston, who was speaking animatedly to her father, Matthew Martin, and Robert Hillman. She turned her head to listen.

"… can you believe that people would do that to a man— ruin his business, just for having an opinion and printing the truth?" the pastor asked. The men shook their heads. Frank just stared at the floor.

"I think all of us who take a stand against this abomination will feel persecution before the end," said Robert, scratching his stubbly chin.

Lydia turned her head back to her grandma who was still scrubbing dishes. She was weary of hearing about the slaves and the righteous cause of abolition. Yes, it was terrible, but what could they do about it besides talk, talk, talk? It was a waste of time. What about these diseases that kept killing babies and children and the people who were starving to death in Ireland?

Lydia heard her father clear his throat. She turned to look at him and met his eye.

"Help Grandma," he mouthed with a nod toward the sink. His brow was wrinkled, and his hands were jammed deep in his pockets. She could see his fingers moving restlessly over the jackknife in his pocket, aching to create something.

Shaking her head to clear her thoughts, Lydia got up and pushed her chair in. She looked for something to do. Grandma, with her usual efficient manner, had nearly finished washing up. Barely a drop had touched her spotless apron.

"I wondered if you were going to sit there until I was finished," she said to Lydia. "Looks like I was right."

"I … I'm sorry," Lydia said with a gulp. "Here, let me go dump out this water," she said, reaching for the pan.

"Wait!" Grandma held her hand out to stop her. "Put this on first," she said, handing her an apron. "I don't want you ruining my dress."

Lydia looked down at the stylish black frock with its pleats and shiny buttons. Although she hated the color, its tailored features and long skirt had caused her to feel grown up today as she took her place with the family. She was glad Will had seen her in it. The last time she'd met him he'd teased her about a flower in her hair. He was two years older than her, but already working in the store–a grown man.

Tying the apron strings quickly, she grasped the heavy dish pan and carefully began walking to the door. It was latched. She looked around but Grandma had gone over to talk with the other women. Not knowing what to do, Lydia coughed, hoping to get Frank's attention. She turned around to make eye contact and saw Ned Johnston hurrying to her rescue.

"Let me get that, Miss Cowper," he said, slipping past her to lift the latch.

"Thank you."

"My pleasure," he said, grinning widely as he held the door open.

Lydia hurried out, nearly missing the stoop step and sloshing dishwater on her shoes. She glanced back to see if he'd noticed, but the door was shut.

"Fiddlesticks!" she said under her breath. The warm water soaked into her stockings. She walked over to the tree line and threw out the contents, holding the pan at arm's length to save her shoes from further drenching.

Before going back in, Lydia paused. The eager smile of the pastor came to mind. Frank had teased her recently that the man, who was nearly 10 years her senior, was sweet on her. The very thought of being paired up with him was repulsive. All that endless praying, Bible quoting, and especially the pious poverty was unthinkable. She wanted a house with painted plastered walls and at least four rooms. She wanted to create stylish clothes on a sewing machine and wear them over a corset and hoops with a pretty hat, and maybe even wear jewelry. And most of all, as much as she loved her family, she wanted to travel. Flat Rock was so far from any place exciting like Madison or Cincinnati.

Chapter 3

The Monday after the funeral, Seth went to his workshop after breakfast as usual, but couldn't seem to get anything accomplished. The house was so quiet! No little feet running across the floor, no giggles or exhausted whining. Even the birds seemed to be silent. He stood with his arms crossed gazing out the window to a gray morning. Thunder could be heard rumbling in the distance as an overnight storm swept off toward Napoleon.

He lit a lamp, illuminating his work bench where white shavings lay from Alice's casket. A carving of a tiny dog stood unfinished amid the scraps. His mouse would never enjoy it now.

He picked it up and stared at it, seeing not it, but Alice's pudgy little hand stroking it, squeaking with delight. He clutched the figure until his hand shook. Then he drew in a ragged breath and threw it violently into the scrap pile in the corner and followed it with other bits of wood cluttering the table. Wary of frightening anyone with his outburst, he grabbed a hoe near the back door and headed to the vegetable patch to attack weeds with his wrath.

* * *

In the hushed cabin, Lydia watched her mother from the corner of her eye as she swept the floor. Jane was systematically going through Alice's belongings: stockings, a pair of shoes, underthings, dresses, a quilted blanket, and a few playthings. The sight of a blue dress caused Lydia to stop her rhythmic strokes. It had been her Christmas gift to Alice remade with material from one she had outgrown. Alice had been crazy about it because it had a little white lace collar Lydia had crocheted in secret, working on it during the toddler's naps. Alice would have been too big for it next winter, but that didn't ease the ache in her throat as she watched her mother carefully fold it and place it in a pile on the bed.

"What are you going to do with those?" Lydia asked.

"Give them to Lorna for little Grace, I suppose," Jane sighed as she added the last of the box's contents to the pile and stood up.

"But what if…?" Lydia's question died on her lips as she looked at Jane. At 41, could Mama even hope to have more children? Was it even safe? She had already lost two pregnancies and now three children. No, it was just going to be Frank and her. Suddenly Lydia wished she was closer to her brother.

There were four years between them, and their interests were so dissimilar. Right now, despite the threat of rain, he was a mile up the creek at his favorite fishing hole, drowning a worm, as he called it. He had hardly spoken since the funeral, and seemed to be avoiding everyone, grabbing some bread and butter before breakfast, then setting out with his pole and stringer.

"Lydia?" her mother's voice broke through her thoughts, and she looked up inquisitively.

"Would you look under the bed and see if there is anything of Alice's under there?"

She put away the broom, walked over to where her mother sat on the bed, squatted down, and leaned over.

"No. Nothing but my …" The sight of her unlatched keepsake box vividly recalled the sight of Allie in her play dress and grubby feet scrambling out from underneath the bed four days ago.

"What did you say?" Jane asked distractedly, looking up from the little white nightcap in she had been gently stroking.

"There's nothing except my box," said Lydia. She pulled it out, stood up and sat with it on her lap on the bed next to Jane. "I caught her getting into it the day she took sick. I wonder what …"

She lifted the lid. Her eyes and fingers sought the familiar items: a length of lace, some ribbon, five matching buttons, a nickel, an arrowhead, a thimble, and drawing of a fancy gown she had clipped from an old *Godey's Lady's Book*.

"Look Mama," her fingers held up a rock she had found underneath the ribbon, "Where did this come from?

Jane held out her hand for the object and brought it close. Her eyes squeezed shut and she let out a little moan and put a trembling hand to her mouth.

"What is it?!" gasped Lydia, quickly grabbing the rock back from her mother. She looked from the rock to Jane, the unanswered question hanging between them.

Jane blinked and two tears coursed down her cheeks. "Alice found it earlier that day while you were out hunting berries. We were at the creek. I was washing clothes, and she was playing in and out of the water. She came running to me saying she'd 'found a she shell like Gammas'". I figured it was just one of those tiny mollusks that are everywhere down there, but it wasn't."

"But…" began Lydia.

"Turn it over," said her mother, gently.

Lydia took her finger and flipped the plain rock in her palm. She gasped. There, raised distinctly from the smooth surface was the shape of a seashell. Its structure was lined with ridges and its edges scalloped. Yet it was the same gray as the rest of the rock. Lydia had heard of fossils and had seen drawings of them, but she had only half believed they were real.

"I think Alice must have wanted you to have it and put it in your box as a surprise. She knows," Jane hesitated, "*knew* how much you love Grandma's collection." She put her arm along Lydia's back and gave her a squeeze.

Jane got up and laid the night cap on the pile. She then gathered it up and took it to the table where she placed the items one-by-one in a basket.

Lydia sat unmoving, staring down unseeing at the fossil in her hand. She was thinking about the ocean – something she had always longed to see. Grandma's mantle was lined with shells she had collected as a girl when she had lived near the coast. How and when did the ocean ever cover this part of the country? Was it Noah's flood? Lydia's mind was filled with questions. She looked over at her mother, one forming on her lips.

But Jane was frozen in place, a tiny baby shirt held to her cheek, weepy eyes looking toward the window, unfocused. Lydia quickly looked away, unwilling to witness the raw grief.

So, Allie had given her the fossil as a gift! Quick to judge, she had responded with angry shouts and worse. A wave of guilt hit her like an avalanche of heavy stones as she envisioned Allie's frightened face.

A loud sniff from Jane brought her back to the present and Lydia stood up. The box clattered to the floor strewing her valuables everywhere. The nickel rolled several feet away before coming to rest.

"I can't believe how stupid I am!" She leaned over and began grabbing items and shoving them back in the box. Tears poured down her cheeks. She wiped them away with the back of her hand, then dashed over and grabbed up the coin. She put it and the fossil in the box, slammed the lid and practically threw it under the bed. Then she sat down, crossed her arms over her chest and began gasping out sobs.

"Lydia!" Jane crossed over to her daughter while wiping her face with her handkerchief. "You mustn't give yourself such names. You know you are smart. You are just … "

"I know," interrupted Lydia, digging for her handkerchief. "I'm hurting, you're hurting. Papa's gone off somewhere. Frank's out in the woods. It's so quiet. It doesn't feel like home anymore because there's no Alice. No Alice! Lydia's words came out in a torrent, like a storm-swollen stream rushing down the hillside.

Jane stood facing her, one hand placed lightly on her shoulder, searching her eyes and nodding.

"I just feel so … so furious!" Lydia flung out with venom. She lowered her eyes, afraid to go on.

"Tell me why," was Jane's patient response.

Standing up, Lydia began pacing the floor, taking long strides as she spoke, head down, arms and legs animated.

"Because," she spat. "I was mean to Allie and now she's gone. Because I have no patience and I'm clumsy. Because you are always so calm and I'm always so irritated. Because Papa waited too long to fetch a doctor. Because we live so far away from everywhere! Because Frank is never around and when he is here, he's not really here. Because you are getting too old to have another baby and that makes me sad. And…" she stopped and turned to face Jane. Her voice sunk to a whisper. "Because God let Allie die even though I prayed and prayed." Tears streamed down her cheeks as she looked into her mother's eyes.

Jane looked back at her, her mouth quivering slightly, tears rimming her eyes.

"Why, Mama?" What harm was there in allowing a little girl to live and grow up? Why? I'll never understand God. I try, but I just can't. I can't." Lydia crossed her arms protectively and walked silently out of the cabin.

* * *

At the creek, Frank sat leaning against a tall sycamore, mindlessly peeling off loose bits of bark. His cane pole was on the ground, its end protruding out into the water. The line sunk dejectedly in the calm stream. The fish weren't biting today. He grabbed a handful of the sandy soil next to him and let it filter through his wriggling fingers as he watched. A couple pebbles remained, and he pitched them as hard as he could upstream. He saw them plop into the sparkling flow, making the skate bugs scatter. He didn't care if he scared the fish or crawdads. He didn't much care about anything, to be truthful.

Everything had changed. He avoided the cabin because that's where he so keenly felt Allie's absence. He couldn't stand to eat next to her vacant chair and the hushed cabin seemed to be listening for the missing child's laughter. Even the woods weren't an escape because every interesting bit of fauna and flora he discovered made him want to take it home to show her. He'd already discarded a four-leaf clover and a snail he had unconsciously stuffed in his pocket. His pockets were empty now, just like home. Just like his heart.

* * *

Inside the silent cabin, Jane gaped at the door Lydia had just gone out of — full of that cold fury that was more frightening than her shouts. She looked down in her hand and saw her damp handkerchief and methodically folded it up and placed it in her pocket.

Strong. She had to be strong. Throughout their 18 years of marriage, she and Seth had mourned lost pregnancies and two other children – babies, both battling for life from the start and not living beyond a few weeks. Those losses had been hard, but this was different. Alice had been real — skipping, jumping, giggling, and asking Jane countless questions. She was a member of the community, loved by all who knew her. And it had all happened so quickly. In little more than 36 hours, Alice's spirit had filled a happy, healthy child and left behind a lifeless form.

Thoughts of her living daughter broke upon Jane as she stood, still staring at the door. What was to become of Lydia — her independent, strong-willed, woman-child? She was bright and capable of excellence in any enterprise, yet prone to pride and mistrust in others and, worst of all, in God. Jane had tried her best to guide her into a solid faith— grounding her in the Bible, setting an example, praying for her, but she was still so vulnerable to the world's call, yearning for things that do not last.

With a heavy sigh Jane reached for her sunbonnet on its peg by the door and tied it carefully under her chin. What she desired was another woman to talk to. Lydia needed to sort out her dark thoughts alone and there was plenty of food in the pantry if anyone got hungry.

She threw a few sticks on the fire and grabbed the basket of clothes. Her eyes landed on the blue dress Lydia had sewn for Alice. Jane lifted it out and then decided not to give it away. She would save it for a granddaughter someday. She tucked it in a box of clothes under her bed. On her way out she found Seth hard at work in the garden, told him of her plans, and set off.

* * *

After she dropped the contents of her basket off to a delighted Lorna, Jane turned toward the Martin's homestead. As she swung the empty basket, her other hand felt empty without Alice's fingers in it. Alice always visited Rebekah with her, delighting in watching her spinning wheel turn while nibbling a cookie.

Jane's throat ached with the memory. Ignoring it she called out as she approached the door. "Bekah! It's Jane. Are you home?"

"I sure am. Help yourself in. I'm spinning and can't stop," came the muffled reply.

Rebekah was just a few years older than Jane, but her children were grown. Her youngest child, Maggie, had been Lydia's best friend. She had married Charles Walton last fall. His family had helped form the Neil's Creek Abolitionist Baptist Church south in Jefferson County and lived near there.

Jane settled herself near Rebekah. She soon felt her tension ease as she talked of Alice and her worries about how grief was affecting the family. Her friend dispensed her usual wisdom and understanding, while her fingers and foot rhythmically continued their dance with the dyed wool. Then Rebekah shared news of her family and told Jane that their son-in-law Charles had asked them in a letter to consider getting involved in helping runaway slaves.

Jane's heartbeat quickened. "Getting involved! How? Bekah! Are you serious?"

"Matthew was dumbfounded when Charles asked him," Rebekah said, her hands flying over her spindle and wheel. "We had no idea Maggie and he were doing more for the cause than just writing letters and donating money. Apparently nearly the whole church is actively hiding them or guiding them to other places. Of course, they keep tight lipped about it. The children and outsiders can't know because there are fines and such if they get caught. Although they say most people just look the other way. Still, it's a risk and I don't mind telling you I'm worried for Maggie and now us."

"Us? Does that mean Matthew has decided to join in?" Jane had asked, keeping her voice steady.

"Well, nothing's set in stone, but he's talked it over with Rev. Johnston, and it seems Brother Ned has already taken steps in finding cells of abolitionists north and west of here who might be open to the idea. He says they need hiding places, 'stations,' they call them, north of the river so they can get them out of reach as quickly as possible. They try to avoid the towns to keep them away from the lawmen. It seems our Flat Rock is just the type of place they are looking for. So …" Rebekah had breathed a heavy sigh, "we are prayerfully considerin' it."

Chapter 4

A week later found Seth in the creek bed a mile downstream from the cabin gathering large rocks to repair a neighbor's chimney. Ruby stood patiently hitched to the wagon, already heavy with stone. Seth grunted as he used a lever to raise a stubborn specimen. He paused and straightened up when he heard the clip clop of a horse's hooves upstream.

Shielding his eyes from the afternoon sun, he saw the tall lanky form of Will Perry riding around a bend on a big mahogany gelding that put Ruby's dull black coat to shame with its shine. Light brown hair curled around Will's collar and his tanned face and light gray eyes were shaded by a wide brimmed straw hat.

"Mr. Cowper?" Will called as he slowed the bay to a halt.

"Yes, Will. How can I help you?" he said, laying the lever on the wagon seat.

Will climbed off the horse and met Seth's eyes. "Pa sent me to find you. He was told by John Lanham, the post carrier, that Mr. Tielmann, the undertaker in Napoleon, needs some coffins and would like to put in a rush order."

Seth's brow furrowed. *A rush order? Had there been a horrible accident?*

"What's happened?"

"John says it's cholera. Says it's killed an adult and three little 'uns in the past week and others are comin' down sick."

Seth slowly nodded his head. Cholera seemed to crop up in nightmarish waves every summer without warning, taking old and young in its wake. An idea struck him. "Do you reckon that's what killed our Alice?" he said aloud.

Will's gaze went to the horse's reins in his hand and began fidgeting with them. "Well Mr. Lanham says they can't keep nothin' on their stomachs and their innards turn to water and soon they just waste away. The doctor is at a loss as to how to stop it."

Seth sighed. Perhaps the doctor couldn't have helped anyway. He had to stop blaming himself. He shook his head as if to shoo away the thought and looked at the young man, admiring his patience. "How many and what size does the undertaker want?"

Will fished a slip of paper from his pocket and glanced at it. "He said he'd buy four three foot, two four foot and three six foot to have on hand."

"I tell you what, Will. I'll ride over first thing in the morning to get the lumber I'll need. Tell your father to have the boards already cut if he can. He knows what I'll need for that order. He can make good on that deal we made."

"Yes Sir, I will, Mr. Cowper,"

Will nodded at him and Seth watched as he set his boot in the stirrup and swung into the saddle.

"You're a grown man now, Will. Call me Seth," he said smiling up at the youth.

"Sure thing, mister ... um... Seth. See you tomorrow." Will turned the horse around and headed back up the creek and out of sight.

* * *

On his way home, Will spied Lydia ahead of him at a turn in the path. He halted the gelding and watched silently as Lydia held her skirts up and walked gingerly among the rocks imbedded in the sandbar. Every few steps she leaned down and turned over a few stones. A fly landed on her cheek. "Go away!" she spouted, while flapping her hand at her face. Her fingertip brushed her nose, depositing sand on the tip.

To cover up the laugh that rose to his throat, Will urged his horse forward into her line of sight. "Well, hello, Lydia. What ya lookin' for?" he called.

"What?" said Lydia, turning around and dropping her dress in one motion. She looked up, meeting his eyes.

Will grinned down at her. "Ya got somethin' on your nose," he said, raising his eyebrows in amusement.

"Oh, bother," she said, grabbing her handkerchief and dabbing at her face.

"What're ya huntin' for? Worms?" he guessed, swinging down from the saddle, and walking toward her, holding the reins.

"No. Alice found a fossil here before she got sick, and I was hoping to find another one. It looked like a perfect seashell," she said quickly putting her hands behind her back.

"Oh, those. We have a spot over at our place where I've found lots."

"Really?! Did you keep them? Can I see them?"

"Woah. Slow down, Lydia," Will said with another grin, looking down into her eager eyes. "Didn't reckon you'd be so thrilled about old rocks."

"But they're fascinating! I have so many questions."

"Like what? asked Will, avoiding her eyes this time.

"Like how and when did the ocean ever cover Indiana?! Do fossils prove Noah's flood? "How did the creatures get set in the rock like that?

"Well," he said, turning to stroke the nose of his horse, which was nuzzling his back as if urging him to hop on and head home. "Never took you for someone so interested in science. Pa likes it too. He's even got a book about it."

"Really? What's it called?" asked Lydia, eagerly.

"I can't remember. It's long. Something about the history of creation."

Lydia's brow furrowed. "Does it talk about the Garden of Eden and Adam and Eve like in the Bible?"

"I've never read it, but I don't think so. Pa's not ..." Will stopped. He knew his father would not be happy if he let the locals know of his secular views, "... much of a Bible reader."

"Will, I would love to see that book and your fossil collection," she said, catching his eye and holding it. Her keen dark eyes burrowed into his until he felt the blood rising in his cheeks.

Will sighed and tore his gaze away. "Well, your Pa's coming over tomorrow mornin' to pick up some lumber. If you ride along, I'll show you the book and fossils if I get a chance."

"I will, Will," she said. He looked at her again and returned her smile at the sound of the double use of his name. Lydia was backing away. "Bye, Will Will! I gotta run. Mama will wonder what's happened to me and the water."

She hurried over to where she'd left a pail and started toward home, waving enthusiastically as she went.

"Goodbye, Lydia," Will said, thoughtfully stroking the gelding's velvety nose. He stood still watching her hurrying away, her pink sunbonnet bobbing through the green until she disappeared.

* * *

Jane closed the Bible with a sigh. She'd been searching through its thin pages for nearly an hour and the dishes still weren't clean. Where was Lydia? She'd sent her out for fresh water before she sat down to read, and she should have been back long ago. The girl had been distant and distracted since her outburst the other day. Jane knew it was best to leave her alone to sort it out, but she missed her cheerful chatter, especially now that the cabin was so quiet and empty.

Her thoughts were full of worries despite her best efforts. Jesus had said in Matthew, Chapter 7 that today's concerns were all that she needed to think about. Still, her little family was struggling, and it was hard to stay positive. In addition to Lydia's sulky moods, Frank avoided the cabin as much as possible. He rambled in the woods and creeks in the long-lasting light, coming home only for meals and chores. He was growing so fast. The man inside him was beginning to emerge, evident in his growing body and in his insightful words when he talked to them about his day.

Seth? Well, he appeared to be handling his grief fairly well, but she knew he was restless. She often peered into his shop and caught him idle, hands fingering a piece of wood and staring into space. She had yet to find an opportunity to tell him about the Neil's Creek proposition.

The sound of Lydia's footsteps hurrying for the door broke Jane from her reverie.

"Mama, I'm so sorry I took so long with the water," she said, breathlessly, carrying the nearly full pail to the fireside. Water had splashed as she came in, but Lydia was already grabbing a rag to soak it up before her mother had even noticed. She stepped outside to wring it out on the ground, washed her hands and dried them, and then sat beside her mother.

Jane looked into Lydia's face. The sullen look was gone, and she saw that her daughter's cheeks were pink and her face glowing with excitement. Jane smiled.

"Mama, can I go with Papa to Perry's store tomorrow when he picks up the lumber?"

Jane's brow furrowed. "What lumber? He's not needing more lumber that I know of."

"Well, Will Parker told me that he was going there for lumber in the morning."

"When did you see him?"

"At the spring. I was lookin' for fossils when he came along on his horse. He stopped to talk and said Papa was comin' tomorrow for lumber. I want to come with him because Will's going to show me some fossils and a book he has about them. Can I please go, Mother?"

So, this was the source of the pink cheeks and enthusiasm, thought Jane. She knew Lydia was sweet on Will and while he seemed like a nice young man, she and Seth had decided between themselves that since his family were not church goers, Will would not be a good match. She didn't want to say no, however, wishing to keep Lydia from her dark mood, but she also didn't want to encourage a relationship with Will.

"I need to talk to Seth about this first to see what this is all about. I'm not so sure I can spare you tomorrow. You know we need to do the washing and ironing."

"But we can do that in the afternoon! Please?" she said, leaning forward on her elbows, her hands clasped in a pleading manner.

"Lydia, I won't discuss it further until I speak to Seth. Now let's get that water on to heat and get these dishes cleaned," Jane said standing up from the table and heading for the bucket.

"Yes, Ma'am," said her daughter, staring at her clasped hands and biting her lip.

* * *

Hours later, after delivering the heavy load of rock, Seth halted Ruby just inside the darkened barn and looked around. He noted with satisfaction that Frank had already milked Annie and had cleaned her stall, fed, and watered her. The chickens too seemed to have been fed, although their water bowl was too full, spilling over on the ground and wetting the hay. Frank's mind often wandered from his task and Seth had to keep a close watch on him. He started to unhitch Ruby from the wagon when he heard the creak of the door and saw Jane step in.

"Hello, Sweetness," he said, a smile spreading across his face. "How is ever'thing?"

She stepped in front of him, stopping him from tending to the horse and smiled back, reaching her arms around his middle, and giving him a squeeze, her nose pressed into his broad chest.

"My, you must have worked hard today. Your shirt is drenched!" Jane said, pulling away from him, her nose wrinkled. "You need a dip in the creek."

"Movin' heavy rocks around is hard work. I gathered them for a long while and then I unloaded them at Mayer's. That chimney repair's going to be hot work too," he said, leading the freed Ruby to her stall.

Jane followed. "Lydia said Will Perry told her you had a lumber order to pick up tomorrow," she remarked, removing the horse's bridle while Seth began brushing her flank.

"Oh, that's right. I nearly forgot. I've got my hands full for sure," he said, pausing to let Ruby swish away a fly and then continued his grooming. "The Napoleon undertaker wants me to make nine coffins and needs them quickly."

"Nine?" Jane looked up from stroking the mare's neck. "Why so many? What happened?"

"Cholera," said Seth, shaking his head. "There have been several deaths, and more are sick. I think that's what happened to Alice. Accordin' to the postmaster, who spoke with the doctor, they are struck down just like she was."

"Oh, those poor folks! It's unbearable to think of others going through this."

"Regardless, I've got to stop the rest of my work and get that order filled. There may be more needed. I'm sorry, Jane. I know you were countin' on me to help more with the garden now that there's so much to put up."

"Lydia and Frank will have to help more," she shrugged, handing him the pitchfork. '

"I was thinkin' on that," Seth said, leaning on the tool for a brief respite. "It's about time Frank learned a trade. I appreciate the fish and game he's been getting for the table, but he needs more skills. Could you spare him some so I could teach him on these coffins? They're simple and don't have to be picture perfect."

"I'm sure we'll manage. But Lydia's got her heart set on going with you to Perry's in the morning and putting off the washing. Seems Will wants to show her his fossil collection and such."

"Well, if you can't spare her, she will just have to have her heart broken," I guess, said Seth. "I'll tell her we all must pitch in right now. There will be plenty of time for fossil gazin' later on."

"I guess I'd better go in and dish out supper. I have so much more I want to talk over with you, dear; there's just not enough hours in a day," she said.

"How about same time, same place tomorrow?" he said, winking at her as he led Ruby out to her picket line.

"Yes Sir, Mr. Cowper, sir," she said winking back as she headed for the house.

* * *

The next morning Lydia was up with the sun. She quietly slipped out the back door, as if heading to the outhouse. Instead, she went into the barn where the first rays of the sun were creeping through the cracks in the logs and the top of the Dutch door. She found the milking stool and pulled it to where the beams were brightening a dusty corner and sat down, fishing in her deep apron pocket.

"Dear Will," she wrote with a stubby pencil on the back of an envelope she had purloined from the kindling box. "I couldn't come to the store today because I'm helping my mother with the wash. I desperately want to see your book and fossils. Could you meet me at our spring tomorrow around 4 and bring them? Please write back and let me know. Give your reply to Frank and don't let Father see. Hope to see you tomorrow, Lydia."

She folded the note into a tiny square and slipped it into her pocket and sighed. Last night at supper she had asked about going to Perry's, but her father had calmly said, "No, daughter, you need to stay and help your mother. I won't be able to help her with the garden much either. because of this rush order and I need Frank to help me." She'd had to bite her tongue to keep it still.

Lydia still felt bitter about it. She gazed at the fresh morning and imagined Will's expectant face when her father's wagon pulled up to the store. She shook off her thoughts when the barn door creaked open.

"Wondered where you'd gone," Frank said, walking over to her with his contagiously wide grin. "I need the milk stool, Lyd."

"Well, I need you to do me a favor, Frank," she said, standing up and holding out the note.

* * *

Frank silently stepped out of the sizzling sunshine and into the darkened store. Will was standing behind the counter, wrapping a parcel for Rev. Johnston. The tall thin pastor was talking about God and Will's need to attend church. Will was vainly attempting to change the subject, but the preacher persisted. Frank wiped a sweaty palm on his pant leg and eyed the outside door where his father was settling accounts with Mr. Perry. He cleared his throat.

"Frank! I didn't see you there," said the reverend, turning around and meeting his eyes. He walked forward and placed a hand on Frank's shoulder. "How are you and the family doing without little Alice?" he asked, patting him gently.

"Okay, I reckon," Frank shrugged, nervously glancing over at Will, whose eyes were watching the pair.

"Well, you are all in my prayers. Say, is your father outside?"

Frank nodded.

"Good. I need to speak with him," the pastor said, stepping toward the door.

"Don't forget your purchase, Rev. Johnston," Will said, holding out the package.

"Oh yes," said the preacher, grabbing it and heading out the door.

Will came around the counter and smiled down at Frank. "Thanks," he said.

"For what?"

"For distracting the preacher and getting rid of him! He wouldn't shut up about going to church."

"It really would do you and your family good to go, I think."

"Where's Lydia?" Will said, ignoring the comment and looking toward the window.

Frank paused to make sure he could still hear his father's voice outside, then took the folded note from the depths of his pocket and held it out.

"She couldn't come, but she asked me to give you this," he said pushing it into Will's hand. "I don't know what it says. She wouldn't let me look at it, but she said you're supposed to write a reply and give it back to me."

"Really?" Will said, and Frank took note of the excitement of his tone. "Okay. I'll write back and give it to you before you leave. Thanks," he said clutching the note in his hand and turning back toward the counter.

Frank watched the older boy surreptitiously for a moment, as he sat on the high stool and unfolded the envelope. A slight smile spread on his lips as he read. Realization dawned on Frank. He pivoted and grabbed the door handle.

"See ya," he mumbled, waving as he stumbled outside.

* * *

Seth spied Ned as he stepped out of the store and waved to him. Seth had just finished pressing some money into Peter Perry's hand. The lumber order had taken up nearly all the wood he'd left at the sawmill less than two weeks before. Paying something for the sawn lumber was only fair since the merchant wouldn't have any left to sell.

Ned headed toward him, and Mr. Perry made a hasty retreat to the mill, stuffing the money inside his pocket.

"Have you found some carpentry work?" Ned asked, shaking his out-stretched hand.

"Yes, pastor. But unfortunately, it's for coffins. Several folk up Napoleon way have died of cholera and more are sick. I'm thinking that's what took our little one," he said, fanning himself with his straw hat.

"Oh, that's a shame. I hadn't heard. I will lift them up in prayer, as I do you and your family right now. Losing such a lively, sweet child has got to be hard to bear, Brother."

"Yes," Seth said, clenching his teeth to keep from tearing up at the thought of his silent home

"Listen," Ned said, leaning close to Seth's ear. "I need to talk to you and Jane in private over an important matter involving the church. Could you stay over at Cinda's after Sunday meeting and have dinner there and we'll talk it over? She already knows about it."

"Sure," Seth said. "Lydia and Frank too? They're members, you know."

"No. Just the adults for now," he said, leaning closer and nearly whispering.

Seth's eyebrows raised in surprise, but he nodded at the preacher, who gave him a knowing glance and put his fingers to his lips. "This is just between us. Understand?"

He nodded again and before he could blink, the man started walking quickly toward the creek bed, package tucked beneath his arm.

"What was that all about?" Peter Perry said, coming up behind Seth who had turned to watch the pastor's hasty retreat.

"Oh, just church business."

"Then it's not my business. Come on, let's get that lumber loaded."

* * *

After hanging the newly strung onions in their places in the cellar, Lydia climbed up the ladder slats and scrambled back into the house. She carefully replaced the cover over the hole in the floor and went to wash her hands. She was finally alone. Jane was out back clearing the onion plot. Banging and scraping sounds were coming from the workshop. Quickly she found the scrap of wrapping paper in her pocket that Frank had handed her under the table at dinner and reread it.

"See you then. Will," was all he had written, but it was enough.

Now she had to find a way to get to the creek at the right time. She glanced at the pocket watch her father religiously kept wound and placed on the mantle until needed. It was 3:25. She then checked the water pails. They were nearly empty, just as she had hoped. She poured the remnants of one into the wash basin and grabbed the other and headed for the door, meeting her mother just outside.

"Mama, we're almost out of water. Would you like me to fetch some?" she said, holding up the pails for proof.

"Why yes, thank you, Lydia. You've been a great help. I think I may lie down for a little while before starting supper. First the laundry and then the onions in this heat and then tomorrow we'll have to tackle the weeds again if we're to ever keep up with them."

"May I soak my feet awhile? That cool water will feel so good." Lydia's heart thumped hard in her chest as she waited for an answer. She looked away from Jane's steady gaze.

"Why yes," I guess you've earned it," she said, reaching out and playfully tugging her braid. "Don't stay too long now," she said and went in, pulling her sunbonnet off.

* * *

37

He was late. Ma had kept him busy stocking the store, then he had chopped firewood. When he finally went in to wash up, he saw it was 3:40.

Thinking fast, he grabbed the loaded rifle from its hook over the door and poked his head in the lean-to kitchen where his stepmother was kneading bread.

"Ma, I'm gonna ride down the creek and see if I can get us some squirrels for supper. You know how Pa's been wanting some fried up with gravy."

"Okay, Will, that will be fine."

Will hurried to the picket line and untied Andy. He had already secreted the book and a bag full of his best fossils in his saddle pouch, which he now slung over the gelding's back and quickly notched. Fortunately, Pa was inside sorting the afternoon mail, so he avoided any questions.

The shoes on Will's horse made an urgent clop, clop as he trotted Andy downstream to the Cowper's spring. He slowed to a halt before the last bend in the creek where it turned toward the Cowper homestead. The gurgle of water made a pleasant sound up ahead as the stream rushed over a small waterfall before spreading into a shady fishing spot.

He climbed down and tied the horse to a sassafras tree on the bank. He then rolled up his pants legs, untied his pouch and headed downstream with it. The spring-fed water was cold on his feet. He went slowly, hoping to surprise Lydia like he had before.

* * *

Lydia had practically run to the creek with the buckets, determined to get there early so she wouldn't miss Will. She had already filled the pails and set them high up on the bank. Then she sat on a dry rock that jutted into the water, pulled her skirt up and plunked her feet in. She let them dangle into water that came nearly to her knees and kicked against the current.

"Oh, I come from Alabama with my banjo on my knee. I'm goin' to Louisiana, my true love for to see," she sang. She had learned the song last fall from a girl she met at a church picnic over in Letts. Soon she lost herself in the catchy tune and was just shouting out the chorus when Will rounded the corner. Lydia's blue work dress and pinafore were covered with dark splashes where her feet had stirred the water in her enthusiasm. She bobbed her head back and forth as she sang.

Will chimed in, laughing. "It rained all night the day I left, the weather, it was dry…"

"Will!" Lydia shrieked, scrambling up and smoothing down her skirts. "You stop sneaking up on me like that. You nearly scared me to death!"

"But I like seeing the real you, Lydia. You're always so prim and proper trying to be a lady. It's nice to know you can let your hair down and have some fun."

"But letting my hair down would be shameful," she protested, looking right at him from her elevated position.

"As if sneaking off behind your Ma and Pa's back to see me isn't shameful?" he asked, his eyebrows raised, a roguish dimple showing in his cheek.

"It's just… I don't think they would understand. They are so protective. But I know you won't do anything to me — just scare and embarrass me! Now, let me see what you've brought," Lydia said, stepping off the rock and sitting down near the water buckets.

She could feel her cheeks growing warmer as he climbed out of the water and walked over and looked down at her. She held his gaze and let a beguiling smile play around her lips as she looked up at him. He handed her his saddle pouch and lowered himself to sit beside her.

* * *

Frank had seen Lydia swish past the window with the buckets, a smile breaking over her face. He had turned from his scraping and watched her disappear through the woods. What was she up to? Was she going to meet Will? He knew their parents would not like her meeting a boy alone, and he had apparently helped her deceive them. He was ashamed for his part in it and swallowed a lump in his throat. It seemed always to be there now since Allie died. He spied a squirrel scampering from tree to tree and grinned at its carefree gamboling.

"Frank? Frank!" his father was nearly shouting.

"What, Papa?" he asked, turning quickly from the window.

"I need you to concentrate on that board and keep at it or we'll never get finished. Please keep your mind on your work. We mustn't waste our time."

Frank looked at the pile of boards waiting for him to smooth. He picked up the wooden planer and laid it carefully on the left and drew it back. It hit a rough spot and he made some sawing motions to get it unstuck.

"Frank! No!" said Seth, banging the hammer down on the table and rushing to Frank. "I told you not to jerk it over the wood! That will not smooth it. You will make it rougher," he said, grabbing the planer from Frank's hand, which was frozen in place on the grip. Now watch me again." He set the tool down in the same area of the board and masterfully swiped it down the board in a graceful motion.

Frank stared at the board. Why couldn't he do it right? He wanted to please him and make him proud, but it was hard. His mind kept wandering to the woods, to Lydia, to Alice, to the fried corn and turtle Mama was making for supper. The coffins would just be buried in the ground. What did it matter how smooth they were? He knew making things that were nearly perfect was important to Papa, but he honestly couldn't make himself care that much.

"Now you see? It's not that hard," Papa was saying, putting his hand on his shoulder. "Maybe if you recited poetry or sang while you worked, it would help you concentrate, and the time'd go faster."

"I could sing 'Yankee Doodle,' I guess," sighed Frank, picking up the planer.

"That a boy," his father, said, patting him again on the shoulder. "Let's see if you can get that pile smoothed before supper."

* * *

Lydia hurried into the barn with the sloshing water pails. She feared she had stayed too long at the creek with Will, looking through his fossils. There hadn't been time to read any of the book, so she had boldly asked Will if she could borrow it for a week — promising to meet him at the same time and place next Tuesday. He'd seemed reluctant but had finally agreed to her pleas.

Now Lydia looked quickly around the tiny barn for a place to hide *Vestiges of the Natural History of Creation*, a slim book she'd been able to tuck into her side pinafore pocket. Will's fossils had piqued her curiosity and questions swirled in her head she was sure the book could answer. She scampered up the slats on the wall that led to the hayloft and slid it under a pile of musty hay in a corner. She said a swift prayer that the mice wouldn't find it and hurried back down to the dirt floor below.

* * *

Two hours later, Seth slipped into the barn to check on the livestock. A summer storm was brewing. After watching Frank all day, he didn't feel he could trust him to do the chores satisfactorily. He noted that the animals had been fed and watered, but the shutters weren't secured against the wind and rain. Shaking his head, he walked outside and closed and latched them.

"Seth, where are you," Jane was calling from the darkening barn.

"Out here," he said, opening the door and walking in. "I was closin' the shutters. Frank didn't do it, even though I reminded him," he said, shaking his head.

"He *is* a bit of a scatterbrain," said Jane, picking up her favorite hen, and stroking its russet feathers.

"I hope that's just a phase," said Seth, pulling Jane close and petting the top of the hen's head with his forefinger. "All day long I found him staring into space, off his task." It took him hours just to smooth the boards for three coffins, and I have six more to do tomorrow! It would have been a lot quicker just to do them myself," he said, raking his fingers through his beard distractedly.

"Now, Seth," he's young and you must be patient with him. He'll learn. He's not used to indoor work."

"He can sit for hours readin' and writin' and cipherin' for his schoolwork though," Seth complained. "I could never do that."

"Well, Frank is not you. And Lydia is not me. They are themselves, and our job is to help them become who God made them to be."

"Now you're sounding like Brother Johnston," teased Seth, gently poking his forefinger at her pert nose. "Speaking of the pastor. He wants to meet with us at your mother's after church Sunday — without the children."

"I'll bet I know what that's about," said Jane, putting down the chicken and shooing it away.

"You do?" Seth asked, eyebrows raised.

"Yes. It's what I've been wanting to talk to you about. Ned's already talked to Rebekah and Matthew about it. He wants to get the church involved in …"

"In what?" Seth urged.

Jane sighed deeply and looked into his eyes for a moment before whispering, "Helping runaway slaves."

Chapter 5

Sunday after dinner at her mother's cabin, Jane quickly got up from the table, determined to clear away the dishes before her mother did. Like Lydia, 'Cinda was very efficient in whatever she attempted. She was methodical and focused, never getting distracted by talking with folk as Jane did. Seth and Pastor Johnston lingered at the table discussing the probable statehood of California. The far-flung territory was rapidly increasing in population and importance since gold was unearthed. Now the debate on whether it would be a free or slave state had begun.

"Mark my words, they will never be satisfied until they've pushed their abominable slavery into every territory and eventual state," declared the pastor. "They won't stop unless we stop them!"

"Yes, but how do we do that, Ned?" asked Seth. "We can't force them, except by law, and there are just too many on their side in Washington. Even many Congressmen from the North side with them because they're afraid if the blacks are freed, they will come up here and take away jobs. And let's face it, they will!"

Jane silently sat back down at the table with a cup of coffee. A rare breeze was coming through the window at her back. She closed her eyes for a moment, enjoying the sensation. She opened them and made eye contact with her mother, who smiled slightly at her and cleared her throat at the first opening in the debate.

"Well, if any of you are interested in what *I* think…" said 'Cinda.

"Oh, yes. Of course we are, Lucinda," said the pastor.

"I believe people won't do anything by force — especially if it's going to hurt them financially, which ending free labor definitely will. I think we must continue to strive to change their hearts, but also their minds. Make them see, not only how owning human beings goes against God's moral law, but also how changing into an economy that matches the north, and the rest of the civilized world for that matter, is beneficial to them in the long run — financially, I mean."

"You speak with much wisdom, Mother Cinda," Seth remarked after a pause and a slow nod. "Yes, people will care when it starts hittin' 'em in the pocketbook."

Jane smiled at him, always pleased when he could voice approval of her difficult-to-please mother.

"That's the trouble," added the preacher. "With the demand for cotton so high, folks are gettin' as rich as kings. They don't want change. Their overhead is so low — free laborers they feed scraps to and barely clothe! Why we spend more on keepin' a horse than they do a person, and we treat it a darn lot better too!"

"Pastor!" Cinda gasped.

"Oh, I'm so sorry about my language, ladies," the pastor said hanging his head for a moment. "It just makes my blood boil. I feel so useless about it all."

Jane, who had listened silently with her dark eyes darting back and forth between the speakers, swallowed the last of her coffee and cleared her throat. "I thought that was what we were here to discuss, Rev. Johnston."

"Of course, Jane," said the clergyman, patting her hand. "I'm sorry I've gone on so long. The California question just reminds me that the problem is just going to get worse. But…" he paused, looking around at them with a slight smile, "I think the time has come when we can join together and do something at last."

* * *

"I just don't know about this, Jane," Seth was saying as they made their way home, hand in hand, up the creek bed.

Jane looked up at him. His light gray eyes were narrowed, and his brow furrowed in thought. He walked with his head lowered, focusing on steering them around the biggest puddles in the shallow stream. She gave his hand a squeeze. "What's bothering you about it most?" she asked.

"Well, it's not the right or wrong of it, if that's what you're thinkin'," Seth said. "Moses' parents hid him from the soldiers who would kill him at Pharaoh's bidding. It's a way of actually helpin' people and hittin' the purses of their owners, like we talked about. But I'm worried about you and the children. If it was just me, I wouldn't care, but if I were caught and jailed who would provide for you all?"

She started to answer, but he shook his head. "And even if they didn't hold me long, there would surely be a big fine, and we can't afford it. We could lose our house, our land — everything we've worked so hard for!"

She stopped, causing Seth to pause as well. "Listen," she began, forcing him to look into her eyes. "Don't you think God would be on our side in this — that he would provide and guard us? Don't you trust Him?"

"Of course I do. But…" his voice trailed away and he shut his eyes to gather his thoughts. "I know God *can*. I just don't know if and how and when he *will*. And that scares me, Jane."

* * *

The heat and dust nearly choked Frank as his head rose into the stifling haymow. Mama and Papa were at Grandma's for a meeting of some kind with the preacher and Lydia was lying in bed with "women's complaint," as she called it. Now was a good time to find out what Lydia was hiding up here. He had caught her scrambling down the ladder on two occasions.

Newly mown hay was already stacked high, filling the air with its sweet earthy scent. Frank began searching methodically in the corner nearest to him, scuffling his feet through the loose piles, feeling behind the neatly twined bundles. Finally, he spied something black and hard peeking under the golden strands and grabbed it with a triumph, "Yes!" Frank absolutely loved books.

"Ves… Ves-ti-ges of the Natural History of Creation," he sounded out slowly, reading the title. He frowned. He had no idea what "vestiges" meant. What he wouldn't give to own the big fat dictionary that sat on the teacher's desk at school. He hurriedly flipped through the book, fearing to hear the creak of the barn door's hinges below.

There were no illustrations, and the author was called "Anonymous." Frank flipped back to the first chapter, "The Bodies of Space." The writing was full of big words he did not know, frustrating him. He stopped at Chapter 4, "Commencement of Organic Life - Sea Plants, Corals, etc." He found a strand of hay laid between the pages, guessing Lydia might have used it as a marker.

Lydia had allowed him to look over the fossil Allie had left her. Now he skimmed the pages for more information and found it. "…fossils reveal animals that are different specials than those that now exist."

"Yeah. That's because they drowned in the flood," he whispered. He sat down and leaned against the wall and read on. He soon became absorbed in descriptions of extinct fish fossils found with large, spear-like teeth. The book recounted the findings of the bones of mastodons — elephant-like animals that were twelve feet tall. The author theorized that life on earth progressed from simple to complex, starting with sea plants and ending with mammals over a long period of time.

"What are you doing?!"

Frank jerked, slammed the book shut and sat upright. He had lost track of time, completely lost in his thoughts. Lydia's face, flushed with heat and anger, was glaring at him from the top of the ladder.

"I found this book," he said, holding it aloft as if he needed to provide evidence. "Is it yours?" He knew very well it wasn't but decided to play innocent.

Lydia, who had pulled herself up, took three long strides and leaned over, snatching it from his hands. "No, it's not mine, as I'm sure you know. And I know you didn't just find it! You were snooping around, looking for it, I'll bet."

"Well, what if I was?" Frank said, scrambling to his feet. "I didn't like helpin' you sneak around behind Ma and Pa's backs. I spied you goin' off to meet Will the other day, so when I saw you climbing up here, I knew you were up to somethin', so I figured I'd find out what." He crossed his arms, scowling at her, nearly eye-to-eye.

Lydia's eyes widened and she stepped back before replying in a somewhat shaky voice, "How did you know what I was doing? You read my note, didn't you?"

"No. I said I wouldn't, and I didn't. But I'm not stupid. I knew something was up between you two because of the notes. Then when I saw you hurrying off with a ridiculous smile on your face, I figured it out."

"Did Papa see me too? Do you think they suspect anything?" she asked in a breath.

"No, he didn't see you. But if you keep it up, they'll find out. They always do," he said, remembering lies he'd told, and discretions uncovered.

Lydia seemed to shrink before him. "I just wanted to learn more about fossils and Will lent me his father's book. I've got to be really careful with it," she said, looking down at the slim volume and wiping away modicums of dust and hay. "I honestly couldn't make much sense of it."

Frank sighed, "Well, I didn't get very far, but chapter four talks about fossils and Anonymous says that life went from seaweeds to mammals over lotsa years, not in a couple a days like the Bible says. Papa won't like that for sure."

Lydia giggled. "Anonymous isn't a name, Frank. That means whoever wrote it isn't putting his name on it. He's keeping it a secret."

"Well, I reckon so. I thought it was an odd name, he admitted, grinning. "It was interesting about the fossils, though. I'd like to see Will's. What do you think Anonymous says about how Adam got here? As far as that goes, how did the planet even get made to begin with? It didn't just appear out of nothin'. God made it."

Lydia stared down at the book for a long moment. She breathed a deep sigh and placed a hand on Frank's shoulder. "I'll tell you what. If you promise not to tell, I'll let you read it as long as you take care of it and keep it hidden up here. Don't get caught with it because then I'll have to explain where I got it. I have to give it back to him Tuesday."

Relieved, Frank stuck out his hand. "Okay. It's a deal," he said, shaking her hand and grinning sheepishly at her. Suddenly he felt a great wave of affection for her, the only sibling he had left and gave her a hug around the neck. Lydia allowed the embrace and then returned it briefly before climbing back down the ladder.

Chapter Six

"Well, that's the last of it," Seth said as Jane finished helping him lift the last coffin unto the wagon. Nine boxes, still smelling of fresh pine, were stacked high, the smallest ones resting on top. Taking his handkerchief out and mopping his forehead, he looked at Jane. Her brows were knit, and her eyes were shining with unshed tears as she stared at the smallest coffins.

"So many little ones," she said, shaking her head. "So many families hurting like we are, Seth. I wish there was something we could do to help them."

"Let's say a prayer over these boxes" he suggested. Taking her hand, he laid his other on the pile and she followed his lead.

"Father, please bring comfort to the folks who've lost children and loved ones to this sickness. Let them look to you for answers and we ask that this outbreak stop. Bring your healing hand to those who are suffering with it and protect those who are well." He paused for a long moment, then added, in a quavering voice. "God, we still don't understand why you took our Alice. We may never understand. We miss her. We miss her so bad. We ..." Unable to speak, he broke into unexpected sobs.

Instantly he felt Jane's arms encircling him, her tears dropped into his beard, and he squeezed her so tightly he lifted her momentarily off the ground. After a moment, she pulled back, kissed his forehead, and took up the prayer. "And God, please use this loss to make us more loving and understanding toward others. Give Frank his joy back and give our Lydia her faith back."

"Amen," boomed Seth, a smile breaking through as he looked at his bride of 22 years. They had grown up together, cousins who shared the same values and heritage. They had been through so much, eking it out in this virtual wilderness. He was confident they could pull through this recent heartache if they stayed of one mind and spirit. He returned her kiss and released her with a squeeze.

"Well, I'd best be going," he said, securing the boxes with another length of rope. "It'll be slow drivin' with this load. Hope the old girl can handle it," he said, slapping Ruby on the rump as he climbed onto the driver's seat. "Goodbye, Jane. I should be along about supper time, I reckon." He chirruped to the horse and the wagon began to roll.

* * *

Inside, Lydia let the curtain fall back over the window where she had been standing, watching her parents. Her stomach was in knots with the battle that raged within her. She was angry at God for taking Allie and sometimes wondered if he even existed. If he was a God of love, he wouldn't let babies die. Maybe he made the world, but then just left it alone. Yet she knew her Bible and she saw the trust her parents and Frank had and wanted to believe it. She was torn. She looked around at the empty, silent house. Her hands curled into fists and slammed them both hard onto the log walls.

"Why, God? Why?!" Lydia muttered, taking up the broom by the door and sweeping up the dirt Frank had tracked in when he'd come in from doing the chores. This afternoon she would see Will again. Maybe she would ask him what he thought about why God allowed suffering and how he had created the universe. The book had only left her with more questions, and she wanted answers. She needed answers.

* * *

From the barn loft the sound of wagon wheels alerted Frank to his father's departure. He quickly finished the lengthy paragraph and reluctantly shut the pages of the book with a sigh. He knew Ma would be looking for him to start hoeing the garden any minute. Lydia was going to take the book back this afternoon and had allowed him to take one last look at it while their parents were busy. He had read most of the slim volume in snatches over the past two days, skipping over some parts and rereading interesting bits. Perhaps the planet *was* older than it seemed to be in the Bible. Something had to explain the fossils and remnants of ancient life not mentioned in the Bible.

He shrugged as he got up and then scrambled down the plank steps. It didn't matter to him how God did it. The world was vast and infinitely fascinating. He spied the hoe leaning against the barn wall and thought of the weeds that fought against the beans for their share of the sunshine and rain. The beans, hard shriveled seeds in his hand in the spring planting, were near to bursting out of dozens of pods that hung thick under their shady bushes. Even though he'd only recently finished breakfast, the thought of beans cooked with pork fat and his mother's golden cornbread made his mouth water.

"Let's go fight those weeds," he said to the hoe, grinning. He plunked a straw hat on his head and headed for the garden.

* * *

Before opening the door of the house, Jane wiped all traces of tears from her cheeks. Lydia was just sweeping the dirt out the side door when she entered.

"Where's Frank?" Jane asked, heading to the wash basin, and splashing cold water on her cheeks.

"I'm not sure," said Lydia as Jane turned around. Lydia's eyes moved around the cabin as if to find him hiding under the table. "What are your plans today, Mama?" she asked, placing the broom back by the hearth.

"Well, I believe most of the beans are about ready to harvest. If they are, we'll need to pull them up, pick off the pods, and then spread them out to dry.

"If I help with that, may I have a little time to myself at the creek again today when I fetch water for supper?"

"Are you still searching for fossils," Jane asked with a smile, glad to see Lydia occupying herself.

"Yes, and maybe I'll find an arrowhead too. Mr. Hillman collects them and said he'd pay a nickel for any whole ones I find."

Jane stirred the ashes in the fire. "What are you saving up for?" she questioned, always hoping to learn more of her daughter's heart.

"Oh, I don't know," Lydia shrugged.

"Well, we'll see if I can spare you when the time comes."

Jane opened the door to Seth's workroom and peeked out the window. She nearly gasped when she spotted Frank hoeing vigorously in the garden.

He rarely took the initiative in doing chores. One hand still on the doorknob, she smiled as she watched him work. The hem of his pants showed three inches of his ankle, and his shirt was tight over his thickening upper arms. She would need to buy cloth for new school clothes soon. He would turn 13 next week and her heart ached, to see how quickly he was growing into a man.

* * *

Fred Tielmann rushed out of his shop room door in Napoleon to greet Seth just as he was climbing down from the wagon. "Thank God, you've brought them," he said, grabbing Seth's hand and shaking it vigorously. "I've got two waiting and I'm expectin' to hear any minute about another one needin' a box."

Seth cleared his throat, taken back by the offhand way in which the undertaker spoke of the dead. "Well, I got them here just in time, I see," he said, hurrying to help Fred who was already at the wagon, loosening a knot in a rope.

"Yes. Sorry to be so blunt, Mr. Cowper, but it's the 'dog days,' ya know, and these bodies won't keep. Gotta get 'em in the ground, especially with this sickness goin' 'round. It ain't healthy."

"Is the cholera gettin' worse, Mr. Tielmann?" Seth asked as he pulled the first tiny coffin from the top of the pile.

"Well, Doc says there's two more cases come down yesterday. Some've got well, but the weakest just can't seem to recover. There's talk of folks leavin' town until it passes."

"We're pretty sure that's what took our little Alice a few weeks ago, though I can't figure out how she got it when she hadn't been around any sick folks. The rest of us are right as rain …" he trailed off, shaking his head, "Right in body, Sir, but our spirits are hurtin'."

"Well, I'd imagine so," said the undertaker, pausing in his labor to look Seth in the eye. "I saw your little 'un a time or two, and she was a bright little thing, for sure. You have my sincere sympathies," he said, taking on a more professional tone. "Anyone else down your way sick?"

"Not that I've heard of," Seth said, quickly taking a tool from under the wagon seat and smoothing a rough spot he'd found on the last box. "Say, Mr. Tielmann…"

The undertaker held up both hands. "Please, Mr. Cowper, call me Fredrick or Fred."

"Alright. If you call me Seth," he said, warming to the fussy townsman. "Haven't I seen you at some of the abolitionist meetings held around these parts … Fred?"

"Yes, sir, I'm against that slavery business. Terrible thing it is. Why most of the world has ended it! It's about time we Americans did," he said turning even more red as he apparently prepared to step onto the proverbial soapbox.

"I thought so," Seth said, smiling into the man's crinkled blue eyes. "Neil's Creek antislavery church is plannin' a big meetin' in September and some of our men folk are goin'. Would you like to come with us?"

"Well, I don't know, that's a long trip."

"Matthew Martin's son-in-law, Charles Walton, has promised to put us up for the night if we'll come," Seth said as he started to lead Ruby over to the nearest watering trough.

"If things slow down around here, and I pray to God they will, I'd like that," Fred said, following the wagon to the trough. "Now, let me get your payment and I'd better lay in another order. I don't wanna run out ever again!"

* * *

"Dong, dong, dong," the cabinet clock in the nearby parlor jolted Will out of his daydreams. He had paused in his task of adding a long column of figures in his father's ledger. Will was good at arithmetic and enjoyed keeping his father's accounts for him, but thoughts of a brown-eyed girl with a ready smile and woman's figure kept invading his thoughts. He was to meet Lydia at the creek in just over an hour and he still had to fetch in firewood after he finished adding up last week's receipts. He closed his eyes and shook his head, trying to clear his mind.

Ten minutes later, he closed the books and scurried out the kitchen door to the woodpile.

"Ma?" he called when he came in with the last armload.

"I'm in here," Eliza called from the bedroom.

Will dumped the logs into the wood box and crossed over to the doorway to his parent's room and stuck his head in. "I just wanted you to know I'm nearly done with my chores and remind you that I've made plans to see if I can catch us a turtle or two down at the crick.

"Oh, I haven't forgotten," she said, coming out of the door and smiling up at him. "You sure have taken a notion to huntin' here of late," she observed.

51

"Last week it was squirrels and now turtles. What'll it be next week? Frogs?" she teased.

"I'll have you know that frog legs are good eatin'. Pa says the French love 'em and he had 'em as a boy. Says they taste like chicken."

"I've heard a people eatin' rattlesnake too, but you'll never catch me tryin' it," she teased. "But, I've no objection to some good fried turtle or turtle soup, so I wish ya good luck."

"When's Pa gettin' back from town?"

"How should I know?" she shrugged. "But I'll be fine. Never you worry about me. I got my pistol and Darky. I'll be fine. The black shaggy mutt had been given the name by Peter, reportedly for his shiny coat and lazy demeanor.

"Well, I guess you'll be alright," he said, grabbing his hat and starting out the front door.

"Hey, wait! Aren't you forgettin' something?" she teased.

Will's brow wrinkled as he tried to think. "I don't need no gun - not for turtles."

"No, I mean a sack, ya goose!" Eliza said. "Ya gonna drag 'em here by the tail all the way from the crick?"

"Oh yeah!" he said, pivoting to run to the barn to grab a gunny sack.

* * *

After she'd allowed Lydia to go fossil hunting, Jane freshened up and headed to Rebekah's for another chat. Matthew hailed her from the chopping block as she stepped gingerly through a large puddle in the creek bed near their cabin. Startled, she dropped the skirts she'd been lifting above her ankles and climbed up the bank, sewing basket swinging from one hand.

"Afternoon, Jane. Bekah's busy puttin' up 'kraut, but I'm sure she'd welcome an extra hand, if you don't mind. She swears she can't stop work for a minute these days with all the garden ripenin' up at once," he said, setting up another long.

"Lydia and I spent all morning pulling up beans and hanging them up to dry ourselves," said Jane, loosening her sunbonnet strings as she neared the cabin door.

"Well, you ladies have it hard. The heat in that kitchen is unbearable in my book. At least out here I get a breeze now and then," said Matthew, grabbing the axe.

"Is that Jane?" Rebekah called, poking her head out of the open window and shooing a fly distractedly. The 45-year-old woman was beet red, her graying auburn hair was escaping her up-do, strands hanging limply and clinging to her neck.

"You look like you just took a dip in the creek," exclaimed Jane, coming in the door and laying down her basket and bonnet.

"A bath sounds wonderful right now," said Rebekah, giving Jane a little squeeze on the shoulder.

"Would you like an extra hand? I can get in practice for when my next round of cabbage is ready to put up."

"Would I!" said the older woman. "It's times like these I really miss my girls. You're lucky to have Lydia still at home."

"Yes, but she is not always easy to have around. She's been very moody since Alice's passing and is questioning everything."

"Is she being defiant and wayward?" asked Rebekah, brows knit in concern, handing Jane an empty jar to wash.

"Not exactly. She's just temperamental and angry at God. It hurts to see her waver so much in her faith."

"Well, I guess that's to be expected somewhat. How's Frank?

Jane carefully placed a clean jar upside down in a pan of water warming by the fire and grabbed another to wash. "Oh, Bekah, he is growing like a weed! I swear that boy's head is past my nose now. And he is much quieter and solemner than he was. He seems to have grown up overnight. But his faith seems to be intact, praise God."

"And Seth?" urged Rebekah, ladling chopped cabbage into some readied jars.

"As well as can be expected," Jane sighed. "Fortunately, he's been busy, and that helps a lot."

"And yourself?" she asked, eyes focused on the jar.

Jane didn't respond. Instead, she started wiping up water she'd spilled on the table. Suddenly she felt weak, and the cabin began to dim. She grabbed at a chair to steady herself.

"Jane!" Bekah rushed over, placed her palm on her forehead and helped her ease into a chair. "Are you alright? Are you feeling poorly?"

"Just a bit lightheaded, Bekah," said Jane, gently brushing aside her hand. She sighed. She had to face facts. "You asked how I am. Well," she paused and studied her friend's concerned face. "I haven't said a word to anyone, and I can hardly believe it myself, but I think I'm expecting a baby."

Rebekah's mouth opened and she plopped a sweaty hand on each side of her face and sat quickly in an adjacent chair,

Jane watched her friend's reaction with amusement. Her eyebrows raised and her lips pursed in a mischievous smile. "How's that for an answer?"

* * *

That did it! Will looked down at his clothes and shook his head. His shirt sleeves were rolled up to his shoulders and his pant legs past his knees, but that last quick grab for the elusive snapper had knocked him off balance and he'd nearly fallen, wetting the back of his britches as he stumbled into deeper water. He had hoped to have a big one or a couple of smaller ones bagged before Lydia showed up just downstream. He'd found a big one, but it was on the offense, rushing to snap at him every time he tried to grab its tail.

He decided to try one more time before giving up and heading to what he thought of as their trysting spot. He'd read that once in a book as a place where two lovers met in secret. He smiled at the notion, but stood statue like, staring down at the turtle. It was motionless and had partially pulled in its head. Will reached his hand inch by inch closer.

"Will! Will Perry! Where are you, Will?" Lydia called from around the bend as she came daintily through the shallows, holding up her skirts. The aroused turtle made a mad dash for Will's pink toes. Will emitted a girlish scream, jumped back, and slipped on the slimy bedrock. He went down with a splash and sat up spluttering and dumbfounded, water spilling from his dark blonde hair and beard.

Lydia's mouth opened in surprised and then her brow furrowed in concern. "I'm coming, Will!" she said, splashing rapidly towards him.

"No! Wait there. I'm fine," he said, holding up his palm to halt her. He got gingerly up, running his hands along his hair and beard to squeeze out the water. Every inch of him was soaked. "Well at least he didn't get my toes," he said grinning.

Lydia took a long look at Will and burst out laughing. "You look like a drowned rat," she choked out, holding a hand over her mouth to hide the giggles, which persisted in coming long past what she considered polite. "Frank's been trying to catch that big one for months. He's just too smart to be caught, I guess."

A half hour later, Will gleefully held the flailing reptile up for Lydia to admire. They had worked together to fool the snapper, Lydia distracting him by lying on the bank and dangling a long weed in the water and Will snatching his tail just as the turtle opened his mouth to grasp the tantalizing bait.

Water streamed from Will's pant legs as he stepped onto the bank after thrusting the furious turtle into the feed sack and tying it into a knot. He tossed the wriggling bag further up the slope and sat down next to Lydia, who inched over to avoid his wet clothes.

"We're good team, aren't we?" he asked, looking into her smiling pink-cheeked face. Her sparkling eyes were wide, and she grinned back at him. Her direct gaze was causing stirrings that demanded attention. He began to inch his hand near hers, his pulse quickening.

"I'm going to demand payment you know," she said with a coy wink. Hoping she was going to ask for a kiss, he put his hand gently on hers and began to move his head closer to hers. His eyes were closing when Lydia suddenly stood up and spoke rather loudly.

"I need you to help me find an arrowhead or a fossil. I told Mama I was going to look for them and I'd better bring back something as proof."

Disappointed, but not daunted, Will sighed and stood up, running his hands through his hair and beard again to distract himself. He had to go slowly with Lydia, although she was masking nothing in her attraction to him. He knew enough of her conservative upbringing to conclude that Seth and Jane Cowper would be dead set against any unchaperoned visits such as this one. "Bet I can find one before you can," he said and raced to a nearby stony bank.

* * *

At the cabin, Frank was relishing the solitude. Usually, he found it in the woods at the creek, but Mr. Perry's book had filled him with questions. He was sitting cross-legged on his parent's bed, shirt unbuttoned to let in the breeze from the window, studying the Genesis account of the creation. He had read the first three chapters several times and it had only filled him with more questions. Earlier he had scurried up to the loft for his slate and pencil. He found writing things down always helped untangle them. On the gray surface he had written: "Day 1 - light; Day 2 - heaven (sky); Day 3 - earth, seas, plants; Day 4 - sun, moon, stars; Day 5 - fish and birds; Day 6 - land animals and man; Day 7 - God rested."

He remembered that Will's book had said the fossils showed that animal life began in the sea. He wondered about the other animals. Had they changed over time or had different species died off like the giant elephant-like creatures whose bones were discovered in Kentucky?

He looked at the list again and his brow furrowed. When was water created? He read the first chapter again to make sure he hadn't missed it. Nowhere did it answer that question. It seemed water always been there with God in the darkness that covered the world before the light was created. What was water made of and why had it always been there? He snatched up his pencil and wrote "water?"

Adam and Eve had apparently only eaten plants before eating the forbidden fruit. He thought about the wild and farm animals he and the family ate nearly every day. Was eating animals wrong? His brows knitted and he shook his head. No, that couldn't be right. Jesus had eaten meat. Frank sighed and closed the heavy Bible. Maybe his pa could help him understand.

* * *

It was nearing 6:30 before the Cowper family sat down to supper. Jane had managed a favorite summer dish made from immature beans snapped into bite-sized pieces and cooked with bits of salt pork and sliced potatoes. Seth's favorite, sweetened cornbread, was the perfect compliment. Despite the empty chair, reminding them of the recent loss, Jane was happy that for once, everyone joined in the conversation after the first few bites.

"The cholera in Napoleon has taken a half dozen folk, three of them little ones like Alice," Seth reported. "Mr. Tielmann, that's the undertaker, was gettin' pretty desperate for the coffins I brought him."

"Are more folks sick?" asked Jane, worry clouding her face.

"Yep. He says the doc is still findin' new sick ones and some people are thinkin' about leaving town for a while until it stops."

"But then they'll spread it around to other folk," put in Lydia, wiping her lips carefully with her napkin.

"I wish they knew how people get it," said Frank, getting in on the adult conversation. "None of us got sick when Allie did."

"I hear it's been really bad in Cincinnati again," reported Jane, brows furrowed. She closed her eyes against a wave of nausea and kept them closed long enough for Seth to notice.

"Are you feeling poorly?" he asked, reaching to squeeze her elbow.

Lydia and Frank lapsed into silence.

"Yes," she said without thinking.

"Oh no, Mama!" cried Frank, beginning to stand.

Jane opened her eyes to three sets of eyes gaping at her with concern. She sighed heavily, grabbed Seth's hand, met his concerned gaze, and smiled.

"No, this is a good kind of sickness." Lydia's mouth opened to speak, and Frank's brows knit, but Jane saw a grin was breaking over Seth's face. "I can predict I'll feel much better sometime in late February when your little brother or sister makes an appearance."

Part Two

Bluegrass Region, Kentucky

Chapter Seven

"**H**ey, you!" yelled a gruff voice from outside the door.

Lily was kneeling beside the barred window of the slave jail in downtown Lexington, Kentucky. Her eyes were squeezed shut and her hands gripped each other tightly. Her lips were moving in a fervent prayer.

"You, yaller gal!" said the voice again, even louder.

The girl's hazel eyes opened wide in surprise, realizing the voice was addressing her. She slowly raised her head and turned to look up at a man standing in the doorway.

"Yeah, you!" The man, wearing a mended shirt and faded pants pointed down at her, then turned his head to aim tobacco juice at the wall.

"Mr. Robards wants ya downstairs."

Lily made no move, but remained kneeling on the bare floor, stupefied, her hands still clasped.

"Now!" he barked, holding up the leg irons.

She jumped, startled, and scrambled up to obey.

The man, whom she assumed was one of the jailers, stepped inside and locked the door with one of the many keys he wore on his belt.

"Now stand still while I put on these irons," he demanded.

Lily's heart was pounding, fearful of what might happen next. She'd been locked in the bare room since late morning listening to the sounds of the city. She'd been dumped there after the slave buyer had roughly jerked her off the wagon. Overwhelming shame and fear had kept her from doing more than taking a quick glance at her surroundings as the wagon made its way through the streets. She had always wanted to see the big city of Lexington, but not like this, she thought, looking down at the man, who was twisting the lock shut.

"Who is Mr. Robards, sir?" Lily said shakily as the man straightened up.

"Lewis Robards. He's your new owner until auction day," the jailer said, turning around to unlock the door.

Lily swallowed a lump in her throat at the thought. She had never belonged to anyone but Miss Willson. The woman's sudden death three days ago had thrown Lily's quiet world into chaos and destroyed everything she had come to trust in her short life. She stepped through the door to follow the jailer and stumbled against him.

"Get off me, girl!"

Lily whispered an apology. The man wiped his hand over his shirt sleeve and glared at her. Then his attention was diverted as a man dressed in a frock coat with a sapphire blue waistcoat passed them by in the hallway. Then man stopped and turned.

"Is she for sale?" the gentleman asked. He openly stared at her, his eyes roaming over her face and form. Lily quickly bowed her head and studied her shackled feet.

"Yes, Mr. Jamison. Just takin' her down to Mr. Robards for a look see."

"Fresh off the farm?"

"Just got here this mornin'. Fresh as they come."

"Well, she'll go high then." Lily heard him move on down the passage but kept her eyes on her feet.

Ahead of her, the jailer turned and started down a narrow staircase. Lily tried to keep up with him, but the chains made descending the stairs challenging. Her mind was racing.

"I'll 'go high,'" she mused silently. "Will that mean a good place or a bad one? Will I end up near here or be sold south?" She had no hope of landing where she knew anyone. She only knew Miss Willson's neighbors and their slaves who were sometimes hired to help with harvesting and other tasks too big for Lily to do alone.

"Well, hello, Smitty. Who you got there?" a man drawled.

Lily looked up sharply and followed the voice with her eyes to the bottom of the stairs. A man in a yellow bow tie and a white shirt with rolled up sleeves was standing with his hands on his hips, grinning up at her. The jailer, who'd already made it to the bottom, was peeking around the corner, watching as she stood frozen in place.

"What I tell ya, Mr. Robards?" the jailer said, nudging the man with his elbow.

"She *is* a beauty," the man nodded, gesturing at Lily to continue down the stairs.

Mr. Robards had dark brown hair and a thick moustache and beard. Blue eyes gazed at her steadily from his lightly tanned face.

Lily's heart began pounding as she shuffled past the man, who continued to stare at her. He motioned for her to precede him into a room near the front door. Entering, Lily saw a polished desk covered with stacks of paper, two chairs and a locked cabinet. Sheer curtains covered the window, which faced a street bustling with city traffic.

"Sit down," Robards said, closing the door and pulling the blinds partially down, blocking the harsh sunlight of the May afternoon.

Lily glanced at the finely carved chair beside the desk and carefully sat down on the floor against the wall. She didn't dare meet the man's gaze, so she stared at her hands in her lap. She heard him pull out a chair.

"Get off the floor, girl," Robards barked, pointing to the chair in front of the desk.

Lily scrambled up, using the windowsill for leverage, and shuffled over and sat down.

"Sorry sir, she mumbled.

"What's your name?"

"Miz Willson calls, um called me Lily," she rasped, coughing slightly.

Robard's brows knitted.

"Do you need something? When did you last eat or drink?"

Lily's eyes moved back and forth in thought. "Um, I had some water and a biscuit this morning, sir."

"Here?"

"No, Sir. At Mr. Bowden's. I stayed the night with his cook's family before that man come and brought me here."

"Who's Mr. Bowden?"

"Miz Willson's lawyer. He said I was part of her 'state and he had to sell me to pay off the taxes on her place."

Mr. Robards stood up and quickly walked to the doorway.

"Smitty!" he roared, looking down the hallway.

Lily started at the man's loud voice, then her eyes darted to the window where a horses' whinnying could be heard along with men's shouts. She never imagined a city would be so noisy. Her whole life had been spent on the farm in Jessamine County. She squeezed her eyes shut trying to hold back tears.

She heard heavy footfalls behind her, and Mr. Robards was back with a tin cup of water and a corncake.

"Here," he said, thrusting it at her.

"Thank you, sir."

The man sat back down at the desk and studied Lily intently as she swallowed the cool water in sips and nibbled at the cake. Lily kept her eyes lowered, uncomfortable with his penetrating eyes.

"How old are you?"

"Um. Miz Willson said I turned 13 three days after Christmas."

"How'd she know? Were you born there?"

"Yes sir, my momma belonged to her daddy. My birth was written up in his Bible, Miz Willson said."

"Where is your momma?

Lily swallowed hard. The corncake seemed to stick in her throat. She closed her eyes remembering the day when she'd been in bed sick with fever and Mr. Bowden had come to fetch her mother and the two male field hands for the slave buyer. She could still hear her mother's shrieks and feel the tears dripping on her hot forehead as they had dragged her away.

"She and the rest of the slaves was sold when Miz Willson's daddy died."

"How come you weren't sold too?"

"I was sick and Miz Willson said she would keep me to help do for her."

"What do you know about your daddy?" Robards said, looking at Lily's light skin and eyes.

Lily's lip quivered at the question. "I don't know for certain, but Miz Willson once said she thought she ought to do right by me 'cause we were almost sisters.

"Uh huh," muttered the man, twirling a pencil in his hands thoughtfully.

"What about your mother? Was she dark or light?"

Lily closed her eyes trying to picture the woman who'd exited her life so early.

"'Bout like me, I guess. Her eyes were kinda gray. I 'member that."

Mr. Robards smiled and nodded. Lily was aptly named with her light skin and heritage that was only a quarter black at most. Dollar signs began dancing in his head.

Puzzled at the questions, Lily's mind raced. She'd heard most slaves in Kentucky were sold down south to work on plantations. Hard, backbreaking work. She figured Mr. Robards would ask her about her experience next so she blurted out.

"Sir, I's a real good cook and I can clean house and sew and do ladies' hair. Miz Willson had me doin' all those things since I was little."

"What about outdoor work?"

"Well," Lily looked down at her hands, not wanting to say too much. "It was just a little farm, but I helped care for the chickens, milked the cow, and worked in the garden patch."

"Let me see your hands!" Robards said suddenly, his eyebrows knitted.

Hesitantly she slowly laid both hands on the desk. He picked them up, roughly, examining them closely. She frowned at his touch and at her jagged nails. She had cleaned them before leaving as best she could, but her nervous chewing had done damage. Also, callouses from scrubbing floors and digging in the garden were evident.

"Well, that can be fixed," he said.

Lily noticed he was talking to himself more than to her.

"Smile," Robards ordered, and she knitted her forehead and grinned slightly.

"No! Smile big. Let me see your teeth!" he said, raising his voice. "Open up!

"Now stand up and turn around slowly." Lily jumped to obey, stumbling with the weight of the chains. "Lean over. Now show me your feet and ankles."

Lily's cheeks stung with shame as she obeyed the man's every order.

"Take that rag off your head"

Lily saw Robards' eyes widened as her long honey-colored braid tumbled out of her kerchief.

He stood up suddenly and walked around the desk, facing Lily, who was staring at the door, tears stinging her eyes.

"Turn around," he said, twirling his finger to demonstrate.

"Stop!" he said when her back faced him.

Lily felt his hands on her hair, loosening the bit of string that held the plait in place. Her face burned with mortification as his hands undid her long locks. When he'd finished, she felt his hands stroking the back of her head. Without thinking she raised her shoulders and pulled away.

Quick as a snake striking, Robards slapped her ear.

"Hold still!" he ordered, moving his hands over her hips and then up to span her waist and grope her small breasts.

A whimper escaped her lips and tears began rolling unchecked down her cheeks.

Robards grabbed her hand and pulled her around hard, the cuffs around her ankles rubbed mercilessly. She hung her head, unable to meet his gaze. "Look at me, Lily," he said, cupping her chin in his hands and forcing her head up. "Do you want to work in the cotton fields down south?"

"No, sir," she said sniffing and blinking hard.

"You do what I say, and I can guarantee you that you a better life than you ever had with Miss Willson."

"What would that be, Mr. Robards, sir?" she whispered. Confusion was mingled with hope in her heart.

"We're gonna make a lady out of you, Lily. A fancy lady."

* * *

"Stand still, Lily!" Mrs. Bannister mumbled around the pins stuck in her mouth. It was a week after her arrival and Lily was standing in the seamstress' workroom, arms held out awkwardly, as the woman stuck pins around her arm hole seams. She tried to focus on the clock on the mantel, wishing she knew how to tell time. Mr. Robards had promised to send little Zeb to fetch her back to the jail house at 6 o'clock for supper and she was hungry and ached from being made to stand still for so long.

She was tired of the whole business. She wanted all the uncertainty to be over and done with. After meeting with Mr. Robards, she had been moved to a different building with other women and girls, where she now had a bed and good food. Della, the slave woman in charge, had them practicing doing various hairstyles with each other and then on themselves. They bathed, cleaned and trimmed their fingernails, and applied creams to their face and hands. Also, they were made to practice walking, standing, sitting, and speaking "like a lady," according to the strict Della.

Now they were all being fitted for long dresses to be worn at the upcoming auction. Lily tried to avoid thinking about it, but after dark in their shared bedroom, the other girls whispered across the room about it every night and she couldn't help but overhear.

"Miss Della is Mr. Robard's fancy girl," Peggy had giggled just last night. Peggy was almost as light skinned as Lily with ginger-colored wavy hair. She was bigger and stronger than Lily. Peggy had been a farmhand and the sun had tanned her too dark, according to Della. A special lotion was being applied to her face, arms, and hands.

"What's that?" whispered Tilda from her corner, a petite skittish young girl who cried in the night for her baby brother.

"Well if you don't know now, you're 'bout to find out," stated Peggy frankly.

"When?" asked a voice Lily couldn't identify.

"I heerd Smitty tell Della this morning when he brought our vittles that she had just one more week to get us ready."

"Ready for what?" Tilda asked.

Peggy sat straight up in bed, incredulous. "Why for auction, stupid girl. Ya think they's gonna keep us here forever? They's just fattenin' us up like hogs before the slaughter. They's makin' us look all nice so's we sell high to some man who wants a yaller girl like us."

Lily had squeezed her eyes shut and bit her lower lip. She had feared that all this training and getting a new dress was not a blessing, but a curse. Now, standing still for the seamstress, she knew her fears were real and not imagined. Miz Willson, who had been like an aunt to Lily, had read aloud to her from the Bible and she knew what Peggy was alluding to was sinful and shameful. How could she bear it? An unwelcome tear rolled down her face and she hated it because she couldn't wipe it away without being fussed at. Would supper time ever come?

* * *

"Arms up," commanded Della as she held the newly made blue cotton dress's hem up for Lily to slip over her head. She struggled to thrust her arms into the tailored sleeves that came to her wrists that ended with a bit of tatted lace. Never had she dreamed of wearing something so fine and so long with a skirt of almost four yards of material that came to her ankles. The only dresses she had ever worn were no longer than her calves and made of her mistress' castoffs, full of patches and threadbare.

"Now button up and be careful. That waist has only been basted on for now. Once I tell Mrs. Bannister the fit is good, she'll finish up in time for tomorrow."

Lily painstakingly slipped each button into the neat buttonholes that went from her waist to her collarbone. The lump in her throat at the word "tomorrow" refused to dissolve. The whispered talk at bedtime had only increased her terror over what was in store for her. There was no one to turn to. God seemed deaf to her pleas, silent, sending no words of wisdom or a tangible change in the dreaded future.

"Miz Della," she whispered, reaching out to the older woman with her eyes in her desperation.

"Yes?" Della turning from where she was unpacking another garment.

"I is so scared 'bout tomorrow!"

"I *am* so scared about tomorrow," Della corrected.

"Yes, ma'am," Lily nodded, tears forming in her eyes.

"Well, Lily, so was I when I was in your place a few years back. But I do my best to please Mr. Robards and he treats me well. Just do as you're told and be polite and obedient and you'll be fine."

Lily hung her head and wiped her eyes on the back of her hands, careful to avoid the lace.

"But the Bible says to give yourself to a man outside of marriage is a terrible sin. It's wrong! I'll be so ashamed. How can I talk to God again and face good Christian people?"

"Now honey," Della said, softening as she came close and put her arm on Lily's shoulders.

"Us folk… *We* folk who are slaves," she amended, "don't have a choice. We must do what we're told or be beaten or sold away. And don't think about running away. You'll be caught for sure and be in worse shape than you're in now. We've just got to keep trusting and praying for forgiveness and deliverance.

Lily nodded, but the knots in her throat didn't loosen.

"Now keep your head up. Practice that pretty smile and tilt of the head I taught you and stand straight and proud tomorrow. Don't ever let them see you scared or rebellious and you'll be treated better. Take it from Della," she said, giving her a quick squeeze and stepping away. She looked long and hard down into Lily's eyes, biting her lip. Then she shook her head and straightened her shoulders. "Take off that dress now. I'll be there in the morning in time to see to your hair and apply a bit of color to those cheeks."

Lily did as she was told, but her brows knit, and her stomach churned. She had seen the pain behind Della's eyes.

* * *

That night the room was hushed after darkness fell. Peggy's boisterous talk was reduced to unintelligible whisperings to the girl next to her. Tilda was sniffing loudly, and the other girls were restless. Lily wanted to get down on her knees to pray the way she'd been taught but didn't want to attract attention. Instead, she turned her face to the plastered wall and reached her hand up to touch its coolness. Tears were building, but she tried not to blink for fear the tracks would show. She struggled to visualize her mama's face, but all she could see was it scrunched up in screams of anguish as she was dragged away from Lily's cot. Wouldn't she cry even harder if she knew what Lily was about to become? Her eyes were stinging now, and she quickly lifted the light coverlet to catch the tears.

"God? Where are you? Why are you letting this happen to me? Save me. Sweet Jesus, Lord, help me," she pleaded in her head. "I don't know what to do. Save me from becoming what Della is. Please, please, please."

Chapter Eight

Auction day dawned sunny and warm. From the window of what Mr. Robards called "the waiting room," Peggy was giving a report of what was happening outside.

"There must be a thousand people out there by the courthouse. Buggies ever'where and black and white and rich and poor. I seen a lady with a skirts that musta been five-foot wide and full of ruffles and lace flounces. Top hats on every other man, and dogs, cats, horses, and children runnin' around laughin' like they's at a party."

"Yeah, and we's the spectacle, they's come to see," groaned an older girl who pulled a shawl more tightly over the low-cut gown Mrs. Bannister had made her.

Lily's heart threatened to jump out of her chest. Her hands were shaking so badly that she clasped them tightly and willed them to be still. She longed for the pockets Miz Willson had always allowed her to sew in her work dresses. Maybe if she couldn't see them, she'd be able to resist the urge to chew her nicely trimmed nails.

"That must be the auctioneer! He's climbin' up the stairs to the platform," reported their lookout.

The wall clock's ticking and Peggy's jabbering were incessant. Lily tried to recite the Lord's Prayer under her breath, but she kept losing her place.

"Lily!" Della said as she rushed into the room carrying a box.

Lily dropped her hand guiltily. She hadn't even been aware she was chewing on her pinkie.

Della addressed the room. "The auction is starting. There are many other groups ahead of us. We will be last, the finale, as they say, and you all need some freshening up." She scanned the room. "Liza, you've scratched your ankle and it's bleeding. Get a rag and clean it up. Peggy, your hair is all windblown from standing by that window. Check the mirror in the hall. Mamie, your hem is coming down. I'll have to fix it. Stand up."

Suddenly the room was abuzz with activity. Lily looked herself over and found nothing amiss but a rough fingernail. The noise from the street rose from a cacophony to rhythmic words as the auctioneer commenced the sale with music-like pitches and men started shouting out bids.

* * *

An hour or so later, the front door banged open and Mr. Robard's boots could be heard in the hall. Lily sat up, jerking her hands out from under her thighs where they were tucked away safe from her teeth. Not long after the auction began, the wails of the slaves who had been separated at the auction rose above the noise of the onlookers. The sound unnerved the awaiting girls and even Peggy's tongue was still as she watched from the window, hugging herself.

Della stood up and every eye turned to the door. Mr. Robards peered in, whisking off his tall hat and ran a hand through his beard as he surveyed everyone.

"Good morning my fancy girls," he said stepping into the room. His eyes narrowed and his thin lips pressed together. "The time is nearly here," he said in a solemn tone. "I want a good return on the investment of time and money I've spent on you." He paused. One hand on his hat and the other on his hip, he slowly scanned the room, looking each girl in the eye to make sure they were listening.

"You will smile and put your shoulders back and hold your heads high and proud when you are being sold. You are the cream of the crop, aside from the young strong bucks who look like they can pick their weight in cotton, and I'm counting on you to keep up my reputation here in Lexington. When I advertise I'm sellin' choice slaves at the Cheapside Auction, that's what people expect. If the auctioneer or a buyer wants you to say somethin' or do somethin', you do it. If any one of you refuse or cry or try to run off, it will lower your price and I will personally see that you regret it."

"Della," he said, turning to her. "I'll have Smitty bring you the placards right away with the numbers. Make sure they're put on the right girl and then have them lined up in order just inside the back door waiting for the call."

"Yes Lewis. We'll be ready," she said, smiling at him. He turned to leave and nearly ran into the jailer who was holding a stack of cardboard just behind the door.

"The auctioneer just started bids on the last lot before these 'uns," muttered Smitty, out of breath and holding out the placards.

Robards hurried down the hall and Della grabbed the cardboard. Smitty's eyes grew round as he gaped at his former inmates, sitting prim and proper in their new dresses.

"You may leave now," Della said firmly. Smitty backed out and hurried after the slave trader.

Della consulted the auction flyer and began calling out names and placing a placard with a large black number around the girls' necks with an attached hemp cord.

"Lily?" Della's eyes searched for her, but Lily was rooted to her chair, head bowed, knees knocking, and teeth clenched. Della handed the remaining signs to Peggy and carried one to Lily. Placing a manicured finger lightly under Lily's chin, she raised her head and looked into her eyes. "Jesus sees you. He's with you. Don't be afraid. Now stand up," she whispered.

Lily did as she was told, hands stiffly at her side, fists clenched. She bowed her head slightly as Della slipped a card with "Lot No. 56" boldly printed on it. When Della walked away, Lily looked down at the indecipherable characters and wished Miz Willson had taught her to read. She took a deep breath, bit her lip, and took her place in the line heading for the door.

* * *

Thomas Mercier ran his finger along the top of his cravat and swung the wide brim of his hat back and forth over his face. The 27-year-old hadn't anticipated the heat in Kentucky to be this intense before June, but the cloudless sky allowed the sun's rays to seep into his black overcoat. He wished the auctioneer hadn't left the prized fancy gals for last. Yes, he'd picked up a couple of bargains in two youngsters that would fetch good prices at the Natchez market, but he was counting on finding a comely mulatto girl he could double his money for there. His friend and mentor, Mr. Chastain, had promised to pay half the price for any girl he thought worthy.

"And now, ladies and gentlemen, we come to our final lots, the prime of Cheapside, our fancy ladies," sang out the auctioneer at the top of his voice.

Applause, cheers, and even a few whistles rose from the crowd like a sudden breeze. Thomas plopped his hat back on and grabbed the list of auction offerings from his coat pocket. There were nine lots, numbered forty-nine to fifty-seven. Each one was described the same: "likely young mulatto girl."

He anticipated a line of "likely" girls from which he could pick one with the most promise to invest in and looked toward the slave jail in anticipation. The crowd quieted when a rather tall girl with the number forty-nine on a card around her neck slowly climbed the steps. Her copper-tinted wavy hair was done up in a chignon. The tan plaid dress was stylish and long, showing just a few inches of her ankle. Her light brown eyes stared above the crowd and her rather large, tanned hands were crossed primly in front of her. She was well developed with wide hips and full breasts.

"Look at this lovely slave gal, gentlemen. Her name is Peggy and she's good for anything you have a mind for her to do," the auctioneer said, winking at some men nearest the stage.

Thomas' pulse began to race. If this was just the first lot, should he bid early on or wait and see how high this Peggy would go first. Or should he hope for another just as good down the line? Why couldn't they let him get a look at them all first? He cursed himself for getting to town too late for a private appointment to see the offerings.

"Let's start the bidding at five hundred, shall we?" the auctioneer suggested.

"Five hundred," immediately shouted one of the men in the front. Before the hawker could open his mouth to ask for another bid, another man offered $550.

Flustered at his indecisiveness, Thomas shouted, "Six fifty!" The two men in the front row craned their necks to look at their competitor. He smiled nervously at them then raised his eyebrows at them and stared them down.

"We have six fifty, gentlemen. We can do better than that. Peggy, turn around slowly and hitch that skirt up to your knees." The girl closed her eyes momentarily, but nodded slightly and pulled her dress up higher, showing off shapely, muscular calves. She rotated once and let the dress fall.

"I bid seven hundred," said a new bidder a middle-aged man in a top hat.

"Seven fifty!" sputtered the first man.

"Eight fifty!" the older man countered, spittle shooting out of his mouth.

There was silence. The auctioneer's eyes darted through the crowd. Thomas' mind was racing. The old man seemed determined to outbid them. Best to wait until the big bidders had spent their money.

"I have eight hundred and fifty dollars on Peggy, lot forty-nine. Anyone for nine hundred?" The crowd was still. "Eight seventy-five?" the man teased. No one spoke. The auctioneer banged the gavel on the podium. "Sold to the gentleman in the tall hat, a Mr. Tolliver, if I'm not mistaken. You may sign the bill of sale for her at the offices of Mr. Lewis Robards on Short Street."

Twenty long minutes passed. With just two more girls left up for sale, Thomas berated himself for his indecisiveness. A few of the girls had been undesirable in his opinion, too skinny or with too many African traits like thick lips and kinky hair, despite their light complexions. One slight girl had commenced to crying as soon as she stepped on the platform despite a man in front who loudly admonished her to stop. She had gone for a mere $425 to a surly looking man who joked that she'd be good for breeding, if nothing else.

The auctioneer broke into his thoughts. "And now, gentlemen, lot fifty-six. Meet Lily."

Thomas looked over to see a girl climbing the steps in a bright blue dress. Her light brown hair was braided, knotted, and pinned at the nape of her neck. Like the first girl, she didn't look at the crowd, but stared into the sky. Her flawless face, no darker than his, was enhanced by rosy cheeks, arched dark eyebrows and long lashes framing large hazel eyes. She stood straight with her legs slightly apart and her hands clasped behind her back. He moved forward for a closer look. Her lips were moving slightly as she stared ahead.

"A likely lady, gentlemen. Now what'll you bid?"

Thomas hesitated again. He wanted Lily. He could see she was young but would develop into a beauty when she had matured. However, if he started the bidding, he might start too high. Already some of the earlier buyers had left the crowd in front of the platform to claim their purchases. He was sure she could fetch more than $1,000 in Natchez.

"I bid three fifty," said the surly man, obviously hoping for another bargain.

Thomas cleared his throat and raised his hand. "Three seventy-five," he said.

"Four hundred," shouted the first bidder, narrowing his eyes at Thomas.

Before Thomas could open his mouth to counter the offer, the hawker said, "Gentlemen. Look at that skin and posture. Surely you can bid higher than that. Lily, show them your teeth in a big smile. The girl complied, but the brief toothy grin couldn't hide the fact that it was forced. "Now pull up your skirt and show them your legs and hands."

A brief flash of a skinny calf and long tapered fingers was all Thomas or any of the crowd could see. He was tired of the show and wanted to get on with the bidding.

"She's awful skinny, Barley," one man in the back shouted and then grinned. "I don't think she's growed up yet. Let's see some more skin than that." Several men in the crowd laughed loudly while others averted their eyes and glanced around as if to see if any of the women in the crowd were paying attention.

"Five hundred!" shouted Thomas. He didn't know if baring more of the girl's skin would make the price go higher or not, but he didn't want to take the chance.

The auctioneer looked back to the first man to see if he would raise his bid, but he just stood there, arms crossed. "I ain't biddin' no more until you show us more of the merchandise."

"Yeah," hollered another man, obviously drunk and dressed too shabbily to be able to afford to buy anything. "Show us more."

"Show us more! Show us more!" a small crowd of boisterous young men chanted.

Obviously hoping for a higher percentage of the take, Mr. Barley whispered to the girl and, still looking straight ahead she began to unbutton her shirtwaist. Her hands shook and she fumbled her way through the top two buttons before the auctioneer sighed and quickly undid the rest of them. He held up the top and told those wanting a peek to make it quick.

There were muffled shouts and even cries from some of the bystanders on the outskirts of the crowd around the slave block. Thomas stole a look and saw Lily biting her lip with her eyes closed. A single tear coursed down her cheek. A small white breast, about the size of a green apple poked against the blue fabric. The rowdy men crowded closer and laughed at her underdeveloped chest.

"That's enough!" yelled the auctioneer, telling the girl to button her blouse. "Now, do you want to bid?" he said, pointing at Thomas' competition. "Six hundred maybe?"

"No, sir. She's not worth it," said the man, who turned away.

"I've got five hundred. Anyone want to go higher? She'll mature, gentlemen."

"Five fifty," said a man hurrying to the front. Thomas recognized him as Mr. Tolliver, who'd bought the first girl. Peggy was following behind him, head lowered. Her hands were tied by a rope that was being held by a house servant judging by his clothing.

"I'll go six seventy-five," Thomas said, verbally throwing all his remaining money in the deal.

Tolliver hesitated. He looked at Lily, then at Peggy, then at Thomas, who stared him down, brows raised in confidence. He slowly closed his mouth and shook his head.

"Sold for six seventy-five!" Barley barked, banging the gavel.

* * *

The sun had left the sky while Lily dozed in the darkness of the wagon bed, the crickets and tree frogs lulling her to sleep despite the knot in her stomach. Herr head banged against the uprights of the wagon when the wheel beneath her slid into a deep rut. She jerked awake and tried to remember where she was.

"Dang it, Jethro! Do you have to hit every hole in this road?" said the voice of the white man who had bought her at the auction, retrieving his hat from around his feet.

"I's sorry, Mister Thomas, sir. I reckon we best light the lamp or I's likely to get lost out here in the dark," said another voice.

Lily's arms ached from laying across the backs of the two boys on either side of her. Just a few years younger than her, they had wept unashamedly for the loss of their families for many miles of the trip. Then a motherly instinct took over and she'd pushed aside her own worries and invited them to scoot over beside her for a bit of warmth and comfort. Their leg chains lay tangled with hers in the wagon bed.

Peering through the small opening in the back of the wagon, she could see nothing but a few scattered stars and an occasional tree branch hanging over the road. In the front she could see silhouettes of the two men by the pale moon's light. The man called Mr. Thomas turned and began groping in the space behind him, muttering curses.

"You, gal! Lily!" he bellowed, jerking the boys awake. The trio was only a couple of feet away from his grasping hand.

"Yes, sir?" she said, her voice quavering.

"Feel around in there and see if you can find the lantern. We can't see a thing up here."

Lily pulled her tingling arms from the side of the wagon bed. The eyes of the boys could just be seen, wide and frightened in the dim light glowing through the canvas. Lily leaned forward and began to feel around for a lamp. There was nothing within reach, so she painfully got on her knees, the cuffs of the chains chafing her ankles. She crawled forward a few inches, hands outstretched, trying to keep her balance in the jostling wagon. Still nothing. Slowly she inched toward the opposite corner, dragging the heavy lead ball attached to the chains forward with her.

"Well?" asked the man.

Silent, Lily continued to stretch forward until her fingers touched metal. She hooked her middle finger around the side of a hurricane lamp and, balancing herself on one elbow, held it aloft toward him. She felt a tug and released the lamp and crawled backwards to her spot. As she straightened out her aching knees, she caught a whiff of sulfur and the lamp glowed, illuminating the men's faces.

"Now that's more like it, Mister Thomas," crowed the driver with approval. "Hook it on that nail there in front of ya." Shadows moved around the wagon's interior as the man struggled to find the nail for the lamp. Finally, he settled back. Lily sat up straight, hoping for a glimpse of the landscape, but all she could see was the hunched backs of the two men with an occasional glimpse of the long ears of the mules as they plodded along. She had no idea where they were going or when they would get there. In her heart, she hoped they would never stop.

* * *

The ear-piercing braying of a mule shook Manny from a deep sleep as he lay on his bed of hay in the stable loft. Below him a horse neighed in answer. He sat up, rubbing the dust from his eyes and hair. From the cracks in the flooring, he could hear the creaking of a wagon below as it came to a rolling stop.

"Job!" Manny called, looking around the loft where he spied the stable boy in a patch of moonlight curled up sound asleep. Manny shook him and he immediately sat up with a jerk. "Jethro and Mista Thomas is back. We's got to move," he said, getting up and pulling a shirt over his head before nimbly descending the ladder.

Below in seconds, the teen quickly unlatched the stable doors and pulled them inward, attaching them to posts to allow the mules and wagon to pass through. He blinked when a beam of light from the lantern flashed on him as the conveyance rolled by. When it halted, Manny quickly headed to unhitch the mules, but Thomas Mercier grabbed his shoulder as he walked past.

"No, shut the doors first and latch them. I'll take no chances of those three runnin' off."

Manny looked up and nodded, switched directions, and did as he was told. As he turned back, he caught sight of three heads silhouetted in the lantern light, one big and two small, inside the wagon. Even though he couldn't see their faces, he could imagine their fears. Surely, they were wondering what horrors awaited them, trapped as they were among strangers.

As he went through the familiar chores of caring for the animals and tack along with Job, Manny mulled over his own state. He'd been purchased just two weeks before by Mercier at the boat landing near Carrollton where the Kentucky River meets the Ohio. Manny's owner, Mr. Konkel, had gotten fed up with his attempts to run off and decided to "sell him south" and get a troublemaker off his hands. He'd made him stand at the loading dock with a "for sale" sign around his neck while chained to a post.

Mr. Mercier from Louisiana had paid $600 cash for him after he'd examined him for his soundness. Manny shuddered remembering the shame of being made to jump about and strip half naked for the man to check for scars. At first, he'd been dejected as he sat on the lower deck of the riverboat in chains with several other slaves who worked for the southern planters. They'd told him stories about the heat and backbreaking work field hands had to endure in the cotton. Then his keen mind had begun racing. Yes, their final destination after spending the summer in Kentucky was for the Gulf states, but before they went south on the Mississippi, they'd have to head back north to the Ohio, and Manny was hatching a plan.

* * *

Thomas collapsed into his bed, tucked into a tiny room in the back of the Chastain summer home. He glanced at his pocket watch and let out a groan. It was nearly 2:30 and the sun would be rising in just a few hours. Without a doubt either the rooster's crowing or the creaking steps on the servants' stairs would be sure to wake him all too soon.

He had risen from this spot before light to catch a coach in Frankfort. Jethro had followed in the wagon, able to take a slower pace. Despite his weariness, he didn't fall asleep immediately. Thomas was excited to show Paul Chastain what he had bought. Images of the two healthy boys and young Lily sprang to his mind. He smiled slightly at the satisfying thought as the gurgle of the nearby river lulled him to sleep.

Four hours later he was awakened, not by a chicken or a groaning stair, but by a gentle tapping on his door. Sunlight was filtering through the closed shutters, and he squinted.

"Who is it?" he called.

"It's Missy, sir," said a voice through the keyhole. "Is you up? Ya gonna want a fire lit?"

Thomas heaved a heavy sigh. "No! I'm heading down," he shouted, sliding on his trousers. He glanced at his reflection in the wall mirror. He needed a shave in the worst way. Perhaps after meeting with Chastain, he'd head to Frankfort to the barber. Grabbing his wallet, hat, and an overcoat, he rushed through the door, nearly knocking over Missy who'd waited patiently in the hall for him to exit.

Refusing to use the servant's narrow staircase, Thomas strode to the curving central stairs that ended in the wide passage that divided the two sides of the ground floor. As he neared the bottom, he heard sounds coming from the dining room and headed in that direction. Paul Chastain was just digging into a plate of fried potatoes, eggs, bacon, and biscuits. The aroma nearly knocked Thomas over, reminding him that he hadn't eaten more than a few mouthfuls of cold biscuit and ham on last night's long trek.

Chastain was a 47-year-old who had inherited a fortune in land, houses, and slaves in southern Louisiana. His lifetime of plenty had widened his waistband as well as his wallet. His jowls were filled when he looked up when Thomas hurried in and stood waiting for him to speak.

"Thomas! Good morning. Have some breakfast. How'd it go yesterday? Tabby said she needed three more helpings sent to the stables, so I take it you didn't leave empty handed. Sit down and tell me all about them."

Thomas filled a hot plate from the offerings on the sideboard and sat down next to Chastain. "Where is everyone else?" he asked, glancing around. He tucked a napkin into his cravat and picked up a fork.

"Still in bed," said Chastain, digging out his pocket watch. "It's not even 7 yet. Martha and the girls won't be down for at least another hour. Now tell me everything," he said, swallowing the last of his coffee and reaching for more.

Thomas narrated the highlights of the auction, mentioning the heat, the crowds, and the raucous youths who had demanded to be shown the covered areas of some of the fancy girls. He said the highest price paid at the sale was for a muscular young man at least 6 feet tall and who had been trained as a boxer.

"How much?" asked the older man, eagerly.

"Guess," Thomas said, grinning.

"Nine hundred dollars?"

"Higher," Thomas said, raising a finger.

"A thousand?" Chastain asked, incredulous.

Thomas again pointed to the ceiling.

Chastain laid down his fork, eyes round. "Eleven hundred?"

"Eleven hundred and fifty," supplied Thomas.

Chastain gave a low whistle. "I hope you got better bargains than that!"

"Wait 'til you see," he said, wiping buttery fingers on his napkin.

* * *

Lily scraped the remnants of grits out of her tin cup and licked the spoon before laying the dishes beside her in the hay. She sat with her manacled ankles straight out, unable to sit comfortably with her legs crossed, as she preferred. Her aching back rested against the rough slats of the loft. She sighed. Despite her anxiety over what the day held, there was satisfaction in once again having food in her stomach and a few hours of sleep.

Nearby lay the boys, Joe and George, already back to sleep after gobbling down their breakfasts. Hours ago, as they were settling down to sleep in their temporary quarters, she'd learned that they were cousins raised by the same grandmother. They'd both cried fresh tears telling how she had clung to them when the master arrived to take them to the auction. Remembering her own mother's anguish, she had tried to comfort them as best she could, reciting the 23rd Psalm aloud.

The warm and comforting animal sounds and smells in the stable were lulling her back to sleep when she heard the creaking of hinges and voices below.

"Emmanuel!" called a man's voice.

"Yes sir, Master Thomas," answered another voice from a different part of the building.

"Where's those young uns' I brought in last night?" the first voice asked in the southern drawl Lily now recognized. She hadn't allowed herself a proper look at the man who had bought her but had heard his voice often over the long trip.

"They's still upstairs. Job brought 'em their grits a little bit ago."

"Are they still manacled?"

"Manacled?"

"He means chained, boy," came a new deeper voice.

"Oh yes, sir. I never touched no chains."

Lily heard the boys stirring. She looked over and saw Joe's eyes open wide in alarm. She put a finger to her lips, hoping to learn all she could.

"You want me to fetch them down?" asked the voice she assumed belonged to someone called Emmanuel.

"No, I'll do it," said her owner.

Lily reached over and shook George's shoulder when she heard scrambling at the bottom of the nearby ladder.

"Wake up, master's comin'" she warned.

George and Joe both sat up and the three of them were attempting to stand in their shackles when a man's hat rose through the hole in the floor.

The man's eyes met hers as he stepped off the ladder and Lily immediately looked at her feet, her heart pounding. Was this man about to do to her the things Peggy had whispered about? She closed her eyes and prayed silently.

"Now what's your name?" he asked after a few moments. The voice was loud and nearby, and her eyes flew open. The man was kneeling at their feet, fiddling with the chains that bound them together.

"Lily," she mumbled.

"Oh, I remember you, Lily," he said, his toothy smile showing below his mustache. "I meant these boys," he said, nodding toward them.

"I's called Joe," George said, pointing to himself with a mischievous grin. "And this here's my little cousin, George."

"Nuh huh," said Joe. "I's Joe and he's George."

The man looked at Lily with a questioning look.

"Which is which?" he asked.

"I don't rightly know, Master …" she trailed off.

"You can call me Master Thomas for now."

"Yessir, Master Thomas. The big 'un told me he was George, but he could've been foolin' me."

"Well, it don't really matter, does it? You three will be gettin' new masters in a few months and they can call you whatever they want. Right?" he said, looking at the trio.

"Yessir, Master Thomas," they all said obediently.

Lily looked down at her feet and saw the man pulling away the heavy chain that linked her to the boys. After he removed the ankle cuff he stood up, arms akimbo and looked down at them.

"You three are now the joint property of me and Mr. Chastain, who owns this land here in Franklin County. He and his family live near New Orleans most of the year but stay here in Kentucky from May until September. This is just their summer home. You and Emmanuel downstairs are just some investments we've picked up during our stay here. We plan to make a nice profit from you in the slave markets down south. I am a business partner of Mr. Chastain and I have personally guaranteed him that you will behave yourselves and not run off or misbehave."

He paused and leaned toward them pointing a finger in their faces. Lily wanted to take a step away as she observed his changed countenance "Now if you do and make a liar out of me, I'll find you no matter how long it takes and whip your hides until you bleed."

The man took a deep intake of breath through his nostrils and straightened up. He looked at Lily and the boys long and hard. Lily didn't dare look away. He had said his speech very quietly, but sincerely. "Now, do we have an understanding?" he asked, raising his volume. Lily and the boys nodded in unison.

"Let me hear you say it!" he shouted. Little Joe covered his ears momentarily.

"Yes, sir, Mr. Thomas," Lily responded, leading the way for the boys, who echoed her quickly.

"Very good. Now Mr. Chastain is waiting downstairs to meet you. Brush off the hay and make yourselves presentable. Lily, you've got a smudge," he said, whipping out a handkerchief and wiping her cheek. He then turned to the boys and removed tear tracks from their faces. "Now stand up straight and be polite. If you are good, you'll be treated good. Now follow me," he said heading toward the ladder.

* * *

Down below, the scent of Chastain's cigar mixed with the odors of hay and manure in the stall where Manny scattered hay onto the floor. Overhead he could hear Mercier's boots on the ladder. He leaned over to peak through the slats of the stall and saw bits of hay and dust floating down, caught in the sun's rays from the open windows. Once the buyer was down, he lifted a hand to steady a blue skirt covering cream-colored ankles and feet. Manny's eyes widened as a white girl with a light brown braid descended, followed by two younger black boys.

Once the trio was at the bottom, Mercier looked at Chastain, smiled and said, "Mr. Chastain, these three were guaranteed prime stock at the Cheapside sale. Lily here is about thirteen years old, healthy and a real beauty, as you can see. These two strong boys are George and Joe, about eleven and eight years old. They've been trained to do both inside and outside work and George here seems especially bright." He put his hand on George's woolly head and the boy beamed.

Manny's eyes and ears absorbed it all. "Stupid's more like it," he muttered under his breath, shaking his head at George's goofy grin. White folks loved to butter up the slaves they saw as being especially gullible. "Like pettin' a dog you want to train to fetch," he added silently. He looked at Joe but saw nothing but fear in his eyes that were darting to and fro as if looking for a place to hide.

"How much for them?" Chastain asked.

"Both for five twenty-five. We can easily double our money if they stay healthy and grow taller, which they should at their age."

And Lily?" Chastain took his cigar out and pursed his lips, looking the girl up and down.

Well, sir," Mercier began. "I know she's a bit skinny, but she's obviously just started developing. And look at her rosy cheeks and those eyes and hair. She'll be a real looker in no time. I guarantee you she'll fetch at least a thousand in Natchez."

"How much?" demanded Chastain, reaching over and flicking hay from Lily's shoulder.

"Six seventy-five," said Mercier. "One buyer seemed determined to get her and was up to five fifty. There was only a couple more girls to go, and I was sure she was worth it."

Chastain nodded then stuck his cigar back in his mouth and with his thumb and forefinger leaned forward and parted Lily's lips. Manny could see the startled look in the girl's eyes as the fat man made her open her mouth like examining a horse. Fortunately, the gate hid him from sight as his eyes narrowed and he ground his teeth at the humiliating scene.

"So that's twelve hundred all together, six hundred dollars for each of us," Mercier said.

Chastain stepped back and put his thumbs through his suspenders and looked again at the three slaves. "Well, Thomas, you spent the lot, but I think you did well. Let's see if Ben could use some help down at the smithy. George here could start learning a trade and that would make him more desirable to buyers. Joe could be of use either in the kitchens or the garden, and Lily had best be taught to act like a lady if she's going to be worthy of a rich man. I'll put her in as a lady's maid to Aimee or Yvonne and see if she can learn from them."

Manny heard Mercier let out a big sigh and he looked over to see the man's eyes seeking him out among the stalls. Intent on not being caught eavesdropping, Manny quickly ducked down and began noisily rustling the hay with the pitchfork.

Chapter Nine

The sun's rays slipped through the draperies and illuminated the auburn curls of Yvonne Chastain, age fourteen, buried deeply in a dream under her lavender satin duvet. The noise from a neighing horse in the nearby stable trumpeted through the window and wakened her. She'd left it open a crack, despite her mother's warnings of foul air coming from the river. Her long lashes fluttered open, and freckled arms reached overhead in a luxurious stretch. She sniffed the air with her snubbed nose and caught a whiff of bacon and biscuits and practically sprang out of bed.

Two minutes later she was in the hallway calling for Missy to empty her chamber pot and make her bed. After tying her dressing gown, she knocked on her sister's door and impatiently called.

"Aimee! Are you up? Let me in."

There was no answer. After a few more impatient knocks, she heard shuffling and the door creaked open showing the nightcap and half-shut eyes of her older sister. Aimee was seventeen and practically engaged to their second cousin, Henri Richards. She had reddish golden hair, an aquiline nose, pale skin, blue eyes, and was tall and angular. Fourteen-year-old Yvonne, on the other hand, was rather short and dumpy, with dimples in her pink cheeks and light brown eyes that were almost golden hued in a certain light.

Yvonne pounced on her sister and gave her a hug that almost knocked them both on the bed.

"Sissy, we've got to get dressed and get down to breakfast fast. Mr. Mercier's surely back from Lexington and you know we don't see enough of him. Oh, he makes my heart pound with that moustache and cleft chin!"

Aimee sighed and pulled her cap off and ran her fingers through her hair. "Yvonne! Will you ever get over your infatuation with that man? Why he's barely even a gentleman and he's at least 10 years older than you. You know Papa would never let you marry him even if he did fancy you."

"We don't know that," said Yvonne, sitting beside Aimee on the bed. At least he's more handsome than Henri! With his round cheeks, pink lips, and yellow hair he looks just like a big baby."

"You're wrong. Henri's just handsome in a different way than Thomas Mercier. And he's rich. You know he'll inherit the plantation and all the slaves and other property someday. I'll live like a queen."

"I'd rather be poor and happy than rich and miserable," said Yvonne decidedly.

"You might change your mind once you had to empty your own chamber pot and scrub floors and cook and everything."

"Well Mr. Mercier has money to buy a slave or two. He's buying them here to sell for profit at down home. He's smart and industrious, not lazy living off his family's money like Henri."

The girls' voices were rising steadily in their debate but stopped abruptly at a familiar tapping on the door.

"Girls! Lower your voices at once and get dressed and come down to breakfast," their mother, Martha, said in a loud whisper outside the door. They looked at one another and scattered to obey.

* * *

Lily's eyes widened as she timidly walked through the open kitchen door of the big house. Two women and a girl of about eight, heads wrapped in cloth wraps, were bustling about, scraping dishes, washing pans, and plucking a chicken. She stood mutely in the doorway, amazed at the size of the room, which was larger than Miz Willson's parlor and eating room combined. The serving dishes and plates were beautifully painted with gilt edges and the utensils gleamed with a shine only polished silver can create. No one noticed her standing there until the girl tripped in her scurrying and bumped into her.

"Who are you?" the girl demanded.

The older woman in a ruffled apron turned around at the sink and narrowed her eyes at Lily, who had rebraided her silky tresses into a neat plait and stood nervously smoothing down the skirt of the long blue dress Mrs. Bannister had made. The woman wiped her hands on the apron and walked over to the newcomer.

"Miss, why didn't you knock at the front door? Are you a friend of Aimee or Yvonne?" asked the woman, whom Lily assumed was the cook.

Lily shook her head and looked at the floor. "Mr. Mercier told me to come in here and ask to speak to Mistress Martha."

The cook's brows furrowed in confusion below her red kerchief.

"Mr. Mercier? How do you know him?"

She looked up at the woman and met her eyes. "He bought me at the sale in Lexington yesterday."

"What?" the cook asked, incredulously, echoed by the girl and other woman, who had both stopped to stare at Lily.

"Bought you? But you's white!" the young girl spluttered.

"Hush your mouth, Dora," said the younger woman, swatting the girl on the rear.

"Get back to work both of you," said the cook, still staring at Lily.

"My name's Sally," the woman said, holding out a damp hand.

"Mine's Lily," she managed to reply as she shook the offered hand.

"Well, Lily. I guess I'd better see if Miz Martha is still in the dining room. I'll be right back." The woman turned and walked briskly out an inner door.

Her stomach churning, Lily found her pinkie finger in her mouth. She nibbled on a stubborn hang nail, almost enjoying the pain. What would her new mistress be like? Miz Willson had always been fairly kind to her except when she had company. Then she would speak harshly to her, ordering her around as if afraid of seeming too familiar in front of guests.

Suddenly she realized the kitchen had grown quiet and she looked up to see the girl and woman staring at her – the girl with curiosity and the woman with a judgmental glare. She quickly looked down at her bare feet. They needed a good scrubbing. She had no shoes. Master Thomas had said she wouldn't need any until she was sold at the big auction house in Natchez, wherever that was.

After a moment, Sally poked her head in the door. "Lily? Follow me."

Lily looked up, took a deep breath, and obeyed.

* * *

At the dining room table, Yvonne rested her chin in her hand, her eyes glazing over in daydreams as she chewed her biscuit. She'd missed Thomas and wished she'd hurried downstairs sooner. She heard voices and turned her head to listen.

Her mother was looking up at a pretty girl in a blue dress standing slightly behind her. "How old are you, Lily?" The girl's hands were clasped tightly behind her back.

Yvonne's eyes widened and her mouth flew open. "Who's tha…?" she started but was silenced by her mother's glare.

Yvonne watched the girl's greenish eyes dart over to her and then come back to her mother. "I's.." she began and then restarted. "I am thirteen, ma'am."

"What training have you had as a lady's maid?"

The girl swallowed and looked quickly at the table. "I did for mistress, sewing and mending and fixin' her hair. That's all, I guess. The rest was house and yard chores, ma'am."

Yvonne was listening intently and noted her sister's keen interest as well. "Aimee, Yvonne," her mother announced, "Your father has declared that this creature," she said indicating Lily with a tilt of her head, "must be taught to be a lady by being a personal maid to one of you. Obviously, she'll need a lot of training and a firm hand."

"I'm the oldest," butted in Aimee before Yvonne could open her mouth.

"That's not fair," said Yvonne. You have your own servant at home. Why can't I have one here. It's only temporary anyway, right?"

"Never mind, Yvonne. Your sister is in greater need of one at her age and she will get the privilege, if that's what you want to call it, if she wants it."

"Of course I want her!" said Aimee. Yvonne saw Lily's eyes darting from speaker to speaker. "Tabby never has enough time to help me with my toilette. Besides, she reminds me of Marietta Belleau. Don't you think so, 'Vonne?"

Yvonne stared briefly at Lily who lowered her eyes, her cheeks flushed. "A little bit I guess," she shrugged, reluctant to agree with her sister about anything.

"Alright girls. We will let Aimee show Lily her room and explain her duties. But even though this girl may look like one of your friends, she is *not* your equal. Her mother was a slave, and she is a slave. She is colored and don't you ever let her forget her place. She will be sold as soon as we're back South and likely for some shameful purpose. Remember that and take care."

Yvonne looked at Aimee and then at their mother who was folding her napkin and calling for Tabby to clear the table. Then she glanced at Lily who was standing rigidly staring at the carpet while a tear coursed down her pink cheek. She felt a wave of sympathy for the girl and grabbed her nibbled biscuit and hid it in her hands under the table.

"Lily, I'm Yvonne. You look hungry. Here, have my biscuit," she said, awkwardly holding it out as soon as her mother left the room. The girl started to reach for it, but snatched her hand back when Aimee loudly cleared her throat.

Yvonne turned on her. "Don't say a word, Aimee. She's probably had nothing to eat but a few bites of cold grits. Do you expect her to slave away for you on just that until dinner?"

"You leave her to me. She's mine. Mother said so."

Yvonne pressed her lips together and glared at her sister, her hand still holding the biscuit.

"Oh, go ahead. Let her have it," said Aimee with a flip of her hand. "What do I care? If she doesn't eat it Dora will and that pickaninny's getting fat and mouthy lately."

Yvonne turned to Lily and nodded. The girl took the biscuit but did nothing but hold it behind her back. After a moment Yvonne shrugged and went into the kitchen to question the cook.

* * *

In the stable Manny was saddling a gelding for Thomas who stood watching as he leaned against a stall chewing on a bit of hay. The close surveillance caused him to fumble while fastening the cinch and he grabbed at the lose end clumsily.

"You'll have to do better than that if you want any chance of keeping out of those cotton fields," said Thomas with a grin that put a knot in Manny's stomach.

"Yes sir, Master Thomas," he answered in his best servile tone.

"Just what kinda work did you do for your owner up north?"

"Oh, little bits of everything," answered the teen, now confidently reaching for the bridle. "They was only three of us servants. I chopped trees and split logs for the fires, took care of the horses, cows, pigs, chickens, and such, helped in the garden and with the baccy. All kinds of work," he shrugged.

"Have you ever done house work?"

"You mean like scrubbin' floors and cookin'?" Manny's face scrunched in disgust.

"No. I mean as a butler or valet."

"I've heerd of those things, but I don't know what they do."

"Well, who helped your master get dressed and shaved and took care of his things?"

"Master Konkel dressed and shaved hisself. Sometimes he'd head over to the barber in Milton to hear the news. His wife and the house girl took care of his clothes and such I reckon."

There was a lengthy silence while Manny finished adjusting the bridle. Mr. Mercier gazed at the sky out the open door. Finally, he straightened up and looked at Manny who was holding the reins.

"I'll tell you what, Manny. I look to make a fine profit off you and those other three darkies I bought, but I've a mind to keep you and train you to do those things for me. All the fine gentlemen in the South have valets and I plan to be a gentleman someday. Would you like to keep from being a field hand?"

Manny was nodding vigorously before he even spoke.

"Yes, sir, Master Thomas. I'd like that just fine."

"Well, we'll put you on trial for the next week or two. You'll have to be quick to obey, polite and decent. Why don't you come along with me to town, and you can start now."

Manny looked at Thomas like a dog who had just received a pat on the head. And in his mind, he was already adjusting his plans for escape.

Chapter Ten

wo weeks passed with Lily, Manny, and the boys learning their new tasks. Lily spent her days in the big house learning her lady's maid duties but wasn't permitted to sleep in Aimee's room. Even though it was customary, the girl said it made her nervous having someone "watching her while she slept." Fortunately, for Lily, Aimee was a late sleeper who demanded not to be disturbed before the June sun was high in the sky.

Lily was glad because the early morning hours gave her time for prayer and solitude in the barn loft with its familiar wholesome scents of hay, horse manure, and leather. She relished the frequent breezes that wafted through the openings with hints of honeysuckle and clover accompanied by birdsong. She was homesick. The longing surprised her, but she genuinely missed the daily chores of cooking, cleaning, feeding the chickens, and tending the garden. She also lamented the loss of independence she'd enjoyed in the familiar confines of the Willson farm.

Below she heard Dora bringing breakfast and she quickly scrambled down the ladder to join Manny, Job, Joe, and Jethro who were already sitting on the tackle boxes below. She and Joe missed George, but he was now staying at the blacksmith's forge most nights and they rarely saw him. Job, a couple of years older than Joe, loved to poke fun at him and take advantage of his gullible nature. He was already engaged in it as Lily sat down among them and began to eat.

"At home we's got gators as long as that hay wagon," Job gestured with his elbow lifting his tin of water. "They eat young 'uns nearly ever'day, they do," he said, stopping to lick a bit of molasses off his fingers. Joe's eyes went wide as he gulped down his bite of hoe cake. Lily licked her fingers and then began chewing on her thumbnail. Miz Willson had told her alligators were monster lizards with sharp teeth and claws. She glanced at Manny who was rolling his eyes and at Jethro, who was trying to hide a grin.

"Don't forget the snakes," Jethro said, encouraging Job.

"Oh yeah. We's got copperheads and cottonmouth snakes that are 'bout as tall as a growed man. They's pizen an'll kill ya dead, they will," he nodded for emphasis.

Manny stood. He was nearly as tall as Jethro and looked down in disdain at Job. "We's got copperheads and cottonmouths, and rattlers in Kentucky and we aint skerred of no Lo'siana snakes or gators. We's got bears, wolves, mountain lions, wildcats, and such. Now shut up and get to work."

Job was shaking his head and muttering to himself as they all began to collect their bowls and cups when they froze to a voice coming from the back door.

"Job," called Master Thomas, "Where are you, boy?"

"Here, Massa Thomas," called Joe and Job in unison as they rushed to obey.

Lily saw Thomas put his hands up to stop the onslaught of the two youngsters rushing toward him. "Woah! I called for Job, not Joe."

Joe lowered his head and mumbled an apology.

"Well, I guess they do sound alike. That could be confusing. I'll tell you what. Job's been in the family a long time and Joe's only with us until September. From now on you'll be Jim, Joe."

Joe hung his head and walked away. Lily, hearing the exchange, remembered how the boy had proudly told her that he'd been named for his uncle. She walked over and placed her hand gently on his curly head and he looked up, tears brimming.

"You'll still be Joe to me and George and everybody else back home," she whispered.

* * *

A few days later Manny sat upright and proper as he sat beside Jethro in the driver's seat of the Chastain's carriage. He was wearing the new pants and fitted shirt Mr. Mercier had had made for him as well as a borrowed hat from Jethro. Manny had driven a team of horses before, but Thomas had insisted that the older man come along to help him navigate this trip into the capital city. They were to drive to a hotel in downtown Frankfort, four miles away, to pick up Henri Richards, a relative of Martha Chastain. Mercier had insisted he be on his best behavior because Richards was an important man and he wanted to make a favorable impression.

Manny turned the team near the river as they passed a settlement called Bellepoint, just outside of Frankfort, and then headed towards a covered bridge spanning the Kentucky River. Jethro said taking the team through that two-lane contraption would be a real test of his abilities. Manny had heard tales of a bridge collapsing over that same expanse and curled his toes in his boots in anxiety. He loved water, had grown up swimming and boating on the nearby rivers, but he didn't trust bridges.

Traffic increased as they drove deeper into the heart of the city, and he could feel the horses' tension through the reins. Frankfort was smaller than Madison, Indiana, just up and across the river from his former home, but it seemed bigger with the scurry of a large city and its imposing capitol building fronted with six massive marble columns.

"Here we are now. Just slow and steady," Jethro said as they neared the bridge. "Don't let the horses know you's skeert," he added, patting him on the shoulder.

Manny glanced back at Thomas, but he was absorbed in a newspaper. "Giddup," he hollered when the team seemed to slow as they approached the blackness of the two-lane crossing. He glanced up, his eyes widening as the horses walked right up and into the structure.

"Why it looks just like a barn door!" he marveled, twisting his head this way and that to see the roof and massive timber trusses. "And listen how their hoofbeats echo in here!"

"Keep your eyes on your lane!" shouted Jethro, making a grab for the reins as a wagon loaded down with barrels rumbled past.

"I've got 'em," Manny assured him and focused on the horses who were tugging to speed up, frightened by the amplified din.

Manny didn't realize he was holding his breath until he pulled the team to a stop in front of a three-story building two blocks away.

Mercier folded his paper and hopped out. "Stay there. I'll be right back with Richards."

Jethro climbed down to check on the horses. Manny leaned back against the backboard, relaxing for the first time since he'd entered the city. He craned his neck, staring long and hard back at the bridge, marveling at its craftsmanship and size and wondering if such a thing could ever be built across the Ohio.

"Manny!" warned Jethro. He sat up and then scrambled down to greet the newcomer as Mercier had coached him. Mister Thomas was carrying a valise, followed by a young yellow-haired man in a light blue coat and a shirt covered in fussy ruffles. Manny stepped toward the pair and bowed.

"Good afternoon, Mr. Mercier and Mr. Richards. Please let me take your bag," he said holding his hand out, but keeping his eyes on the gentlemen's shoes. He'd been told no eye contact was allowed unless a gentleman or lady was addressing you personally.

"After you, Richards," said Thomas.

Manny stepped aside letting the two men pass by. Jethro was already settled in the driver's seat, his hands on the reins. Manny secured the valise in the space under the backseat, then stood aside and let the two men enter, eyes cast down. Then when they were seated, he climbed up beside Jethro, barely touching the seat before the horses pulled away.

* * *

"Ouch!" Aimee screeched, pulling her head away from Lily as the boar-bristled brush tugged at a snarl at the nape of her neck. She glared at Lily behind her in the vanity's mirror.

"Sorry, Miss Aimee," Lily said snatching the brush back in alarm.

"You're impossible!" Aimee grabbed the brush and lifted her hair and ran the brush behind her own neck, catching on the same knot. She lifted the fingers of her other hand up to feel and sighed.

"Grab the scissors from my sewing basket and just snip off that tangle. We're running out of time! Henri will be here within an hour, and I've not even started dressing," she demanded. She laid the brush on the table and leaned over so Lily could snip off the offending knot.

"Now my corset," she instructed, standing up and raising her arms in the air so Lily could strap her into the stiff apparatus. Lily had practiced lacing up the garment by using a pillow when Aimee was in her dressing gown during breakfast. She was usually content with a snug fit, but today she demanded Lily tug the strings as tightly as possible while she held her breath.

"Tighter," Aimee hissed through gritted teeth, eyes tightly closed.

When she was satisfied, she stood quietly while Lily slipped several petticoats over her head, tied them, and then gathered an enormous skirt of rose-pink linen in her arms and held it up for her mistress to dive into. As Aimee adjusted the waist and neckline, Lily came around and started fastening the 20 or so hidden hooks in the back of the frock.

Twenty minutes later Aimee was scrutinizing the back of her head with her hand mirror facing the open window that overlooked the street. Lily stood back, holding her breath.

"Well, I suppose it will have to do," she said. Lily let out her breath in relief. She'd been close to tears over Aimee's fractious complaints during the plaiting and pinning of her straw-colored locks.

Aimee moved back to the vanity and looked again in the mirror, then pushed her lower lip forward in a pout. "My ears just will not stay hidden!" she whined, pulling a few more strands over them distractedly.

Lily stepped forward. "Why Miss Aimee, you's got nice little ears. Why hide them? You's got lots of pretty earbobs you could wear," she said picking up her mistress' jewelry box.

"It's 'you've,' Lily, not 'you's,' as I've told you a dozen times. You must learn to speak properly if you ever expect to attract gentlemen. But never mind that. The reason I'm not wearing ear jewels is it is out of fashion this season. A middle part with hair smoothed over the ears is what the *Godey's Ladies Book* shows is all the rage, so that is how my hair will be done."

"Oh," said Lily, placing the box back on the vanity.

"And don't ever touch my jewelry again unless I expressly ask you to," said Aimee, knitting her brows and looking up at her.

"Yes, Miss Aimee," she whispered.

Suddenly they heard the alarming howl of Beau, Mr. Chastain's redbone coonhound. When Beau paused for a breath, the clip clop of horses' hooves echoed from the driveway.

"He's here. Oh, good gracious!" spluttered Aimee jumping from her chair and grabbing up her silk wrap. "Where's my gloves? Where's my fan?" she gasped, searching the room. Lily snatched them up from the bedside table and shoved them at the frantic girl. Aimee began to push her shaking fingers into the gloves as she headed to the door. She grabbed the doorknob and looked down at her stocking feet. "My shoes! Hurry Lily! I had my heart set on meeting him as he walked through the door."

Lily grabbed the ornate slippers from under the bed and put them beside the girl's feet. She held out her arm so Aimee could hold onto it as she lifted her skirts and shoved her toes into them.

"If I miss his entrance, it's your fault. You must get faster, slowpoke," she said over her shoulder as she scurried through the door.

* * *

It was 20 minutes to midnight later that day, and it was all Thomas could do to keep awake. The busy summer day combined with wine at supper and a glass of bourbon had done Thomas in. He waited bleary eyed for Jethro to stop his endless shuffling and start dealing yet another hand. Opposite him was Chastain who was halfway through his second cigar and his third bourbon. Richards sat to his right nursing a fourth brandy. A teetotaling neighbor,

Stephen Evans, sat on his left. Evans, a banker, had sweated bullets once bets started increasing.

Thomas slid his hand across the table and inwardly grimaced at the sight of his hand. Beside him Evans's leg was bouncing up and down, his telltale sign of a promising hand. Thomas stifled yet another jaw-splitting yawn and decided he'd had enough. He wanted nothing more than to turn down his hand and fold. He had lost more than he could really afford already, but he summoned up the energy and shoved his pile of winnings to the center of the table. The bouncing to his left stopped abruptly and he heard Evans take in a quick breath and hold it as he peeked again at his hand.

Glancing up, Thomas saw that Richards and Chastain were staring intently at Evans, waiting for him to make his wager. He made himself lean back in his chair and don a carefree pose. He hoped the others would buy his charade so he could leave the game without a loss.

Evan's eyes darted around the table. "I fold, gentleman."

"Blast it, Evans! Why don't you place a bet for once?" Chastain blurted. After a moment's hesitation, he said, "I'll call your bet, Thomas. How much?"

A weight seemed to drop in Thomas' stomach as he straightened up and leaned forward to count his bet. He went through the pile twice to be sure, then swallowed and croaked, "Eighteen fifty." That was more than he had made in a week as manager of the dockyard. He decided he would refuse any more invitations to engage in gambling. He ought to make a good profit on his slaves, but that payoff was still months away.

The plantation owner counted out several bills and a pile of coins and placed them carefully in the center of the table. He then looked expectedly at Henri Richards who was gazing a bit cross-eyed at his hand.

"Well, gentlemen," Richards said in his rich drawl, "I think you're both bluffing." He ran his fingers through his ash blonde hair and finished with a swipe at the fuzz above his lips that marked the beginnings of a moustache. "I'll raise you another five dollars."

Thomas raised his hands in surrender, then looked at Chastain who was unsuccessfully hiding his concern by whistling tunelessly. He knew the man hated to lose and often kept playing long after he should quit.

The silence was so prolonged that Thomas was on the verge of closing his eyes when Richards broke it by leaning close to his opponent and saying, "You can win this hand without spending another dime, Cousin Paul," he said, grinning.

"How's that?" the older man asked.

"Give me that new quadroon gal you picked up at auction for the length of my stay. If your hand wins, you get twenty-three fifty and a girl who's broken in and not green when you sell her in Natchez."

Thomas jerked up suddenly. "Hey, she's half mine."

"Now Thomas, I know that," reasoned Chastain. "But he's right about having her broken in. I'll tell you what. How about if I lose, I'll give you five bucks for letting Henri have his fun."

* * *

Early the next morning Manny woke from a sound sleep in his pile of straw near the oat bin. He and Job, along with the newly christened Jim, had all abandoned the loft to Lily not long after her arrival. The housemaids and Jethro all claimed beds in corners of the big house, but Lily seemed to prefer the solitude of the hay mow.

He lay still and listened to the subtle noises of the night. The melodic hum of crickets and tree frogs filtered in from outside and near him in the darkness one of the horses paced in his stall. Then faintly from above he detected a high keening note, drawn out and increasing in pitch. There was a moment's pause, and it began anew.

Lily. He sat up now, alert and wary. The younger boys seemed undisturbed nearby, their slow breathing barely detectable. Carefully he got up and stealthily made his way to the loft ladder, the moon's light barely illuminating his path. He put his hand out to find the slats nailed to one of the beams that served as steps. Above him the whimpering had stopped. After a lengthy silence, whispered words, incoherent at this distance, drifted down, rapid, intense, and importuning.

Silently he began to climb. The whisperings continued until his head rose from the hole in the roof that was the mow's flooring.

"Lily?" he said in a loud whisper. The murmuring abruptly stopped in a sudden intake of breath. There was a lengthy silence broken only by a sniff and a rustling noise.

"Who's there?" she hissed from a dark corner.

"It's me, Manny," he answered back in a voice he hoped wouldn't awaken the sleepers below. "Can I help you?" was all he could think to say.

"It's too late," Lily's voice gasped out in another sob.

Manny puzzled over this response. He couldn't see much, but as his hand touched the floorboards of the opening, he began to feel vibrations as Lily's body began to shake.

"Did you get snake bit?" he asked, starting to climb further up in a rush.

"No! Stop, Manny. I don't want you up here."

He froze with one foot on the top slat.

"It weren't no snake that got me. It was Miss Aimee's Henri. I waked up and he was on top of me." There was a protracted pause that ended in a sniff. "He

93

put his hand over my mouth and said he was gonna 'break me in.' I didn't know what he was talkin' about 'til…" her voice faded away to be replaced by keening and more shaking.

Manny's mind raced. He'd heard about such things, but he'd only lived with Mr. Konkel who'd never taken such liberties with his slaves. "You want me to sleep up here from now on?" He paused. "For protection?" he added.

Lily sniffed again. "It won't do no good. He told me I was to come to his room every night he's here or else he'll have me beat. Said he'd won the right in a poker game with Master Chastain. I can't do it. I can't!" she said, breaking into sobs again, almost hysterical.

"Lily?" Manny whispered after she'd quieted again. "I'm gonna go fetch you some cool water in a bucket and a rag and some soap. Would you like that?"

"Yes," she answered in a voice that was barely audible.

A few minutes later he was carefully balancing a bucket on his head while navigating the slats. When he got near the top, he placed the bucket on the loft floor and then hesitated. "Lily, can I come a little closer?" he said in a loud whisper.

"I guess, but just a few steps in. I aint fit to look at right now."

Manny rose and crawled into the loft a yard or so and placed the bucket closer to Lily who was a pale blur in the corner. He spoke to the blur in a low voice. "They's meanin' to sell you to one of them brothels down south. I heered that kitchen gal talkin' about it to the cook. Did you know that?"

There was another long silence. "I know they sold us as "fancy gals," and that meant men would buy us for somethin' like that. But I been hopin' that…"

"Yes, well you can give up hopin'. That's what they bought you for so that means men like Henri'll be comin' to you night and day for what you got tonight. If I was a girl, I'd rather die than live like that."

"I'd rather die too," she whispered, "but how? And aint it a sin to kill yourself?"

"Well, I don't know nothin' about that, but I know I aint willin' to go no further south than this here county. Master Thomas says he'll make me his personal servant and I won't have to be no cotton picker, but I don't care. I aint goin to L'usiana."

"How you gonna do that?" she asked across the dark space.

"When they head back to their home, they's got to get to the Ohio River first to get down to the Missi'ppi. That means they're gonna be floatin' right there on the Ohio, the River Jordan, as they calls it, for several hours, and I's gonna find a way to jump ship and take off to Indiana." He paused a few heart-beats and then added, "And you's gonna come with me."

* * *

Yvonne got wind of Henri's poker prize through the usual route — the servants. She overheard her mother whispering to Tabby not to say a word if she found any of Lily's things in Henri's room and after wheedling the truth out of Jethro, she had the whole story. She admitted to feeling some satisfaction in finding proof that her assessment of her sister's beau was accurate. But along with the increased revulsion towards Henri, she felt a smidgen of sympathy towards Aimee, and compassion for Lily. She wondered how long it would take for her sister to discover the truth.

The following Monday Yvonne sat in the parlor pretending to study her French, a bare foot tucked under her skirts. Every few moments she would peek over her book to watch the tableau of Lily gingerly buffing Aimee's nails while Henri looked on from a cushioned chair nearby. Aimee was prattling on about how she loved the new parlor Henri had designed for his family's home, Holly Hills.

"I had the most delightful letter from your mother just last week," she gushed. "She sent me samples of the curtains and upholstery. That deep gold with the russet dahlias and swirls is just divine. And the recessed columns with the Greek statuary she wrote about. I can't wait to see it for myself. Ouch! I swear Lily, you've nicked my cuticle again," she scolded, drawing back her hand and slapping the girl across the cheek with the other.

Yvonne looked up to see Lily biting her lip and staring at the marble tabletop.

"Now, now Aimee," said Henri standing up. "You're too harsh on little Lily, here." He walked over and laid his plump hand with its ostentatious onyx ring on the girl's sleeve. The familiarity sickened Yvonne and she watched Lily shrink as the hand lingered several seconds —long enough for her sister to take notice.

"Poor little Lily! Well, what about me?" spat Aimee, her blond single ringlets swaying. You're always sticking up for her and praising her. She's mine. I can treat her any way I like." She rose from her chair, nearly toppling a vase of flowers, and reached over and struck Lily on the chin with her folded fan. "She's nothing! She's less than nothing; she's just property and I can't wait for Father to sell her!"

Aimee, her usually pale face now red and streaked with tears," stumbled past Yvonne on her way out of the room. She glanced briefly down at her. "'Vonne? You wanted her? You can have her!"

Yvonne, stunned into silence for once, along with Lily and Henri froze in place, not even drawing breath, as Aimee's heeled boots stomped up the stairs, faded away and ended with the sharp bang of a slammed door.

Chapter Eleven

*I*t was early September when Yvonne told Lily it was time to start packing her trunks for the trip to Louisiana. Immediately Lily's insides were twisted in a bewildering fusion of relief and dread. Even though Henri Richards had left the house weeks ago, Lily still imagined she heard his voice, smelled his acrid cigarette smoke, and felt his hands pinning her to the canopied bed in the guest room. Enclosed in the heavy wine-colored bed curtains in the stifling heat of the upper floor she had felt suffocated. When she'd dared cry out, he stuffed his scented handkerchief in her mouth, nearly gagging her. Just remembering those nights of shame caused her heartbeat to quicken and her palms to sweat.

Leaving this house was all she'd thought about during the weeks since, but she was pinning her hopes on Manny's cleverness and knowledge of the country around a place called Carrollton, where he assured her their best chance of escape would come. He'd insisted she not worry about the details but work on playing her part.

Her job was to be obedient and pleasant and get in the good graces of Yvonne Chastain so the girl would trust her completely as a fully competent lady's maid. Manny's role was to earn the trust of Thomas Mercier and act as an ideal valet and manservant. They had practiced their "Yes, Miss Yvonne" and "Yes Master Thomas" with exaggerated subservient attitudes in the privacy of the loft until they both doubled over with laughter.

Today, the afternoon before the departure, she was opening a drawer of Yvonne's wardrobe as her mistress came in the door, her pinafore corners held aloft.

"There! I've been all over the house and property looking for my things," Yvonne gasped, all out of breath from tearing up the staircase in her usual manner. "Mother is right. I'm hopeless at keeping track of things, Lily. Just look at all this," she said spilling out a pile of items on the bed.

Lily turned and saw two pencils, three hair ribbons, a small purse, a button hook, two folded papers, a book, and a silver bracelet. "Yes, you've found a lot of things, Miss Yvonne. Do you want me to pack them?

"Oh, I only really want the letters, book, and bracelet. In my room at home, I've got lots of the rest. You can have them if you'd like or give them to one of the other servants. I don't care. Now let's see what else is left in this wardrobe." She started opening drawers, tossing some items on the floor: a pair of knitted stockings, a mended glove and its mate, a hair comb with a broken tooth, and finally a flannel petticoat.

"Ugh. I can't stand to even look at those heavy things. Mother made us bring them in case it got cold up here. She's always freezing if it gets below eighty degrees. Seriously, it's been hot here, but nothing like New Orleans. If we didn't get winds from the Gulf, I'd die of heat stroke even in my cotton underclothes."

"What do you want me to do with the things you don't want to take? Leave them here for next summer?"

"Heavens no! Throw them out, give them away, keep them. I don't care," said Yvonne, who began placing her nightcap and gowns at the bottom of the trunk.

"'Vonne!" came a squeal from down the hall. The girl looked up expectantly at the sound of her sister's voice, but Lily quickly started gathering the unwanted items from the floor and bed.

"Excuse me, Miss Yvonne. I need to go out for a bit, if it's alright with you," she said, hoping to avoid the vindictive Aimee who'd made no pretense of her jealousy.

"Sure, Lily. Take your time."

Clutching the pile of discards to her chest, Lily opened the door and caught a glimpse of Aimee, clasping a paper and reading it as she walked towards Yvonne's room. Lily quickly headed off in the other direction before she was spotted.

* * *

Manny closely followed Thomas the next morning as he climbed the stairs to the hurricane deck of the steamboat Blue Wing. Just as he reached the top, the whistle gave a deafening last warning accompanied with blasts of steam clouds that the departure time had arrived. Nearby a pair of slaves were busy maneuvering the boom to raise the platform off the bow. The Chastain family, along with Lily,

Tabby, and Jethro, were standing by the railing. The mother and daughters were waving to some women on the shore.

Lily, Manny noticed, was gripping the railing with one hand and clutching a cloth bag tied in a knot in the other. Last night she'd quietly confessed her fears about the trip and all it portended to him in the loft as they ate supper. Now he quickly met her eye and nodded, a gesture he hoped would encourage her as he felt the vessel pull away into the river's current.

"I got the darkies all settled below," Thomas reported to Paul Chastain who was returning his pocket watch to its place.

"What's it like down there?" Paul asked.

"Hot as the blazes. The stokers were really shoveling it in. Ours are in the stern with a few others and none too happy about it. They keep complaining about the stench from the other darkies and the heat."

"Oh, they'll settle in soon enough. Martha," he said turning to his wife, "let's go down to our rooms and settle in. You too, girls."

The group turned and headed toward the stairs. Yvonne had positioned herself close to Thomas and when she hesitated to gather her skirts to descend, both Manny and Lily bumped into her.

"Lily, give me some room! You're always breathing down my neck," she said, with an eye on Thomas who had turned at the outburst. "Why don't you go find something to do? Put that bundle down somewhere and enjoy the view. You can see lots of animals and scenery. You did say it was your first time on a boat." She turned to Thomas. "Mr. Mercier, would you be so kind to help me down the steps. I feel a bit dizzy just now."

"Why sure, Miss Yvonne," said Thomas, with a bit of a grin. Manny was noticing how the girl was growing out of her childish figure and wondered if his master had too. Thomas turned to him. "Manny, you've been on this boat before, but locked below. Why don't you and Lily explore the Blue Wing? Don't go jumping overboard now," he added, smiling at Yvonne Chastain, who took his arm.

"Why yes, Master Thomas. I sure would like that. Thank you, Master Thomas," Manny said bobbing his head and grinning from ear to ear. He glanced at Lily and winked. "And there's no way you'd catch me puttin' a foot in that river. I don't have no notion of drowning today or any day."

"Thank you also, Mistress Yvonne," Lily said, nodding at the girl with a shy smile.

The pair stood silently side by side as Thomas and Yvonne started down the steps. Manny watched while the couple descended and turned out of sight, then looked at Lily and smiled.

* * *

After several moments watching the red paddle wheel churn up the muddy river water at the stern, Lily took a turn around the deck below with Manny, taking note of the ornate furnishings and décor in the common rooms. Manny said he'd spent his first trip aboard chained by the ankles on the lower deck. Many of the slaves, he told her, didn't need to be chained as they had a deathly fear of water, but his reputation as a runaway had made Mercier extra cautious.

The teen looked around as they stopped to gaze at the view from the bow, then lowered his voice and whispered in Lily's ear. "I been workin' hard ever since to get Master Thomas to believe I've gave up on runnin' off. I tells him being his manservant is like a dream come true for me and I can't wait to see New Orleans and the ocean." He threw back his head and laughed, his white teeth shining in his dark face. Lily smiled up at him.

"I liked the way you was grabbin' on to the rail up there when the boat took off," he chuckled. "You looked white as a ghost. You just keep on makin' them think you's too scared to even think about getting' wet."

Lily went quiet. It was in fact her first boat ride, but she had spent many happy hours splashing in Jessamine Creek, even in deep pools. She wasn't frightened of being on the water, but the motion of the boat had made her feel queasy and a bit dizzy and her stomach still hadn't settled.

"Let's see the bottom deck," she suggested.

"Sure thing. That's there's gonna be our jumpin' off spot. I's got to find Silas and see when he's free for a chat."

"Who's Silas?" she asked as they moved onto the deck.

"He's the man with the plan, Lily. Our first stop on the railroad to freedom."

* * *

"Lily, get up. I need you," Yvonne said, nudging her foot into Lily's ribs.

Lily sat up quickly from her bed on the floor of Yvonne and Aimee's room. Yvonne, white nightcap hovering in the dim room, was leaning over the bed staring down at her.

"Yes, Miss Yvonne. What is it?"

"I want you to go to the kitchens and get me a glass of milk for my stomach," she whispered. "Make sure you look in the dining room and see what Mr. Mercier is doing, then come back and tell me."

In the darkness Lily allowed her eyes to roll a bit. Her mistress was obsessed with Thomas Mercier. She followed him around the boat half the day and wanted Lily to spy on him frequently the rest of the time. The only good part about it was it allowed her to see Manny and exchanged a word or two. When

Yvonne wasn't shadowing Thomas, she was endlessly discussing wedding and trousseau plans with her sister and their mother. Henri Richards had proposed to Aimee in a letter just before they left, and a big event was being planned for the engagement announcement for the fall with a wedding in the spring.

These planning sessions gave Lily time to think about what would happen in the short time they had left on the Blue Wing. She vacillated between prayer and worry. Manny had told her to put the future in his hands but refused to give her any of the details. The speculation of when and how they were to escape filled her with anxiety.

"Well, go on. Hurry up," Yvonne said, interrupting her thoughts with a gentle push.

Lily stood up and hurriedly wrapped a kerchief around her head. She hadn't been in the habit of using one until they got on the boat. So many of the white passengers had asked Yvonne and her family if she was a relative that Martha Chastain had insisted she wear a headwrap.

Slave garb in place, Lily opened the door a few inches and slipped into the darkness.

* * *

The drone of male voices, and the clink of dominoes on the highly polished dining table had almost put Manny to sleep when the cessation of talk jerked his head up, alert. The half dozen men who were gathered around the game near him were all looking at the door where Lily stood blinking in the lantern light.

"Excuse me, sirs. I's been sent to fetch Mistress Chastain some milk," she said, head down, eyes squinting.

"That's fine, Lily. You go right on through," said Thomas, nodding from his chair.

"Is she yours?" asked the man nearest Thomas, eyes hungrily following the girl as she pushed through the swinging door to the kitchen.

Manny's eyes narrowed and he clamped his mouth shut tight as he listened.

"Yes sir," answered Thomas. "Got her for six seventy-five in Lexington three months ago. Went halves with Chastain. Kind of skinny at first, but she's filled out nicely. I expect she'll fetch twelve hundred at least down in Natchez."

"Oh. I thought she was one of Chastain's house girls," said the man, tugging at his beard thoughtfully.

"Oh no. Miss Yvonne just snatched her up as a maid for the time being. Pretending she's a grown lady. I expect she'll be off to boarding school this fall, which will be fine with me. She shadows me like a lost pup."

Lily had stood quietly in the kitchen with a tin cup listening to the last part of the conversation. When she came into the room, Manny stood up.

Thomas, who often forgot about the presence of his manservant, said, "Manny, why don't you see Lily back to her cabin. It's dark out there and we don't want her to spill her milk, now do we?"

"No sir, Master Thomas. I's be glad to help Miss Lily," said Manny with a touch of eagerness to his voice, hoping he sounded like a dog being allowed out for a walk. He turned and followed her out.

* * *

As soon as the pair was out of earshot, Manny gently took Lily's arm and pulled her aside. "Be ready to jump tomorrow," he said quietly after checking the walkway.

"Tomorrow?" she whispered back, dread filling her stomach.

"Yes. There's gonna be a loud ringing of the bell that signals to the captain that somethin's wrong in the engine room. Keep your ears open for that. They'll make all of us slaves go to the bottom deck. Come and find me then."

Lily wondered how her friend knew so much. Her heart was racing, keeping time with the rapid rolling of the paddle wheel behind her. "What time? What about George and Joe?" They're down there. Can't we find a way to help them escape too?"

Manny closed his eyes and let out a hefty sigh. "I don't even know what time. That'll be up to Silas. And Lily, we've been over this before. We've got a better chance with just the two of us. Those boys will slow us down. Besides, do they even know how to swim?"

Lily shrugged silently and a tear rolled down her cheek. She had gotten attached to the cousins, especially Joe, who refused to answer to Jim whenever he could get away with it. Just eight years old, he had allowed her to baby him a bit. She hated to think of him being separated from George, his last link with family, but knew the chances of their staying together were slim.

"I'm sorry, Lily. We gots to think only about ourselves now — especially you. Remember what you're running from?"

"I'll never forget," she remarked through clenched teeth.

"Just be sure and act natural tomorrow. Don't let on that anything's different. Just trust me. This is our only chance. Once we get way down the Miss'ipi, there ain't no way we can make it this far north again."

Lily gulped, then nodded. "Alright, Manny. I'll pray and trust you to lead the way."

* * *

101

Moments later Lily slipped back into the dark cabin room. Yvonne immediately sat up.

"What took you so long?" she hissed.

Lily held out the milk and Yvonne took it and set it on a table distractedly.

"What was Thomas doing in there? Was he worried? Did he ask if I was sick?"

Lily wasn't about to repeat what she'd overheard Thomas say so she just answered, "No, Miss Yvonne. He was playin' a game with some other men. He just told me to go get what I wanted and then I left. That's all."

Yvonne let out a long sigh and laid back down, covering herself up to the chin with the blanket.

Lily sat on the rug on the floor and laid down. Her mind was racing like the second hand on a clock. She tried to slow it down by reciting the Lord's Prayer silently.

"Lily?" came her mistress's voice.

"Yes?"

"Was it cold out there? I swear I'm freezing. Mother says we're nearly to the Ohio. I'll be so glad to head back south."

The Ohio! Lily recalled all the tales she'd heard in private conversations with other slaves over the years. Some called it the Jordan River, like the one in the Bible that the Israelites had to cross to get to the Promised Land. How would they get across that river, she wondered?

"Lily, are you asleep already?"

She feigned a small snore and lay still as a stone until she heard Yvonne give an exasperated sigh followed by silence. When Yvonne's breathing was as slow and steady as Aimee's, Lily reached out a hand and pulled her bag out from under the bed. Her hand reached in and felt the familiar items: a change of underthings, a comb, her pinafore, and the blue dress she'd been sold in. Added to that had been Yvonne's castoffs: pencils, hair ribbons, coin purse, a button hook, knitted stockings, a pair of gloves, a hair comb, and warm petticoat. She didn't know if she would ever use any of it, but the bag, just an old pillowcase Mrs. Chastain had given her, held everything she had.

"God? Dear Jesus," she whispered, "Please help me and Manny get away tomorrow. Help me to be brave and run fast. Send some angels to help us and hide us. And please don't let them send dogs. I is so scared of dogs. Please, dear Jesus. Please. Amen." Tears were welling up in her eyes and she quickly brushed them away and began reciting the twenty-third Psalm until sleep took her.

* * *

Manny's nerves were raw by teatime the next afternoon. He had stayed clear of the lower deck as Silas had demanded, but he didn't understand what the man was waiting for. Twice he'd seen Lily tailing Miss Yvonne around the decks, her eyes darting quickly to his. He had answered with the slightest shake of the head and passed her by without a word.

There was excited talk among the men about news of more gold strikes in California; Austria using aerial balloons to attack Florence, Italy; and the future of railroads, which one man predicted would be the death knell of riverboat travel.

"The steam locomotive can travel much faster than a steamboat, gentlemen," pontificated the man around whom several were gathered on the top deck, including Thomas and Manny. Of course, there's occasional stops for water and at stations, but the speeds are terrific and there's no delays from these infernal dams and locks! Two yesterday and another one coming up here soon. Without them we'd make it to the Ohio in less than 24 hours."

"Without them," put in another man, "we had to wait for floods to get up this river. I find them a marvel, not a nuisance, sir."

Manny nodded in agreement, not that anyone noticed. He had thrilled to see the engineering of the locks that used oxen to pull up the gates to let in the water that raised and lowered the boats. Twice there were boats ahead of them, allowing the passengers to watch the workings from a distance, though several, like this man, had cursed the delay. He looked at the sun, now headed toward the horizon and wondered how and if the locks were worked in the dark. They had never done it in the dark on the trip up the river back in May and he doubted if it was possible.

Suddenly, above the murmur of conversations a bell overhead clanged furiously. Speakers froze in midsentence and looked around for an explanation. The bell's ringing voice sounded urgent, a cry for help.

"That's the bell from the engine room," said Paul Chastain, looking up and pointing to the bell on the top deck. "It's a signal to the captain. Something could be wrong down there."

His remark was overheard by his wife, standing a few yards away. She gasped and put a hand to her mouth and the other women surrounding her began to whisper together fearfully. Everyone had heard of horrific steamboat accidents that killed and maimed scores of travelers without warning when the boilers exploded.

For Manny, the ringing bell dumped a different load of anxiety on him. He knew it wasn't an impending disaster, but the signal he'd been waiting for all day. All the men were watching the pilot house. Manny's eyes followed theirs and saw the captain hurrying from it to the staircase. He then looked around the hurricane deck for Lily. After a few heart pounding moments, he found her near a crowd of women. She was searching for him as well and when their eyes met, he raised his eyebrows to let her know the time had come.

* * *

After five anxious minutes the captain appeared on the top deck and announced that there was concern about a boiler and for safety's sake, they were going to head for shore and disembark to allow the fires to go out and the boiler to be inspected. Lilly was listening closely with the rest of the passengers. Fortunately, he said, they were just a half mile from the lock station, and most of them could shelter in the lockkeeper's house and buildings there until they could continue up the river.

Chastain quieted down his wife and daughters' fears by telling them it was just a precaution. Yvonne and Aimee sent Lily to fetch a few things from their rooms and while there, Lily grabbed her bundle from under the bed. As she turned to leave, she impulsively grabbed Yvonne's slippers and stuffed them into her own bag, quickly tying the knot and looping it around her wrist.

Back on deck, she handed the sisters their things.

"You slaves are not getting off the boat, Lily," their mother said, pointing to the sack. "You, Tabby, Manny, Jethro — all of you will go to the lower deck storage room with the rest of them."

"But, missus, that's right near that boiler! I don't wanna be blowed up, Missus Martha," begged Tabby.

"There's no time to chain all of you and you can't be trusted unshackled on shore so close to the North. No, you'll all stay on board," said Paul Chastain with a tone of finality.

Overhead the crew could be heard readying the platform for lowering. The eastern shore was approaching. Passengers were heading toward the bow, while their servants were running down the stairs. Shouts of "hurry, hurry!" could be heard above the noise of the engine and paddlewheel. Lily headed toward the staircase, feeling like she was in a nightmare. Just as she took her first step down, she felt a hand on her shoulder. It was Manny.

"This is it, Lily," he whispered over her shoulder as she continued downward. "Silas has done it. It will be easy to slip off in all this hubbub. We won't hesitate. We won't say a word. We'll just slip overboard and swim to the other shore."

Down below, the noise from the boiler was deafening. Cries from the stern where the slaves were kept locked up rose and fell. The boat jarred as it hit the shallows and the platform began to lower. Frantic voices overhead mixed with the calls of crewman going about their duties. Amid the chaos, Manny grabbed Lily's hand and led her to the railing.

They both looked around and saw that no one was paying any mind. Manny climbed over the railing. Holding onto the boat with one hand he held the other out to Lily. She reached for it, sat on the rail and he helped her over. Then closing her eyes, she stepped off with him into the water.

Part Three
Southeastern Indiana

Chapter Twelve

*I*n the early morning darkness, Jane put her hand out to feel for Seth before turning over in bed. The empty space stirred her into wakefulness, and she remembered that he had gone to Jefferson County to the abolition meeting. She lay listening to the stillness of the dark cabin. Lydia, Frank, and Bessie, the hound, were silent. From the open window she could hear nature's nightly symphony of owl hoots, coyote calls, tree frog croaks, and cricket songs.

She missed the sound of the restless movements of Alice and her occasional gentle coos, her unique way of snoring. Closing her eyes, she let tears fall onto her pillow, unchecked. She worked hard in the daylight to put on a brave face for her family. It was a skill she'd learned from her unflappable mother, who came from Puritan stock. But how she missed her sunny baby girl! She could see her now on that last morning before she fell ill – splashing around in the creek, getting drenched and grubby, and laughing at anything and everything.

Jane's throat tightened and ached. The tears increased, and she turned her face into the pillow to muffle a sob. She placed her palm over her swelling womb and thought about the new life inside her. Forty-one was more than old enough to be a grandmother and here she was pregnant for the seventh time. She knew women who'd gone through a dozen or more pregnancies and she'd also known women who had died giving birth. It was always a risk, but one worth taking. Life was so precious. How Alice would have loved having a baby to play with!

"Father, protect this tiny one," she whispered. "Let him or her grow and live to serve you and bless this house once again with laughter. Protect Seth and the others as well as they travel and plan together how to help people. If you can use me in this endeavor, please do it. I want your will. I want to be your hands and feet and your maidservant. I love you, Father. Amen."

* * *

The church building at Neil's Creek was relatively new. Seth studied the workmanship of the structure and found it sound. He was seated three rows from the front between Pastor Ned Johnston and Matthew Martin. Robert Hillman, next to Ned, completed the representatives from Flat Rock. There was a hum of excited chatter as men, and a few women, were filing in and finding seats.

"Mr. Cowper?" Seth turned and found the friendly smile of the undertaker, Mr. Tielmann, grinning at him from two rows back.

"Well, hello, Fred," said Seth, standing up and turning around to reach the man's outstretched hand. His pale bald head was reflecting the morning light coming from the nearby eastern window. "So glad you could make it."

"I've brought a couple of friends with me of like mind from Napoleon and Sand Creek" he said, indicating two men to his right who both nodded genially at Seth.

Seth nodded back, grinning, then quickly sat back down when the banging of a gavel from the lectern silenced the crowd. A tall man, whom Seth assumed was the minister of the church, welcomed the group. He reported that there were representatives of five counties present: Jefferson, Clark, Scott, Jennings, and Ripley. "I especially want to welcome our black brothers out of Madison to this gathering," he said, nodding toward the back of the building.

Seth craned his neck along with most of the attendees and saw a half dozen black men sitting in the back row. A few raised their hand to accept the light applause that broke out. To his astonishment there were also men, black and white, standing behind the last bench and leaning in from the windows.

"We welcome you all. But we are not here, friends, to socialize," said the man, instantly quieting the whispers. "We are here to discuss a dark and treacherous task we at Neil's Creek have taken on for God's kingdom, and to solicit your help in that task. Men, women, children, and even tiny babes are captives, bound in chains even, just 10 miles from where we sit today. They are being sold away from their loved ones to the slave markets down in the deep south, where the hope of escape dies. More and more they are running, crossing the nearby Ohio, seeking the help of people of faith and conviction. People like you men and women gathered here today."

Seth closed his eyes and ears momentarily to the speaker. He thought of Jane, Lydia, Frank, and the new little one expected next spring. He pictured them in chains, sold to strangers, and forced apart forever. He looked around at the grave faces near him. He searched his heart and knew he could not turn his back on anyone who came to his door seeking help – whether escaping slaves or these Christian brothers and sisters who were asking for aid.

"Father, help calm my fears. I *will* do this. I *must* do this if I am to follow your will and my own conscience," he prayed silently, feeling a peace wash over him, an unmistakable sign from the Holy Spirit. Impulsively he reached out and grabbed the hands of Matthew and Ned on either side of him. They both looked at him and he met the eye of each of them in turn and nodded slightly.

* * *

As soon as Frank had done his barn chores, he hurried back into the cabin with the milk pail and set it down on the table. He produced four eggs from his bulging shirt pockets and held them up for Jane to see. She stood stirring cornmeal into the boiling kettle making mush for breakfast over the crackling fire. "Look, Ma. Four eggs today," he said, laying them carefully next to the milk.

"What a blessing. I was hoping those hens would start earning their keep again," she said, still vigorously stirring the bubbling mass. "Now I can make a nice treat for your Pa's supper tonight when he gets home. Rebekah says she thinks they should make it back here by dark."

"Where's Lydia?" Frank quickly washed his hands in the basin and then pulled out a chair and sat. He felt grown up being the only male in the house and responsible for everyone.

"Out fetching water, as usual. She should be back by now. I'm going to need more soon, or this mush is going to turn into cement. She dawdles down there more often now, it seems."

Frank thought he knew why Lydia often lingered at the creek. He didn't want to break his sister's confidences, but he feared no good would come from her secret "accidental" meetings with Will.

"Do you need me to do anything special today Ma?"

Jane kept stirring while frequently adding water from a tin cup in her other hand.

"I think we can pick that last patch of corn and put it in shocks. Then tonight when Seth's home we can have a regular shucking party around the fire with persimmon pudding and cream to celebrate his homecoming."

"Really, ma? That sounds fine. I love your persimmon pudding. Want me to pick the fruit too?"

"No, I think Lydia can manage that with a ladder. If she ever gets back here with the water, that is."

Just then they heard Lydia's sure and light steps outside the door. Frank scrambled out of the chair to help her inside with the loaded buckets.

"Sorry Mama," she sputtered, handing him one bucket and bringing the other to the fireplace. Jane quickly pulled the kettle away from the red-hot embers and dipped the tin in the water.

"We'll all be sorry if this mush isn't fit to eat. I'll pour this water in slowly. You stir. It'll take both hands. Let that and cleaning the pot later be your penance," Jane said in a rush, handing Lydia the spoon.

Behind them, Frank sat back down and observed. His mother always said, "It takes two people to make mush," but he'd never paid much attention. As the cornmeal thickened, it took muscle to mix it properly, so someone had to add the meal or more water while the another stirred until it reached the right consistency.

"That should do it. Put it back on the fire now and keep stirring another four or five minutes," instructed Jane. Lydia did as she was told, pausing a second to wipe sweat from her brow. Her mother sat down quickly beside Frank and put her head on her crossed arms on the table.

"Are you alright, Mama?" Frank asked, placing a hand gently on her shoulders.

His mother looked up at him. From her position at the table and the weary look in her eyes, Frank saw, possibly for the first time, how small and fragile his mother was. He thought about her age and condition and anger welled inside him.

"What took you so long at the creek, Lydia?" he asked, looking across at his sister and noticing that the back of her skirt was damp and sprinkled with sand. She glanced over at him. Frank's mouth was pursed tightly, one eyebrow was raised, and his blue eyes were shooting daggers.

"Oh, I guess I got distracted. I'm always looking for fossils and arrowheads, you know."

"Did you find any?" Frank's tone was dubious.

"No. I thought I did, but after digging a bit I found out I was wrong." Lydia shot a look at Jane, who was still resting her head, eyes closed. Her eyes then darted back to Frank with a puzzled look.

"Did you see anybody there?" he asked, enjoying baiting her. He'd been annoyed with Lydia for her continued lies and deceit and for involving him. Now he felt furious at the thought that her frequent dalliances with Will was wearing on their mother's health.

"No, of course not! Who would be at our spring at this time of the morning?" protested Lydia, her face turning an even deeper red than it already was from hovering over the steaming kettle.

111

Frank opened his mouth to answer when his mother suddenly sat up and spoke.

"That's enough, Lydia. Go wash up now. Frank, please get out the bowls and spoons and the maple syrup. I'll serve."

* * *

Seth didn't return until after seven. In the twilight, Bessie was the first to hear the horses' hooves on the creek and alerted everyone with her howls. Before her children could react, Jane slipped out of the cabin, walking swiftly down in the dim light. She felt as excited as a girl about to meet her beau as she headed down the familiar path. She and Seth hadn't been separated since their wedding 22 years ago.

As the colors of the fall day slid into the grays of night, she spotted a lantern's light below in the hollow and the sound of wagon wheels creaking.

"Seth, is that you?" she called.

"Well now, that's quite a welcome, Brother Cowper," she heard the pastor chuckle as he handed down Seth's satchel.

Seth steadied his hat on his head as he stepped away from the vehicle and turned to wave goodbye to the other men.

"Hello, Pastor Ned," called out Jane as she stepped from the trees into the clearing. "Evening, Matthew. I suppose Robert's already been dropped off?" She grasped Seth's hand and gave it a warm squeeze.

"Yes, Sister Cowper," the pastor said, sitting carefully back down beside Matthew. "We are all glad to be back home. It's been a long journey, but very informative and encouraging. We'll have much to discuss over the next few days and weeks."

"Goodnight, friends," Seth called again, beginning to head toward home.

"Say hello to Mother and Rebekah for me," called Jane as she turned to follow.

The couple took several steps hand in hand in silence. When the horses' hooves began to clatter again on the creek bed, Seth stopped. He turned to Jane and embraced her. She nuzzled his neck with her forehead and kissed him on the cheek.

"My how I've missed you," Jane began, only to realize that her husband was saying the same thing simultaneously. They both chuckled and held each other a bit longer, breathing in the familiar scents and feelings of each other's bodies.

"Any signs of our new little one yet?" Seth asked, placing his calloused hand on her abdomen.

"Seth, it's only been two days since you saw me last," she almost giggled. "I do think I've felt some stirring. I keep thinking how excited Alice would have been at the idea of a baby in the house."

That thought sobered them both and they continued their walk home in near silence. Then Jane spoke up. "I've got so much to tell you, but it will keep until tomorrow. Tonight, I've got a surprise! Guess what's keeping warm for after supper? She barely paused before blurting out, "Persimmon pudding! The hens are laying again, and Lydia picked a half bushel of fruit."

"Well, if that just doesn't make this the best homecoming ever," said Seth. "I'm going to have to go away more often."

"No, you don't," Jane replied, squeezing his hand again.

Their conversation came to a halt as they neared the cabin. Bessie rushed out yapping, followed by Frank who was talking a blue streak. Lydia stood quietly in the doorway, a lantern held high, illuminating a welcoming smile. With Seth by her side, home felt like home again.

Chapter Thirteen

"How much longer do you think you can keep this up?" Frank asked the next morning as he waited for Lydia by the outhouse, knowing she could hear him through the chinks. Lydia stood frozen with her hand on the latch. She'd just been about to exit, the two empty water pails stood waiting by the door. She closed her eyes wishing Frank would just run off to hunt or fish like he'd done for weeks after Allie died.

"Shush! Pa will hear you in the barn."

"I don't care," he hissed. "You'd better come clean about these secret meetings with Will or stop it altogether. Ma looked near to faintin' yesterday before you got back with the water. You need to help her more instead of foolin' around at the creek."

Lydia's rushed out the door, grabbed the pails and marched down the path toward the spring. Her mouth was set, and her eyes narrowed as she pushed past Frank who turned and followed her. Halfway to the creek a twig cracked under his foot, and she turned around.

"Leave me be! Go away and quit bossing me!" she shouted and continued on her way.

Frank didn't stop but caught up with her and grabbed for her elbow. She whirled around and looked directly up into his eyes as he was standing slightly uphill from her. Her mouth was opening for a retort, but then she froze as if startled by his uncustomary aggressiveness. Her gaze, like a doe caught in a rifle's site, calmed his ire down a notch.

"Listen, Sis, I just can't stand the thought of Ma and Pa hurt again. You know they'll never allow you to marry Will, if that's what you're thinkin'. And if you're thinkin' of runnin' off and doin' it anyway, why that's even worse. You know they're gonna find out. You can't keep this up. The stress is killin' me and I've got school to think of startin' Monday."

Lydia, who had been listening carefully to her brother at first, now took her free left hand and pushed his shoulder away from her.

"Oh, so I'm stressin' you. Poor thing. Wish all I had to think of was school. What about what I want? Does anybody care about that? I'm nearly 17 years old and I've got nothin' to look forward to but chores day after day and then helpin' with the baby when it comes. Maybe I want my own house and my own baby. Will says his pa's got land promised to him once he's married and he'll be a full partner at the store and mill. Now leave me alone. It's none of your business what I do."

Frank was stunned by the shove and the torrent of words spewing from his sister. He didn't move a muscle as she whirled back around and headed down the path and out of sight.

* * *

Will didn't show at the spring. Lydia never knew if he'd be there waiting or sneak up on her while her guard was down. Their once-or-twice-a-week meetings in the late afternoon had increased to at least four a week on average. Sometimes he'd be there in the early morning like now. She filled the buckets and then sat down on the dewy bank.

So far, they'd kept their encounters secret from all but Frank. Will said his stepmother had teased him about having a girl when his excuses about hunting became inadequate. Lydia had begged him to keep mum, saying it was more romantic when it was just between the two of them.

The truth was more prose than poetry. She loved the attention from Will. She had allowed him to hold her hand and even put an arm about her shoulders as they sat and watched the tiny fish chase each other around. But she had artfully avoided any further physical contact and Will had been the gentleman she'd hoped he'd be. Still, she knew her parents would disapprove and pressure her to end it if the truth was discovered.

Yesterday morning she was telling him how happy she felt. "I think there may be a God after all. My best dreams are coming true Will, with you and the baby coming."

He had quickly responded, "What's God got to do with it?" When she had looked confused, he'd added, "I mean I've liked you for a long time. I just finally got up the nerve to do something about it. And your ma expecting a baby? Well, that's just nature, not God."

She was somewhat shocked at his response, even though his reasoning fit her own. "So, you don't believe in God at all?" she asked, somewhat incredulously. Will had dropped her hand and stood up suddenly. "Oh, I don't know, Lydia. Pa's kinda hated God and religion ever since my ma died havin' me. My second ma was never raised in the church, so I never grew up believin' like you did. It just doesn't make sense that one being could create the world and do all those miracles like it says in the Bible. If a god did make the world, he just went off and left it or maybe he died. All I know is he's not lovin' or carin' like they say. Look at all the pain and death in the world. Look at your little sister and my ma."

Lydia had just sat in stunned silence. She had had similar thoughts herself many times but hearing someone else saying them was different. Will noticed her expression and knelt back down, patting her shoulder nervously. "Now, don't go tellin' anybody what I said. Pa would lick me for sure. He doesn't want to lose friends or customers around here because of his beliefs, or lack of them. Please, Lydia. Swear you won't tell a soul."

She had promised, but the conversation had stuck with her ever since. The confrontation with Frank had only disturbed her more. A rustling in the leaves broke into Lydia's musings. She thought it might be Will and excitedly scrambled up and brushed grass from her dress. Instead, she turned around to find her father coming out of the woods.

"There you are," he said, his blue eyes meeting hers. "Your mama thought you'd fell in," he said, teasingly. Lydia quickly grabbed the buckets. "Oh, Papa, I'm so sorry. I let the time get away from me and now I've made you come down here to fetch me."

"That's alright, Lydia. I had a notion for a fresh drink from the spring and a splash of cold water to get the sleep out of my eyes. That travelin' can wear a man out. Wait for me a moment and I'll carry a pail for you."

* * *

Will's eyes wandered to the clock on the mantle for the third time since he'd sat down to breakfast. It was too late. He sighed inwardly. He'd planned on sneaking out to meet Lydia at her morning visit to the spring as usual at 7:00 sharp, but the wood box had been empty, and he'd been asked to fill it and do several other chores until his father had called him into breakfast. He knew Lydia wouldn't wait too long for fear of alarming her parents.

"What do you think, Will?" Peter Perry asked, laying down his newspaper and taking a sip of coffee. His father had been droning on about something he'd read, but Will hadn't been listening.

"About what?"

"About these goings on in Michigan," answered his stepmother.

"I'm sorry, Pa. I wasn't payin' attention," he admitted.

"Well this slave who was owned by a family across the river from Madison a few years ago run off with his family and was livin' in Michigan," Peter began, his voice steadily climbing in pitch. "A couple of years ago they was discovered and the owner and several others went there to drag them back to Kentucky. When they got up there the slaves holed themselves up in their cabin and when they busted in, a bunch of people from the town stopped them and had them arrested for trespassing and breakin' and enterin'! Since then there's been lawsuits between the folks in the town and the owners in Kentucky. Worst of all, them negro-lovin' Yankees got them away to Canada, where they can't be touched. It ain't right! It's highway robbery," he pounded his fist on the tablecloth, making the dishes rattle.

"There's some old federal law against helping or hiding runaways, but it's totally ignored up north. They keep talkin' about personal liberty laws and *habeas corpus* and all that. The Kentucky Congress has been demandin' Washington pass stricter laws, but nothin's bein' done. The Kentucky papers my kin send to me are just full of letters of irate owners demanding action and advertisements for help findin' runaways. It's criminal the way these pious folks are all sorry for the darkies and point fingers at slave owners but think nothin' about stealin' a man's most valuable property."

"Now, Peter, try to calm yourself," said his wife, patting his hand. "There's nothin' you can do about it, so don't fret so."

"Yeah, Pa. What can we do up here?" asked Will.

"I tell you what," he said standing up and tossing his napkin on the table." If I get wind of anybody round here helping anybody's property run off, I'll grab 'em myself and turn 'em in. The law's the law and I will obey it and not turn a blind eye to those who don't." He left the room, leaving Will and Eliza in silence.

Will stared down at his half-eaten breakfast, now cold and unappetizing. He thought of Lydia. He knew her parents and church were abolitionists, though he'd never discussed slavery with her, being one of those topics that was avoided whenever possible by most people.

"Will?"

He looked up at Eliza who was gazing at him expectantly and shook the thoughts from his head.

"You sure are daydreaming this morning, Will. Are you finished?" she asked, indicating his plate.

"Yes, Ma. Sorry I couldn't finish it."

117

"Well, if I know you, you'll be starving by midmorning. We've got a shipment in yesterday when you were off wanderin' and you need to restock. Perhaps I'll save some of this bacon and a Johnny cake on the back of the stove for you when your appetite returns," she said ruffling his curls playfully as she carried the plates to the kitchen.

* * *

"Friends, there will be a special meeting for church members only held here fifteen minutes after services conclude today," Pastor Johnston announced at the end of the service the following Sunday.

Frank looked up. He had been staring at his hands while trying to focus on the sermon. He glanced at Lydia who shrugged disinterestedly when she met his eye. Turning to his parents, he saw that Pa had grabbed Ma's hand as they stood up to sing the final hymn. His brows knit in puzzlement as he tried to figure out what the meeting could be about. He'd joined the church and been baptized last fall, but church meetings had always been about things like money and theology discussions. Not much had interested him yet.

Seth and Jane bowed their heads and Frank followed their lead. Lydia did so too, but he noticed her toe was tapping with nervous energy. He had avoided her as much as possible after her heated demands. Frank still fretted that she was heading for heartbreak either by losing Will's favor or gaining it and thus causing strife in the family.

When the people had been dismissed, Frank and Seth normally helped carry benches to the storage shed behind his grandma's house. Now they stood around with other members, waiting for the visitors to leave. Frank had counted 17 people, which included a new family that was settling on land next to the Martins. They were outgrowing this room for sure. Perhaps the meeting was to discuss the need for a building.

Soon the members began drifting back in and taking seats. The children were left outside. He could hear them laughing and rustling through the piles of leaves that were beginning to pile up under the tall maples beside the house. Mentally he counted heads and came to 12, including the pastor. His stomach growled with hunger. He hoped this wouldn't take long.

Mr. Martin, Mr. Hillman, and his father gave a brief account of their trip to Neil's Creek. Each man told of how the meeting had inspired them further to help end slavery. Seth relayed how awed he was at the acts of bravery he'd heard about from the free black men who had spoken. A group of them in and around Madison were working with people across the river to get them safely to Indiana and then leading them to safe houses farther north.

After Seth sat down, the pastor stood and faced the members. All had been still, listening intently. Ned lowered his head and didn't speak for several long moments. Frank was almost afraid to breathe, it was so quiet, both inside and out.

"Friends, we've always been a church that has been firm in our beliefs against the enslavement of human beings," the pastor began, hands clutching the lectern. "Our church covenant declares this belief. Now is the time to decide if we will put our faith into action. The free blacks and the white church folk south of us need safe places, havens, sanctuaries for these men, women, and children who are fleeing their masters, running to freedom; freedom that should be guaranteed in this country where President Jefferson wrote that 'All men are created equal.'

"Our Flat Rock community, hidden away from the main roads and towns, so near to surrounding counties is ideal, these men say, to be a part of what some have called the 'underground railroad'. If you've never heard of it before, it's a sort of code name for the system of helping slaves escape. There are conductors who help move folks from place to place, and there are stations. These are places, homes and outbuildings, where these folk can stay a night or two in hiding, get food, shelter, clothing, guidance, and prayer to continue their journey. Folks who can't help by being a conductor or station keeper can provide food, clothing, and the like, or money to purchase them. They can keep a watch out for those who are seeking out these runaways, and they can help also by just keeping quiet about the activities of others.

I want all of you church members to pray fervently these next few days to ask God how he would want you to help in this endeavor. When you have decided, just approach me privately and let me know. This is not an undertaking to be spoken about. Silence about our own activities and ignorance about the work of others is important if we are going to be successful. There is a risk of financial loss if an owner finds out you are involved in helping to steal away what is legally, but wrongfully called his property. There are laws on the books that make it a criminal offense as well. This is truly a serious task, and I ask each of you, even the young folks in our midst, to take time and prayerfully consider the role, if any, you wish to play."

Frank found his heart was pounding with excitement as people in the room slowly started to file out. Everyone was solemn and hushed, deep in thought as if a funeral had taken place. He stood up and Seth put an arm around him. Jane grabbed Lydia's hand and they walked out, nodding at Lucinda and Ned at the door as they stepped into the autumn sunshine.

* * *

The Cowper family barely said a word to each other as they slowly walked home. Each carefully stepping over and around mundane obstacles in the well-beaten path, as if afraid to make unnecessary noise. Lydia hands gripped the edges of her shawl and she stared at the ground as she walked. Her thoughts were as scattered as the fallen leaves. Uppermost in her mind was a sense of importance. The church leaders had seen fit to include her and Frank and a few other young people in a momentous mission. She, Lydia Jane Cowper, could finally do something valuable, maybe even save someone's life.

She turned around, surprised at how far ahead of the others she'd walked. When they came near, she broke the silence. "Mama, how many people do you think our cellar could hold? How would they keep warm in the winter? Should we start making some quilts? I'll bet we could use the haymow…"

"Shush, Lydia. Let's wait until we get home. Not here. We can talk at dinner," interrupted Seth.

She halted her steps and the rest of them paused. She turned around and looked at each of them. Her parents' eyes met hers in that steady, calming manner they had. Frank glanced at her and then looked away. Lydia's heartbeat quickened. She loved them so much. She had hurt them with her anger, her rebellious spirit, and even her deceit, though she was sure Frank hadn't betrayed her. All three were gazing at her now, expectantly. Suddenly, in her imagination she could see Alice in her father's arms, pulling his hat off and playfully putting it on her own head, giggling.

Lydia felt her throat tighten and ache. She squeezed her eyes shut to hold back the tears and turned. A sob escaped her throat, and she began to run up the path, her skirts and shawl billowing behind her.

"Lydia, wait!", she heard her mother call after her, but she didn't stop.

* * *

Jane and the others stood watching as Lydia disappeared. Her throat ached in sympathy.

"You want me to fetch her, Ma?" asked Frank. "I can guess where she's gone off to."

"No, thank you Frank. I will find her. Sometimes a woman just needs another woman to talk to when our minds are too full."

"Seth, you and Frank go ahead and serve yourself some of that leftover soup I have keeping warm. There's some cornpone in the cupboard you can have with it." She handed Seth the Bible and handbag she carried and shooed them on.

"Take some and leave some," she called, smiling at Frank, teasing him as usual about his big appetite.

"Yes, Ma. I will."

Jane watched as their figures, one just a few inches taller than the other, disappeared around the turn ahead. Then she gathered her skirts and turned her feet toward the creek bottom. A robust wind wafted through the trees, bringing chilly air and the earthy smells of autumn with it. The end of the unbearable summer heat always seemed to refresh her spirits. Fall was her favorite time of year, the colors, the scents, the abundance of the harvest, and the clear blue skies.

The path began getting steeper the closer she got to the creek. Fearful of falling, Jane grabbed at saplings along the way to slow her pace. Suddenly she heard loud wailing up ahead and knew she had found Lydia. She could see her now through the trees, sitting at the foot of a big sycamore and wiping her wet cheeks furiously with her handkerchief. Her shoulders lifted as sobs shook her upper body. Jane's maternal heart ached for this woman-child. Lydia's grief for her sister had outwardly swayed between verbal fury and self-loathing, followed by a cold silence that smacked of indifference of Alice's fate, God, and life itself.

Jane said nothing. She just quietly walked over and sat down beside Lydia, who pulled her into a tight embrace and continued releasing what had been building in her over the past months.

Chapter Fourteen

Seth's eyes were focused on a length of board he was sawing in half, held tightly in the vise on his workbench. His thoughts, however, were as scattered as the dust mites filling the late afternoon sunbeams that slanted through the window. For five days he and Jane had been seeking the Lord's will regarding the work of the church. They prayed together in the privacy of the barn after the noon meal every day and encouraged Lydia and Frank to do the same. Today they both had come to an agreement, feeling a deep peace that assured them of the Holy Spirit's guidance.

Movement outside shifted his attention as Lydia labored into the clearing carrying the water pails. He studied her face. Yes, the defiant look was gone, replaced with a quiet contemplative visage that seemed to come from an inner struggle that he couldn't understand. Jane claimed to have suspicions about their daughter's current mood but declined to share them aloud.

His thoughts stayed on Lydia through several more repetitive cuttings when Frank burst through the lean-to door.

"Hello Pa," he said, carefully laying his stack of textbooks at the end of the long workbench. Seth turned and smiled at him.

"It looks like you're bustin' to tell me something, son. Did something happen at school?"

Frank smiled and lowered his eyes. "Yeah, Pa. Today after Mr. Kelly tested me on my Latin, he asked if I'd help with one of the little boys. Jakob just started school last week and is learning his letters and sounds so he's behind all the rest."

Seth nodded to show he was listening while he measured another length of board. Warmth filled him at the enthusiasm in Frank's eyes as spoke.

"Well once I found he knew the letters' sounds, I showed him how to put them together to make words. He sounded out p-a-n and m-a-n and then f-a-t and h-a-t and afore he knew it he was reading! He let out a whoop and Mr. Kelly looked at me all sharp. I feared he would punish Jakob or both of us, but when I said, 'He's reading, sir,' he just smiled and went back to his recitation class."

Seth put down the measuring string and looked deeply into Frank's eyes and put a hand on his shoulder. "You helped open a new world for that boy, son. Well done. Be sure and tell your ma and grandma. They'd love to hear that too. Now go do the barn chores, then wash up for supper. Your ma and I have come to a decision about the church's mission and want to talk it over with you and Lydia afterwards."

"Yes, Pa. I'll be quick," Frank said, still grinning, as he hurried into the house.

* * *

Lydia stood up after forcing down the last bite of corn cake and gathered her dishes. She'd hardly said a word at supper, but no one seemed to notice as Frank prattled on about school. Normally feelings of envy would creep in at times like this, especially when she noted her parents' rapt attention. But tonight, she was able to smile and be happy for her little brother's excitement. She wanted to feel that inner contentment too. If there was any jealousy, it was in Frank's found passion in teaching. He was developing a goal, an aim, a vocation. While she still felt adrift and rudderless.

She'd poured her heart out to God and her mother over her guilt and grief about the loss of Alice, but she'd she remained silent to both about Will, her feelings still conflicted. He still showed up at the spring, but Lydia's guilty conscience often had her finding excuses to cut the visits short. Wednesday she'd taken to going to the spring earlier or later than usual to avoid an encounter, like she'd managed today.

The raised voice of her father broke through her thoughts as she filled the kettle methodically. "Come sit down, Lydia, the dishes can wait. We're having a family meeting, remember?"

Lydia silently sat back on her chair, crossed her hands in her lap and looked expectedly at Seth along with the others. She felt her pulse quicken as she saw her father grab her mother's hand and she leaned forward to listen.

"Lydia," he said, meeting her eye and nodding and turning to her brother, "Frank, your mother and I have listened to your ideas about this undertaking of the church and prayed for God's guidance, as I know you have also. We have decided and feel God's approval that with the baby due in just a few months, for now our role must be supportive. We don't feel we can take anyone in just now, but we can help by preparing and sharing meals, sewing, and doing whatever else is needed."

Lydia felt a wave of disappointment. Sharing food and clothing wasn't heroic – just something they'd do for any needy neighbor. "But why can't we …" she began.

She felt Jane's small hand tap hers lightly. "Perhaps once the baby is born and *if* it is healthy and *if* my energy returns, we can think about taking someone in, Lydia. We can manage until the baby is old enough to speak in sentences. Then he or she could betray a secret, Lydia. We must think about what is best for everyone concerned."

"I admit, it's not what I was hopin' for," put in Frank. "I rather liked the excitement of having visitors from places I've never seen, but I guess I could deliver messages, keep a lookout for bounty hunters, and gather more game and nuts from the woods."

"Why yes," said Seth, "there's plenty for everyone to do and we'll learn more as time goes on. I'm thinking my wagon could be of use since I haul wood and furniture all around these parts."

Lydia was silent, but her mind was racing. Her fingers started drumming on the table. "Every one of them will need new clothes after travelling all this way from Kentucky and maybe even farther," she said aloud, excitement building in her voice. "They'll need everything from underclothing to coats and in all kinds of sizes. We could even dress the men as women and the women as men as a disguise."

"I think we could take up a collection from the church to help buy the material and thread because we also need to sew things for the baby," added Jane, her face flushed. "I gave everything to Lorna weeks ago and I won't ask for them back."

They all enjoyed a laugh over that.

"Well, one thing's for sure," said Seth, "It's going to get a lot more interesting here in Flat Rock from here on."

Lydia stood back up to start the dishes and Frank gathered his books and a candle and climbed to his loft to study. As Lydia cleared the table, she listened to her parents talking, marveling anew at their steadfast faith. How did a person develop that kind of trust in a god who seemed so unpredictable and often cruel? How could God be loving and uncaring at the same time? That was what Will had said. She didn't understand it either, but neither could she go so far as to believe there was no god at all. "I wish somebody could help me figure it out," she mused.

* * *

"I just stopped by your mother's to talk more to Ned about our decision," Seth reported to Jane as he came in from the back door and hung his hat and coat on a peg. Jane nodded from the rocking chair near the fire. Her hands busily pushed a needle in and out of quilting she had spread across her growing lap. It had been several weeks since the family meeting that launched their work for the runaways. Lydia was similarly engaged, sitting on the bed, leaning against the wall, her needle poking in and out of a tiny gown.

Seth washed his hands and dried them and then sat at the table where he'd been cutting leather. He was trying to piece together his first pair of shoes. A believer from the Zenas church had stopped by last week to teach him the craft. Frank was at school for the day.

"Is there enough light for you to work over there?" Jane called to Lydia. "The clouds are so low and heavy out today.

"Yes, Mama. I can see just fine," said Lydia.

Jane had laughed when Lydia volunteered to sew a gown for her new sister or brother, recalling again how she had given all her baby things away. "You just never know what sweet surprises God has in store for you, Lydia," she had said, handing her the soft yard of bleached flannel.

Her heart swelled as she glanced again at Lydia's industrious stitching. Her daughter's spirit was seemingly settled into a place of peace after confessing her anger and lack of faith over the past few months. Jane blinked at the quilting. More often than she liked to admit, it was getting harder and harder to see clearly. Seth's watch ticked rhythmically from the mantle, her rocker squeaked in a counterpoint and Bessie's dreamland yips at her feet occasionally punctuated the peaceful afternoon.

A heavy sigh caught her attention. Seth's brows were knitted together, and his fingers were wrapped around two pieces of leather while his other hand was attempting to poke them with a tool. While Jane watched, fascinated, he dropped the leather and turned toward her.

"I don't think I can manage this cobbler's trade without a last. That fella from Zenas told me so, but it sounded so simple to just sew some pieces of leather together."

"Can you make one?" Jane asked.

"I think so, but it will take time. I'll have to measure someone's foot and then carve a likeness of it out of a solid block of wood. Then it will only be one size. To do it properly you need several different ones to make shoes for big and little feet alike."

"Well, with the harvest almost put up, there should be time for that soon, I'd imagine" assured Jane. "But I've been thinking about Frank. Seth, he loves studying so much. It's just a shame he can't go on learning when he's done studying here."

"I agree, Jane," Seth said, pausing to take a drink of water from his tin cup. "But I don't see how that's possible. It would mean boarding him somewhere far off and that takes cash. We've got enough to last us awhile, but jobs will be scarcer now that winter's setting in."

"Yes, I know," she replied. "Well, God says to "Ask and you will receive," so we're going to do just that."

"Yes, we surely will, Jane," Seth agreed.

* * *

The following week Will walked along the creek pretending to look for turtles. He'd taken along a sack and his rifle as an excuse for leaving the store to Eliza for the afternoon. Pa had been called to Versailles for jury duty and planned to spend the night in town. He hadn't seen Lydia for several days and worried she was avoiding him. Sometimes she wouldn't be at the creek as expected, and when she was, she seemed changed. He wondered if what he'd said about God a few weeks ago had been the cause.

Judging by the sun's position, he figured it was about the time she usually showed up with her water buckets. Just then chattering broke out in a big oak on the other side of the creek. Two squirrels were facing off on a limb, halted in their frenzied acorn gathering. Quietly he pulled the loaded rifle against his shoulder and took aim and pulled the trigger.

At the instant the gunpowder fired, one of the critters dropped to the ground and a scream went up from around the next bend. Will was so startled he nearly dropped the gun.

"Lydia? Is that you? Are you alright?" he shouted, starting toward the direction of the scream. Hurrying ahead he caught a glimpse of her work dress through the trees.

"Yes, Will," she called to him. "That gun going off all of a sudden just scared me to death, that's all. I had no idea you were there."

He slowed his steps and found her clutching her chest as if trying to stop a racing heart. A filled bucket was by her side, and another was sinking into the shallows near the spring.

"Look what you did," she said, looking down at her drenched skirt and wet feet. She put her hands on her hips and gave him what could only be called a mother-like glare.

Will came closer, afraid now of her anger and not wanting to alienate her more. She stood frozen in a tight-lipped expression, and he looked down at his feet, speechless.

Lydia took one look at his hangdog appearance and giggled, giving him a gentle shove. "Well, did you get him? If your bullet didn't kill him, my shrieking probably did."

He looked up into her laughing face. Her brown eyes were snapping, and her cheeks and lips were apple red. The temptation to grab and kiss her was overwhelming. He swallowed hard and managed to choke out. "Yeah, I think I did. Wanna help me look for him?"

* * *

Lydia allowed Will to take her hand to help her cross the steppingstones to the far side of the creek, now deeper than usual with the recent fall rains. She'd planned on continuing her recent practice of keeping their contact brief, but the sudden bang had knocked all resolve from her mind. They searched together at the base of the tree. Lydia was the first to spy the furry gray tail among the brown leaves, pushing them aside with her toes.

"Right through the eye, Will. You're a good shot," she said, picking it up by the tail and holding it aloft. Will reddened at the compliment but said nothing as he snatched it out of her hand and put it in the sack. "You're really good at store keeping and figures and such too. It's a wonder you haven't swept some girl off her feet by now," she added, teasingly.

He stood silent facing her in the afternoon light, smiling shyly. The creek flowed noisily nearby, mingled only with the soft sounds of falling leaves. A ray of sun pierced through the clouds and flooded Lydia's upturned face in its beam.

"Lydia?" Will whispered, reaching for her hand. His hand was warm, and her pulse quickened. He held her eyes. "You're the only girl I dream about."

Will's gaze was so intense and full of unspoken longing, it frightened Lydia. Her smile faded, but she didn't withdraw her hand. She was sure Will could hear her heart pounding in her chest.

"Lydia Cowper, will you be my girl, for always? Will you marry me?"

She hesitated. She had dreamed about this moment for months, imagined it happening in scores of places and circumstances. Will's eyes were open wide in expectation. She swallowed, then opened her lips to answer.

* * *

Back at the cabin, Frank was in the loft studying when a knock disturbed the quiet. He stood up and looked below to see Seth open the door and usher in Mr. Martin who swiftly entered and removed his hat, nodding to Jane. Her lips were at the end of a wooden spoon, testing her ham and potato soup, the aroma of which drifted up to the loft. Frank's stomach growled in response.

"Matthew, how nice to see you. How's Rebekah? Is anything wrong?" his mother said, sitting down.

"No, Jane. We're all fine. I've come to show you a letter I just picked up from Perry's. It's from our Maggie, down at Neil's Creek."

"Here, have a seat, Matthew," Seth said, pulling out a chair. "Is anything the matter with her family?"

"I don't think so, Seth," he said unbuttoning his coat and sitting down. But both of you, just look at her letter. It's odd, that's all. I can't quite figure it out."

He pulled an envelope from his coat pocket, removed and unfolded the paper inside and laid it on the table.

Seth and Jane both twisted their heads to read the brief note silently.

"What does she mean, 'I'm sending you some parcels soon, three large ones. I trust you will be ready and have room to store them,'" puzzled Jane.

"That's the part I'm confused about. It's too early for Christmas gifts. If she had something else, why didn't she send it along with me when we visited a few weeks ago?" he shrugged.

"Mr. Martin, may I see the letter?" asked Frank, swinging his feet from the loft and onto the slats that served as a ladder.

"Why, sure, Frank," Matthew said, holding the paper out to him and looking up as he handed it to him. "How old are you now?"

"I turned 13 last month, sir," Frank said, reading the letter a second and third time.

Frank handed the paper back to Matthew. His brows knit in thought, and he rubbed a finger behind his ear, a habit he'd had for years. He looked at his father.

"Pa, didn't you say the runaways might come to us up through Neil's Creek?"

"Why yes, but…"

"Don't you see? Maggie's telling us she's sending some runaways up to Flat Rock! Three large parcels must mean three grownups."

Understanding dawned on the faces of the adults. Frank couldn't help grinning.

"When did she post the letter, Matthew?" asked Jane, excitement evident in her voice.

"Let's see," he said, glancing at the letter and then flipping over the envelope. "She's dated it November 11th, but the postmark is the 13th."

"That was three days ago," interjected Frank.

"Why that means they could be here any time!" Matthew said, starting up from his chair. "I'd best get home."

Jane handed him his hat when he finished buttoning his coat. "It might be wise to stop by and see Ned on your way. Perhaps, he'll know more or can give you some direction," she advised.

"I'll do that," he said heading to the door Seth was holding open for him. He turned back and sought Frank's eyes. "Thanks, Frank. You're a smart young man the way you figured that out so fast." He nodded and then went into the late afternoon sunshine.

* * *

Down under the oak tree, a long pause had followed Will's question. Though her lips had opened to answer "yes," Lydia's mind suddenly tumbled with visions of her parents, her grandmother, Frank, Pastor Ned, and the anonymous black faces that had filled her imagination of late. If she left home to marry Will now, she wouldn't be there to help with her mother with the baby or the clothing and supplies for the runaways. She couldn't even tell Will about it.

"Will," she began, looking straight into his expectant eyes. His steady gaze distracted her momentarily. "Will, I care for you, and I believe we can be happy together. But I …"

"But? But what, Lydia? You've made it clear you care for me, and I just told you there's no one else I care for. What is it?"

It pained Lydia to see the hurt in his eyes, so she hurried to finish her thoughts. "But I'm not ready yet. You know my mother is expecting a baby in a few months and she's older and may have trouble. I need to be there to help at home."

"We don't have to get married right away," he argued. "I want to build us a house first. I have a place all picked out. You'll love it. We can announce our engagement and get married in the summer, or a year from now. I can wait."

Things were happening too fast for Lydia. An unexpected anxiety hit her in the pit of her stomach at the thought of telling her parents she was engaged to an unbeliever.

"Listen," she said, putting a hand gently on his shoulder and looking up into his face. "I'm just not sure I'm ready to make you that promise. Please give me a few weeks to think about it. You know my parents don't even know we've been seeing each other. Give me some time to sort it all out."

Just then the distant bang of a door being shut echoed from the direction of the Cowper cabin.

"Sorry, Will. I've got to go. Don't forget your squirrel and your gun. You'd better get another one or there won't be enough for your supper." She gave him a quick peck on the cheek, their first kiss, she realized and practically ran back to the bank and over the steppingstones.

Will stood inert as she swiftly filled the spilled pail and start up the path. Lydia looked back just once, as she took the first turn. His hands hung at his side as he stood where she had left him. Her throat started to ache. She blinked back tears and headed toward home, her heart pounding in her chest.

Part Four

The Ohio River Valley

Chapter Fifteen

Lily struggled not to gasp as she plunged into the depths of the muddy water. She'd had the foresight to tie the pillowcase around her wrist or it would have been lost in the virtual shock of the cold water. Eventually she forced herself to relax and began floating upwards. The cacophony coming from the boat could be heard as she neared the surface and she prayed neither she nor Manny would be seen. Her head broke through, and she forced her mouth shut, suppressing a cough.

When she opened her eyes, she saw Manny several yards ahead of her, half-way across, silently motioning for her to catch up. Lily began paddling towards him as quickly and quietly as she could, only to find herself hampered by the weight of her bag. She stopped after a few strokes and frantically looked behind her. There was still some activity on the boat, but no one seemed to have yet noticed their abrupt departure.

Treading water, for a few seconds, she slipped off the pillowcase and shoved the material between her teeth, leaving her arms free to propel her to shore. The murky water kept trying to fill her crammed mouth, but Lily determinedly pushed forward using strokes akin to the skating bugs on the creek back home. She spied Manny's outstretched hand and soon grasped it. He pulled her towards him.

"Grab onto my shirt and just float along behind me," he ordered. "I'll soon have us out of here."

Lily did as she was told and momentarily relaxed her muscles as he pulled her weightless through the water. Soon Manny's feet found purchase on the riverbed and after taking a step or two he whispered for her to let go. Her feet soon touched ground and she began to follow Manny into shallower water.

"Stay crouched down," he hissed, as she stood up to force her floating skirts back down. "They'll see us!"

Immediately Lily hunched over, taking the heavy bag out of her mouth and grabbing the knot tightly. She then followed Manny, who leaned over almost double to the bank. He looked around for a sturdy bush or sapling to help pull them up when an otter splashed into the river nearby, making them both jump.

"Good Lord, that gave me a fright," Lily whispered, holding her hand at her throat.

"Shush! I'm thinking," Manny hissed. "Let's head up to that grassy spot so we won't leave footprints," he nodded, wading back downriver a few feet.

Overhead the shadows were long as the sun sank before them. The night creatures were beginning their warmup. The noise from the steamboat was diminishing as the fires died down and the boilers cooled along with the frantic nerves of the passengers, most of whom were now on the opposite shore.

Manny stopped and grabbed a low-lying branch from a willow tree and hoisted himself out onto the grassy bank. He got on his knees and stuck out his hand and helped Lily up, her skirts dripping and clinging to her legs.

"Get down. We'll crawl into the trees and set a minute before we take off."

About three minutes later they were about 10 feet from the shore, behind a brace of sycamores. Lily's heart was racing. As it slowed, she became aware of how cold her wet clothes felt with the night air coming on and the sun nearly set. She looked at Manny. His eyes were closed, and she knew he was listening for any sound of pursuit. She felt relieved that the initial stage of escape was over, but she also knew the danger was just beginning. She quickly whispered a prayer of thanks and for continued success and then looked up again at her fellow refugee.

"Let's go," he said, a steely determination filling his face.

* * *

"How long 'til we can board again?" asked Thomas to no one in particular. He and several men were braving the cool night air on the porch of the lockmaster's house. He stood restlessly fingering the change in his pocket and staring at the Blue Wing.

"Only the captain and his darky engineer know that answer," said a tall thin man lighting a pipe and leaning next to him on a porch column. "I hate the delay. I have another steamer to catch in Madison and if I miss it, I might have to stay a few days in that Yankee river town. I'm headin' to Owensboro. Where you headin'?"

"Home. Near New Orleans."

"Oh! What a city that is," the man broke in, shaking his head. "New Orleans makes Madison and Louisville look like villages. You're a lucky man, sir. No Yankees that far south. None of those abolitionist crazy folks stirrin' up trouble."

"That's why I'm anxious to get moving," explained Thomas. "I've heard this area's full of slave stealers and I own half of three slaves on that boat and one outright," he said, pointing to the river. "I wasn't worried while we were moving. But now we're stopped, just a few miles from the Ohio with nobody to keep an eye on them."

"Why the concern? Ain't they chained up?"

"Two of them are and two of them aren't. They're a manservant and a lady's maid. In all the rush to get off, I just ordered them down to the slave quarters. They're both scared to death of water, like most blacks, but still." Thomas paused. "I've got a bad feeling about my boy Manny. He's just too clever for his own good. I thought takin' him ashore with me where he could take off into the woods here was worse, but now I don't know."

Thomas and his new friend both shook their heads and lapsed into silence. Thomas listened to the voices from the boat and tried to discern what was happening. They had been ordered to keep their distance initially, but the engines had quieted considerably.

"Mr. Mercier?" a soft voice with a southern drawl broke into the night.

Thomas turned to the door and saw Yvonne Chastain's head peeking out. It was nearly dark in the shadow of the trees in the yard, but the light from the house lit her auburn hair. He rolled his eyes, sighed, and turned to her. Before he could give a polite greeting, she stepped out onto the porch and hurried over to him, clutching a wool shawl that was wrapped around her shoulders.

"Oh, Thomas! I didn't know where you'd gone off to. I was so scared. Weren't you? Mother had to sit down and put her feet up. She said her heart was about to burst outa her chest from the fright of our escape. Mrs. Munson, that's the lockkeeper's wife, she brought her some brandy for fear she would faint."

"I certainly hope your mother will regain her composure, Miss Yvonne. We're perfectly safe here," replied Thomas, amazed he'd gotten a word in.

"But what about Lily and Tabby? And the others? They're on the boat! They could be blown to bits!"

Before Thomas could answer, the tall man, who had looked with interest at Yvonne, said, "Now don't you worry, miss. Just listen to that engine." He paused. "See how much quieter it is now they've quit adding fuel? It'll be fine now. When it's all cool, they'll inspect it and we'll be on our way again."

"Thank goodness," Yvonne said, nodding politely at the man and then turning to Thomas.

"Won't you come inside, Thomas? Father was wondering where you were, and Mrs. Munson is serving up tea and cakes."

"Yes, Miss Yvonne. I guess I will. I need to have a word with your father." He allowed her to take his arm and together they went inside.

* * *

Manny watched as Lily stood and wrung water from her skirt. Her dress clung to her chest and shoulders and her long hair hung damp and limp down her back. Her eyes were wide and questioning, waiting for him to make a move.

"You got any kinda cup or bottle in that bag o' yours?"

Lily looked down at the soggy pillowcase in her hand and shook her head.

"Well, that woulda been handy. What *do* you have in there?"

"Some clothes and stuff Miss Yvonne was throwin' out. I wish they was dry. I'm getting' gooseflesh out here all wet."

Manny could sympathize because his pants and shirt were in the same condition, and he didn't have any extras.

"Give us about ten minutes of runnin' and we won't feel the cold anymore. You up to making a long dash for it?"

She nodded. "Where we headin'?"

"That all depends. For right now, just trust me and follow."

Lily nodded again and rolled up and tucked her bag under her arm.

Manny put a finger to his lips. "We don't want to stir up any birds or critters. We're too close to shore. Let's just creep along a bit further before we take off. He crouched down and Lily imitated him, taking stealthy steps further into the woods. The sun had set, and the gloaming was taking the color out of the world and filling it with grays and blacks. Manny's ears picked up muffled voices from the further shore, tree frogs and flowing water striking against the lock.

Out of the darkness a sound lifted above the others. From a distance, but still distinct, he heard, "Manny, Manny! Where are you, boy?"

"Lily? Come outa hiding now. The danger's past."

It was the voices of Thomas and Mr. Chastain. Manny looked back at Lily, whose hands were clutched to her mouth, her eyes screwed tightly shut as if she could make herself disappear by wishing it.

He grabbed her hand from her face and hissed, "Run!"

Lily's hand in his, Manny took off, avoiding saplings and undergrowth that would slow them down or cause a rustling motion that might attract attention. In his mind's eye he could almost see the two men searching the boat and coming to the right conclusion about their missing pieces of property. Silas was a genius. Not only did he time the fake boiler emergency right at sunset, the evacuation of the steamer on the opposite side of the river gave them the advantage of time and distance. Immediate pursuit was impossible.

He smiled as he dashed through a stand of cedar trees, getting his bearings in the familiar territory. He didn't have enough breath to relay all this to Lilly and assuage her obvious terror, but his own confidence in their success was bolstered. "Don't be afraid, Lily. We'll make it. I know it."

"I'm prayin' so, Manny," she gasped out as they started up a steep slope "And you were right. I aint cold no more!"

* * *

On the Blue Wing, Thomas' gut and throat ached and both hands were clenched in fists as he stood in the doorway of the hold and stared at the two dozen or so slaves that sat huddled in the corner. Mr. Chastain, holding a lantern in one hand, was roughly questioning each of his slaves for information about the runaways. His hand was raised over the cringing Tabby.

"Don't lie to me, Tabby! I know you slaves love to talk behind our backs and plot to trip us up. You were with Lily in the house and on this boat more than any of these others!"

"Yes, Master Chastain, but never alone! We was always about with you and Missus or the girls on this boat. And she never talked much at the house, that Lily. Not very friendly, 'cept to those little boys and Manny when they was out in the barn. I seed 'em laughin' and cuttin' up whenever I was the one that brung 'em their vittles," she paused for a heartbeat. "At least at first."

Chastain looked back at Thomas, who stared back at him. Both of them knew why Lily's mood had changed. Had Henri's "breaking" caused her enough desperation to flee?

He moved the lantern slightly, lighting up Jethro's face. "What about you? You worked a lot with Manny. Did he ever hint he was planning to run off?"

Jethro didn't hesitate. "No, suh. He was always askin' questions about drivin' a team and how to be a good manservant to Massa Thomas. He seemed real eager like, always wantin' to know more about Lo'siana and such."

"Oh, yes. He had us all bamboozled, the stinkin' thief," shouted Thomas into the room. Chastain froze at the venom and volume in his voice and the slaves ceased their whisperings and whimpers. "He's stolen himself and Lily away from us – fourteen hundred dollars, he's robbed us of! Almost all my hard-earned savings, thrown away at the bottom of this blasted river"

"Now, now, Thomas," soothed Chastain, stepping over legs towards the door. "We don't know that they've drowned. If they wanted to just kill themselves, they could have jumped overboard way back downstream. But no, they waited until we were this close to the Ohio and then jumped. Perhaps they planned this whole thing and they're alive and well and halfway there now."

"You think they swam to shore? Everyone knows slaves are terrified of water. And how could they have known we'd have an emergency and have to evacuate?"

"Well, they couldn't have," mused Chastain, "but maybe they saw the opportunity and just took it and danged be the consequences. Let's get some help and lanterns and a skiff to take us across to the other shore and see if we can find any evidence that they're alive. Maybe the lockkeeper has some dogs too."

Thomas just nodded, closed the door, and followed Chastain and his lantern to the bow, past the still sputtering boiler.

Chapter Sixteen

*E*arly the next morning Manny crept quietly out of the cave where he had led Lily last night after their wild career through the darkening wood. He stealthily stepped from one place of concealment to the next, heading northwest. At the edge of a homestead, he paused. After listening for activity for a full five minutes, he strode quickly to a small outbuilding, reached up and yanked at a horseshoe hung over the door, then let himself in. He swiped a tin cup and a hunk of corn cake that he tied up in a handkerchief. As he was walking back into the cover of the woods, the wham of a screen door slamming shut caused him to flatten himself instantly among some tall tobacco plants. He then crept into a dense growth of ferns covering a gully that led onto Samuel Fearn's field. Thankfully it was dry with just the dew drenched ferns dripping on him.

The rising sun's beams reached through the foliage. He wiped droplets off his face with his shirt cuff and waited to hear if there were any signs of detection. He ran his fingers over the dripping ferns and licked his fingers. He was so thirsty. The only water he and Lily had found was from a spring they'd passed by on their flight to the cave. There had only been enough time to scoop up a handful each. That had been hours ago. They'd reached the cave stumbling through the darkness in the middle of the night where they both had crept back as far as they'd dared in the darkness and fell asleep, depleted.

Manny had been wakened by the sound of Lily retching and shaking like an aspen in a storm. He needed to get back to her with some water but would have to backtrack to the spring they'd passed if he didn't find another water source. He knew Mr. Konkel's well was only about 2 miles away, but the risk of being caught was too great. Konkel kept a greater watch on his property than Fearn did. What they needed was a good rainstorm, but only God knew when that would happen. Judging by the soil beneath him, there hadn't been rain here in over a week.

As he lay hidden in silence, his mind drifted back to the other times he had felt this free. This was his fourth attempt at escape. He'd been bought by Konkel from a relative when he was nine years old after his mother died. At 11 he'd hidden in the corn crib, meaning to run for the river after dark, but the family dog had sniffed him out before sundown. Then at 14 he had stowed away on a steamboat that was boarding for a crossing to Madison. An untimely sneeze midstream had given him away. That escapade had earned him a whipping.

Undeterred, last May he'd hidden in the cave that was their current shelter. For three days he'd foraged for food and was caught by a neighbor of Konkel's when he ventured out. His master had been livid. Since he was short on cash, he decided he would punish Manny the best way he knew how. He'd "sell him south".

Manny smiled when he remembered the smug look on Konkel's face when he'd looked at him last, shoving the $600 in his pocket and muttering "good riddance". Now here he was again, less than an hour's walk from where he started. He hoped fervently that this was his last try, but Lily's desperate plight had tripped up his plans and complicated them. He had more to think about than himself this time. It was time to find some water and get back to the cave.

* * *

A rooster's crow jerked Thomas awake in the predawn light. He fumbled for his pocket watch and squinted but couldn't read it. Cursing, he felt for the candle and matches Munson's wife had placed on the table for him when he'd stumbled behind her into the room after midnight. Once the candle was lit, he opened his watch case to learn it was 5:43.

Last night's change in his fortunes had left him feeling a mixture of anger, fear, and grief over the probable loss of his best purchases from this trip. Though he'd been training Manny to be a manservant, he'd always have the option of selling him for a good profit if it didn't work out. Lily was sure to have at least doubled his money in the special auctions back home. Worst of all was that Lily was half owned by Chastain who silently seemed to blame him for letting her mix with Manny.

Most of his anger was directed at the teenage boy. It was obvious now he was too clever to be anything but trouble. He had fooled them all with his false

139

eagerness to learn skills beyond that of a field hand. Thomas had thought the promise of an easier life in the South than what he had known in Kentucky would be a deterrent and wipe out any thoughts of risking escape.

A search of the west bank of the river last night had revealed enough evidence to show him at least one of the slaves had survived the plunge into the Kentucky. The rolling terrain, thick undergrowth, and the lack of moonlight, manpower, and dogs had brought the hunt to a halt before it had really begun and he and Chastain had silently rowed back to the east bank, deep in thought.

Chastain had questioned his family for clues as to the runaway pair's plans, but they all confessed to have no prior knowledge. Yvonne vacillated between tears for Lily, whom she was convinced had drowned, and anger that she had been so gullible to be duped into believing that she was too afraid of water to ever jump overboard. Aimee, on the other hand, seemed calm and almost pleased at the loss of her former servant girl. Chastain, of course, blamed Manny and Thomas' lack of supervision of a slave who had a history of running.

"Blast him!" Thomas hissed through clenched teeth, keeping his outburst in check so as not to awaken anyone

He reached for his wallet and began counting his money. Munson had promised to find him a slave catcher with dogs to hire this morning. Chastain had said he would contribute a little to the cost but would be leaving with the Blue Wing with his family and his property when it left midmorning. He'd promised Thomas he could rejoin the family either in Madison or Louisville if either of the runaways were caught, but he wasn't willing to delay his trip down the Mississippi more than a few days.

After counting his bills twice, Thomas sighed deeply in frustration. Out of the $2,500 he'd brought to Kentucky, he had $290 left to live on, hire a slave catcher, offer reward money, and possibly buy passage on another steamer, if he missed his previously purchased conveyance. No matter how it turned out, this change of fortune would impoverish him for a time.

* * *

The Blue Wing looked majestic in the morning light that filtered through the tall sycamores along the bank. Its ornate carvings and garish bright colors seemed to mock Thomas. Soon the steamboat would be on its way to the Ohio and then west to meet the Mississippi and he would be left here in Kentucky. Chastain had insisted on talking about the runaway situation with him over breakfast on the boat, delaying the early start he had planned.

After a conversation over biscuits and bacon, Chastain gave him five $20 bills. Thomas stood to leave and shook his partner's hand, promising to write, though the lack of railroad lines through much of the South made it unlikely that any letters would get there ahead of the steamboat.

As he turned to head to the docking ramp, he heard a shout from the door of the dining room. "Oh, Mr. Thomas!" Yvonne came rushing up to the table, her auburn hair pinned up in two looped braids behind her ears. Her cheeks were flushed, and he could see traces of tears on her lashes. She stopped a few feet away and stood looking at him, a crushed handkerchief squeezed in her gloved fist. Her pale-yellow dress complemented her skin and hair, and Thomas couldn't help but be flattered by her attentions.

"Surely you weren't going to leave without saying goodbye to me — I mean Mother and Aimee and me?"

Ashamed, he fumbled with his hat and said, "Well now, I'm sorry, Miss Yvonne, but if there's a chance of catching those two runaways, I've got to hurry. They could be miles from here by now."

"I know. I'm so furious with Lily. Do you know I discovered just now that she must have stolen my slippers? I know they were under my bed when we left the boat. I wonder what else she took from me and put in that old pillow sack of hers?"

"She stole your shoes?" her father asked in disbelief.

"She must have been planning then to run off," put in Thomas, who was feeling a rising sense of urgency. "I've got to go now, sir," he said to Chastain. Keep a close watch on George and Jim."

He turned back to Yvonne. "Goodbye, Miss Chastain. Give my regards to your mother and sister." Thomas headed towards the door.

"Won't you write to me, Thomas?" called Yvonne.

Thomas just gave one last wave of his hat and hurried to the dock.

Once off the boat he spotted the lockmaster on the bank and headed straight for him. Josiah Munson stood watching the big oxen work to open the lock, overseen by a tall black man with a whip. ⸳

"Get that team moving, Moses! We've got five or six boats backed up and more on the way, I'm sure," he shouted down.

"Yes, suh. I's tryin'. I think Billy Boy's goin' lame," he shouted back, pointing to a long-horned black steer balking on the yoke.

"That's the last thing I need to hear today," Munson muttered, snatching his watch out of his pocket to check the time. He started toward the path that led to the oxen when Thomas caught his sleeve.

"Excuse me, Mr. Munson. I can see you're busy, but you promised to help find me someone to help hunt down my property this morning."

141

"Oh yes, Mr. Mercier. I planned to take you myself as soon as things were running smoothly here, but as you can see, that's not happening. I can't leave for at least another hour and not that if we must switch steers. Our backup ox isn't fully broken in and I can't risk leaving the place untended."

"What can I do, then?" asked Thomas, his stomach churning.

"Walk a mile or two up that road," Munson said, pointing north to a dirt track through the trees and you'll come right into Carrollton. Ask anybody you meet where to find the sheriff or one of his deputies and they'll help you out."

Frustrated, Thomas turned back to the lockmaster's house to fetch his trunk. This was the type of job he would have given Manny. The thought infuriated him and doubled his determination to find the boy and give him the whipping he'd promised him back in May when he'd bought him — just a couple of miles from this lock. His hands tightened into fists, and he practically ran up the path.

* * *

Lugging his travel trunk up the road to Carrollton had worn Thomas out before the hunt for Manny and Lily even began. His anger at Manny hadn't subsided but had grown with every step. By the time he put it down near the porch of the first business he came to, his face was beet red, and he wished he could throw the bulky trunk into the river that wound in and out of his vision on his left. He took a deep breath to calm himself, then removed his hat and stepped through the door.

The small, cluttered room seemed to contain everything from candy to corn knives. It was poorly lit, with the sun's rays filtering through leafy branches and merchandise hanging from the ceiling. Thomas blinked as his eyes adjusted, then he heard rapid footsteps approaching from behind a curtain partition and a balding man with a bloodied butcher's apron appeared.

"Goot mornin'," the man said in a thick German accent, nodding to Thomas while wiping his hands on the apron. "How may I help you? Forgive the stank. I'm cleaning some fish I bought this mornin' and salting it down." He looked at Thomas' fine clothing with a hopeful expression.

Thomas hadn't even noticed the odor. Having practically grown up on the docks of New Orleans, he was immune to any distaste over it. He smiled at the man briefly, then cleared his throat.

"I'm looking for the sheriff or someone who can help me find a pair of runaways that took off last night down by the lock."

The man pursed his lips and looked down. "Are they your property sir," he asked, looking towards the window.

Thomas followed his gaze but saw nothing of interest. The wind was stirring the leaves, giving him glimpses of the nearby river. "Yes, well partly mine. We think they jumped overboard and made for the western shore."

"That's hard to believe they would jump," said the man. "I've heard negroes are afraid of water."

"Yes, well that's what they wanted me to believe, anyway. But they're gone and last night we saw some traces on the far bank, so we think they've gone that way. Do you know where the sheriff or a deputy is or someone I could hire with dogs? The dark last night made it impossible to start hunting and I'm on my own here to find help."

"Say, where you from?" asked the man showing interest. "I thought I noticed a southern accent. Tennessee maybe?"

"No, sir. I'm from Louisiana and I bought these slaves here in Kentucky and I planned to take them home with some others and probably sell them for a good profit. Now they've run off and I've got to find them," Thomas said, his voice rising with his anxiety. "I paid nearly a thousand dollars for the pair of them, and I can't lose that much money!"

"Are they men or women?"

"One man and one woman – both young. The girl looks white, light brown hair and fair skin, but she isn't. Have you seen them?"

"No, sir. You could ask around, though I imagine they'd stay clear of town. Probably hiding in the woods somewhere."

"Where can I find the sheriff or a man with dogs for hire?" asked Thomas, getting impatient at the delay.

"Well, the sheriff might be over at the courthouse," the man said pointing east. Someone there maybe could help you. You might want to print up some notices for a reward or place an advertisement in the newspaper."

"Where would I do that," asked Thomas.

"Well, there's the *Carrollton Eagle*, just down the street. They could probably print you some flyers and run an advertisement. But if you're wanting someone to help you hunt, you'd best cross over to Prestonville, just across the Kentucky River since that's where you said the two were heading. They might have gone as far as Trimble County by now. If they've gone across the Ohio already, you'd best look up the Jefferson County Sheriff in Indiana."

Thomas felt like a teakettle about to explode. So many decisions to make and Chastain had left him to make them. He didn't know where to turn next and time was getting away from him. He closed his eyes and held up his hand to stop the storekeeper before he barraged him with more suggestions. "Just tell me how to get to the courthouse. Surely someone there knows where the sheriff is. This is a matter of theft in this county, so that's surely the best place to start."

"Theft?" asked the man, his shiny forehead wrinkling in confusion. "Did they steal some of your property too then?"

"They ARE my property!" shouted Thomas, unable to contain himself any longer. "They've stolen themselves away from me and I intend to get them back and make them pay!"

"Yes, sir. Sorry, sir," said the man who scribbled a name and address on a scrap of paper and shoved it at Thomas, who snatched it and turned around and headed for the door. He saw his trunk sitting askew where he'd left it and shouted back at the man. "Please bring my trunk in and keep it for me until I return. I'll pay you for your trouble." Then he hurried out of sight.

* * *

Thomas's frustration increased as the day wore on. The courthouse was empty except for a clerk who looked up from his ledger when Thomas rushed in and asked for the sheriff. He just pointed silently out the window with his fountain pen at a nearby building. Thomas walked to what looked like a one-room shack. A sign over the door read "Carroll County Jail and Sheriff's Office". Hope rose in his chest. He opened the door and started talking eagerly to the official inside.

The man held up his hand and Thomas paused.

"Whoa there, slow down. I'm not the sheriff here. Sheriff Allen is out of town transporting a prisoner, a runaway, to New Castle in Henry County."

"Does he catch many runaways?" Thomas asked eagerly.

"A few. If the patrollers don't catch them first," the deputy's replied.

"When will he return?"

"I expect he'll stop by to see his folks before comin' back. They live over near Campbellsburg. He'll probably get in around sunset, I'm guessing."

"Can you help me search for my two runaways? They jumped in the Kentucky and swam to the western shore about sunset last night and I've got to have help." The man's laidback manner irked Thomas, who was growing more impatient by the moment.

"I'm sorry, sir. I've got a prisoner here," he jerked his head in the direction of the back corner of the room, "and I can't leave him unguarded.

"Isn't there another deputy?"

"Not on the payroll. We've got some men we can hustle up in an emergency to deputize around town." Thomas opened his mouth, but the man cut him off.

"But a runaway slave is not an emergency. A runaway's not a threat to the citizens of the county and that's the only time we're allowed to hire help."

Thomas turned and slammed the door. He looked at the sky. The sun was nearing its zenith, and he was getting nowhere.

He stopped by the newspaper office and managed to put in an order for 20 posters, the minimum they would print, at a dime each. The printer promised to have them ready before closing at five. The newspaper was only a weekly and wouldn't be out for several days, so he declined spending more of his precious money, though the editor pressed him vigorously.

After talking again to the storekeeper and buying a bite to eat, he connected with a man living by the river who let him borrow his boat for two bits. With a growing sense of urgency, Thomas swiftly paddled it across to Prestonville and tied it off at a little dock.

He practically ran to the first house he saw and knocked. Failing to get any help after the first four homes out of no more than a dozen, he was losing heart when the braying of hound dogs greeted his knock at a slovenly looking shack a bit distant from the other homes.

"Shut up!" a gravelly voice barked back at the hounds, who instantly stopped and changed their song to an annoying whine. The door opened about three inches and Thomas saw a rheumy eye peer at him through the aperture. Before he could open his mouth, a voice rose above the canine whimpering. "What'cha want? I aint buyin' nothin', stranger, so you might as well move on."

Instinctively Thomas reached out his hand to prevent the man from shutting the door.

"Wait. I'm not selling anything. I'm looking for someone to hire for a job."

The pressure on the door eased and it opened a few more inches to reveal a man in his late forties, dressed shabbily with tobacco stains in a gray beard. Two coonhounds poked their sniffling noses around the man's legs to check out the stranger. Thomas knew they smelled the dried fish he had wrapped in a handkerchief in his pocket. A good sign.

"What kinda job?" the man asked, skepticism written across his face as he looked Thomas over.

"I'd like to hire someone with tracking dogs to help me find two runaways. They jumped off our boat at the lock last night and swam to this side of the river. It was near dark when we discovered it, and we couldn't track them further. Can I hire you to bring them and start looking now? I can pay well."

The man's eyes opened wide with interest.

145

"Oh, I can't do any galivantin' around with my rheumatism like it is, but my son sure can. He loves trackin' down coons and such out in the woods all over Hunter's Bottom.

"Hunter's Bottom?" asked Thomas.

"Yeah. That's what we call this stretch from here to Milton downriver. Good land between the river and hills you know. Lots of nice farms and big houses with 'bacco and hemp and such for sellin' down south."

"Is your son home? Can he come right away? I'll pay four dollars for the day."

"Well, that's mighty temptin'," said the man, "but Eli is hired out for the day cuttin' 'bacco. He won't be home until suppertime, which is near dark. I wish youda showed up earlier. He aint makin' but two dollars for that back-breakin' job."

"Could I go find him and bring him back home?" asked Thomas.

The man looked up in disbelief. "No sir. He's workin' for our neighbor, Mr. Duncan. You can't just yank him off the job and leave Duncan high and dry. The 'bacco can't wait. Ya gotta cut it when its ready or you could ruin your crop. Don't ya know that?"

"No sir. I'm from Louisiana. We don't grow tobacco there. Cotton's our crop."

"Well, you're a long ways from home, aint ya mister — didn't catch your name"

"Mercier. Thomas Mercier."

The man frowned. "Well, Mr. Thomas. I'll never get my tongue around that last name of yourn. But if you'll come by early tomorrow mornin' about eight o'clock. I'm sure Eli will be glad to take Sonny and Daisy out huntin' for that four dollars.

* * *

That afternoon Richard Daly dipped his oar lazily in the Ohio on his way back home to Kentucky. He was feeling quite content. His carrots, sweet potatoes, and onions had sold out at the Madison market, and he'd pocketed another half dollar toward his goal. His master, Samuel Fearn, was benevolent, allowing him his own little house and garden, and, best of all, the freedom to grow and sell his own produce and pocket the profits. Richard was saving up the sum of $100 that Fearn had promised would purchase his freedom.

His mind turned to his wife Kitty and their children, who lived just upriver at the Hoagland place, and smiled. Tomorrow was Sunday and he was sure Master Fearn would allow him to visit Kitty and the kids. How he was ever to earn enough to buy them from the Hoaglands, he didn't know, but for now, things were going well for him at Hunter's Bottom.

Richard lifted his oar and let the boat's momentum carry him to the group of saplings where he kept the craft tied up. When it hit land, he jumped out and pulled the skiff well onshore, hid it as best he could among some bushes, grabbed the oar and headed up the familiar path to the big house. He had chores waiting and beans to heat up for his supper.

About an hour before sundown, just when he'd finished milking and feeding the livestock, he stopped dead in his tracks. The horseshoe that hung over his backdoor was upside down, not in the lucky "U" shape he'd always heard was proper. He walked closer to examine it. Perhaps a nail had fallen out.

Then Richard's eyes grew wide. He suddenly remembered telling some fellow slaves a few years ago at a corn shucking party that he could get them help if they ever ran away and the signal would be to flip that horseshoe. He knew where they'd be hidden. All the slaves in that area knew of a cave back in the woody hills that was the preferred hiding place for runaways, contraband, and secret trysts. Up until now, no one had used his lucky shoe. He hurried back inside the barn with his bucket of milk and handed it off to Tom, the other field hand.

"Here, take this in, would you?" he asked.

"Why can't you? I've still got the two horse stalls to muck out?" he asked.

Rich looked around to make sure they were alone. "I got the signal. Somebody needs help at the caves," he whispered. Tom's lips puckered in surprise.

"I don't know how long they've been waitin' and I'm gonna head right there and check it out," Rich added. "Make excuses for me. If anybody asks, tell them I'm goin' huntin'. That's true enough, aint it?" he grinned. Tom nodded and took the bucket.

Inside his shack, Richard started gathering some supplies. His mind was racing along with his pulse. He was already planning out the escape, a big grin on his face. Although no one had used the horseshoe signal before, this wasn't his first time helping people steal themselves to freedom and he loved the risk and excitement of it. Out of nowhere a good day had turned into a great one. He grabbed his shotgun along with a bag of stuff he'd gathered and headed out.

* * *

Back at the cave, Lily's insides were in knots from worry, nausea, and dehydration. The cold windless air had kept her clothing damp and the extra things she had laid out on the ground hadn't fully dried. Manny had managed to bring her a half cup of water and a few bites of corn pone, but she doubted if she could keep it down. She hadn't felt so miserable since those nights when Henri

147

had forced her legs open and held her down with his handkerchief stuffed in her mouth.

Fresh tears came at the shame of the memory, and she nearly retched again. Lily tried to recite the Lord's Prayer, but she couldn't focus on anything.

Suddenly she heard Manny's whispered voice from where he was stationed nearer to the cave's narrow opening. "Lily? Are you awake? Are you decent?"

She sat up, startled. "Yes, Manny. Is somethin' wrong?"

Manny, half bent over, but with a smile that she could see even in the near dark, said, "I'd like to introduce you to a friend of mine."

Lily, looking past Manny to the mouth of the cave, saw a shape silhouetted against the dying light. It was coming closer, and her heart started pounding, despite herself.

"This here, said Manny, sitting down near her, "is my friend Richard. He's gonna help us."

A man in shoes and well-patched clothes swept off his hat.

"Nice to meet you, Lily," he said, sitting down next to Manny. "Let's risk a little light."

Before Lily could offer a greeting, she heard a match being struck and the smell of sulfur. A bright flame lit up the man's brown face. He opened a little door and transferred the fire to a tin lantern on the floor beside him.

Lily, so long in the dark of the cave blinked several times before her eyes adjusted.

The man named Richard was looking at her intently. "Manny says you've been feelin' poorly. It's no wonder, you're not much more than a child an' cold an' hungry. Here, drink some of this water and have some of these crackers I brung ya."

Lily nearly teared up again at the kind words of sympathy and held her hand out for the promised water. As she brought the canteen up to her lips, a glimpse of Manny's concerned face added a new layer of misery to her thoughts. Her sickness might jeopardize their escape plans. She closed her eyes and took a long gulp, forcing it past her parched throat to her queasy stomach.

"Richard has a wife and children on another farm, and he says he's helped other runaways make it across to Indiana," Manny said as Lily began nibbling a cracker.

Richard studied Manny as he settled onto the floor. "It's true, Manny my boy, it's true. But before I can help you, you've got to tell me how you ended up here in the first place with what looks like a white girl. The last I heard; Mister Konkel had sold you off to Louisiana folks. I couldn't believe my ears when I heard your voice comin' outa this cave."

"Well," said Manny with a sigh. "It's a long story."

"Well, brother, I've got the time and hopes you two does too. Let's hear it."

* * *

While Manny was telling their story to Richard, Lily nodded off. A snore from her filled a pause in the conversation and Manny covered her with the dry blanket Richard had brought. Afraid of disturbing her he had motioned for Richard to douse the lamp and they had crawled closer to the mouth of the cave. Now, lit by faint moonlight they sat in the dark, the sounds of tree frogs and cicadas filling the gaps between their hushed voices.

"You's lucky, Manny. There aint been no pattyrollers askin' about you today that I knows of. I been gone to Madison most of the day, but I never heard nothin' bout no runaways on either side of the river. Mornin' come, it may be a whole different story, especially if your owner puts up a reward or hires somebody like Wright Rea."

"Who's he?"

"A slavecatcher in Jefferson County. That's across the river, but he's greedy and slick enough to try to catch runaway folks over here. He don't care if he's helpin' one escape or helpin' fetch him back to Kentucky as long as it fills his pockets."

"Does he got dogs?"

"I don't rightly know, but there's plenty of folks that does and will rent them out to slave catchers and pattyrollers for a price. It's all about the money. You and I and that poor gal in there are commodities and folks'll go a long way to see we aint lost to 'em."

"How come you's still here in Kentucky, Richard? You say Mr. Fearn lets you go over to Madison all the time to sell your vegetables and hire out for the day. Why haven't you stole yourself off?"

"'Cause I got my wife and little 'uns to look after. It aint just me. A man alone can hide in the woods and hollers eatin' off the land and escape easy with some help, but women and children make it a whole lot harder — almost impossible if they's too little or weak to walk far. I'm savin' up money to buy my family, so we'll be free and clear and maybe even live in Georgetown or some such place."

"Georgetown?"

"That's the name of the free black neighborhood in Madison. There's freemen livin' in fine homes with their families, although some have left 'cause of getting' caught or suspected of stealing away folks like you."

"I'm worried about takin' Lily, I admit," Manny said, shakin' his head. She's been sickly since we got here and I'm afraid she might be expectin' a baby."

"That little girl?" whispered Richard, the shock evident in his tone.

"'Fraid so. A family guest visited them in Frankfort back in June and forced himself on her more than once. She was bought for the fancy girl trade down south she says. I just couldn't leave her behind to face that."

"Iffin she is goin' to have a baby this winter, we've got to get her out of Kentucky and far from here quick like." Richard sighed. He was stooping down to exit the cave and looked back into the darkness. "I've got to go. I'll make some excuse in the mornin' to Mr. Fearn and start makin' some connections to get you two across. In the meanwhile, you stay put and quiet. I'll be back with more water and food later. Make sure Lily gets enough to drink and pray for some rain that'll wash away any trace of you."

"Thank you, Richard. I'll lay low and let Lily do the prayin'. She's a big believer in prayers."

Chapter Seventeen

Richard managed to get a few hours of sleep before he was roused from bed by Tom, wanting help with the morning chores. After that, even though it was Sunday, his master had asked him to examine the tobacco and get rid of all traces of pests. The time was nearing for cutting and he was searching for hornworms. The bright green insects were masters at camouflage and could ruin the crop. Richard checked a few more plants, which showed no sign of infestation, when large drops of cold rain began pattering on the yellowing plants. He looked up. Dark gray clouds were swallowing up the September sunshine and a gust of wind set the aspens to quiver as if in fright. The bright late morning sunshine, necessary for spotting the pests, dimmed.

"Here comes that rain we been prayin' for, young 'uns," he whispered with a grin, thinking of the frightened teenagers huddling in the dark of the cave.

Before he got halfway to the shelter of the empty tobacco barn, the clouds burst in a downpour that soaked through his cotton shirt and washed the perspiration off his face and neck. Once inside the barn he looked through the gaps to see that the clouds were quickly covering the whole sky. A good soaking rain was just what the tobacco, his vegetables, and the runaways needed.

The downpour provided him an excuse to leave off farm chores for a time to do some of the necessary leg work needed to get Manny and Lily out of Kentucky. Since it was Sunday, asking to visit Kitty and the children would lead to no suspicion. He took off at a run at the first hint of a slackening in the rainfall and headed for the big house to report to Mr. Fearn.

An hour later he was saying goodbye to Kitty, Dick, and Cora. They'd been able to have a quick bite of leftovers together from the Hoagland's dinner in Kitty's cabin. He'd filled her in about Manny and Lily. Sympathetic, especially to Lily and her possible condition, Kitty had promised to make a tincture of peppermint for the girl's nausea.

Richard, a tarp thrown over his head to keep off the rain and his paddle in hand, hurried down to where his skiff was hidden and pushed off into the Ohio. He prayed he could find the Rev. Harris or one of his sons at home. Chapman Harris, a hulking free black man was a preacher and a secret helper to runaways crossing the river. He farmed and preached in Eagle Hollow, just a couple of miles upriver from Madison. Harris had connections to other free blacks and white abolitionists in the area who would help get runaways moved out of the clutches of slave catchers like Rea.

* * *

For what seemed hours to Manny, Lily had been standing and flapping her extra clothing in the still air, attempting to dry them out. The incessant sound and inactivity made him feel like a coil ready to spring, and without knowing it he'd begun to shake one of his legs rapidly as he sat staring at the distant cave mouth.

"Manny, is you alright?" asked Lily in the darkness between them. She paused her swinging to listen for an answer.

"Yes, I'm fine. I just can't bare all this sittin' and waitin'. I can't even stand up and pace in here without hittin' my head. I feel so useless. I wanna get outa here and *do* something!

"Well," Lily began flapping again, "Miz Willson always said 'Idle hands are the devil's tools,' but I's always found my idle times, like on Sundays when Miz Willson let me off mosta my chores, was a good time to get things figgered out. I liked to go wadin' in the crick and cool off and then just sit on the bank and talk and talk," she said giving the petticoat a final shake. She spread it carefully on the ground and grabbed the slippers and began swinging them in circles.

"Who'd you talk to? Was there other slaves there?" asked Manny over the sound of rushing air. His leg had stopped shaking as he listened for her answer. Lily, thus far, had not been much company.

"Oh, no. Just me since I was a little girl, when they sold my mama and the rest of the slaves off."

"How comes they didn't sell you too?"

"I was bad sick on the day the buyers came and they didn't want me. Miz Willson said she'd keep me 'til I got better, but by then she said she couldn't get by without me helpin' her on the farm. She hired out folks when there was jobs too big for just the two of us, but she never bought another slave. Slaves are 'too dear' she'd say, meanin', I guess, that she couldn't afford to get any more."

"So, who would you talk to then?" asked Manny, growing impatient.

"Sometimes the farm animals or a yeller cat we had, but mostly to God."

"Did Miz Willson take you to church? How'd you grow up prayin' to God so much?" Manny had listened quietly earlier while Lily had recited the Lord's Prayer and thanked God for the cave and for their food and water. Then she prayed for George and Joe, then a Della, Tilda, and Peggy and some other names he didn't know, the Chastain's slaves, and finally, to his astonishment, Aimee and Yvonne. After that, she started praying for Richard and for their protection from dogs and slave catchers, and finally for rain to wash away their tracks.

"Miz Willson told people she felt it was her 'Christian duty' to teach me about God. She read verses from the Bible every night before we went to sleep and taught me to recite the Ten Commandments, the Lord's Prayer, and some other things."

"She did all that while not payin' you any wages and keeping you as her slave? She don't sound to me like she practiced what she preached. I heard Jesus said to 'love one another.' How can you do that if you're keepin' people chained up?" asked Manny, his voice rising.

"Oh, she never chained me. Most times she treated me like a niece or younger sister, but I did get a few whoopin's when she was feelin' bad and fractious."

"Fractious? What's that?"

"I don't know. That's what she called it. I guess angry and irritable. Kinda like you right now," said Lily, smiling.

"Do you really believe what she taught you from the Bible," asked Manny, changing the subject.

"Well, I try to. One verse she taught me came outa Proverbs, the 'Book of Wisdom' she called it. It went, 'Trust in the Lord with all thy heart; and lean not onto thy understanding. In all thy ways ack … ack-know-ledge him, and he shall direct your path.'* So that's what I try to do, trust."

Manny opened his mouth to question her further, when the rumble of thunder reached his ears and froze the words on his lips. Lily stopped swinging the slippers and they both listened intently for sounds from outside. Lily dropped the shoes and started walking swiftly to the entrance. A flash of lightning lit her face just as she was reaching her palm out to feel for rain. Suddenly cold drops hit her with a blast of wind, and she pulled back inside.

"Manny, God's done come through again. Fetch me that tin cup!"

*Proverbs 3:5-6

* * *

Less than a mile east of the cave, two rain-soaked hound dogs were sheltering with Thomas and their owner under a big elm tree. They had gotten underway late, but Sonny and Daisy had picked up a scent trail quickly near the lock and Thomas' spirits rose as he and Eli struggled through the brush to keep up with the dogs.

But before they'd gone a mile or so west, distant thunder and wind presaged a storm. Their pace didn't slow until the first drops started to fall, and the thunder increased in volume. Then Sonny's tail went between his legs, and he started pressing his nose into his master's pantleg. He refused to go on, despite every command. Daisy seemed eager to continue, but as the ground and the hunters became saturated in the increasing downpour, she began losing the scent and started heading back the way they had come.

Now at the height of the storm, they had given up momentarily and both men and dogs were standing dejected, thoroughly soaked, and shivering in the rush of cooler air. There was an uncomfortable silence built up between the two men, broken at last by Eli, who had to shout above the tumult.

"I'm sorry, mister, but Sonny is a big coward when it comes to thunderstorms. I'm afraid we'd better call it a day and head back. He won't be worth nothin' as a tracker until he's gotten over it. Besides, this hard rain will've washed any scent off anyways and they'll start following the runoff instead of the tracks. If it had just been a light rain, they woulda found your runaways in no time."

Thomas' irritation on hearing this exploded. "Well, then give me back my money if you're not going to go on. I'm just wasting my time with you, and I've got to get them before they find a way to cross into Indiana. There's no way I'll find them there and I'm running out of money."

"What? No way am I giving you your money back. Besides I left it with Pa and he's likely got it hid. I gave up the chance for another two dollars today hangin' 'bacco at Duncan's. Why don't you just get on your way and hunt for 'em yourself? Or are you too high and mighty to go crawlin' around in the woods like us folk?"

Thomas' fingers curled into a fist, and he made a step towards Eli, only to stop short at the sound of Daisy's low growl. He glanced at the dog and saw bared fangs and raised hackles. Before he could react, he heard a click and looked up to see a small revolver pointed in his direction, held by the steady hand of her owner. Eli's eyes were steely with determination and Thomas held his hands up in surrender, then pivoted and walked away in the direction the hounds had last been headed.

Chapter Eighteen

The steady pattering of raindrops calmed Manny's nerves so much that after an hour or so he drifted off to sleep and was softly snoring. Lily had first drunk her fill from the cool fresh raindrops that dripped from the cave mouth, sharing the tin with Manny, and then when he drifted off, she sat near the entrance to watch a pool of the lifesaving liquid form in a depression nearby.

Once she thought she heard the baying of hounds in the distance and her pulse raced. Then the tattoo of the raindrops quickened their rhythm accompanied by a flash of lightening and the boom of thunder a few seconds later. Her ears strained to listen, but all sound was drowned out by the downpour. The wind picked up and splattered her with rain and she let out the breath she'd been holding and scrambled further inside.

After her eyes adjusted to the dim light, she picked her way along the cave floor to the space where Manny lay sleeping and sat down. She felt around for the dry blanket Richard had provided and wrapped it over her shoulders. The raindrops had chilled her again and she reached hopefully for the spare clothes and slippers. They were still damp, but much drier than they had been.

She sighed and picked up her skirt and began fanning it. It was the blue dress she'd worn on the day of the auction and the memory of that day and the girls she'd been sold with came back painfully. The thought made her forget her churning stomach and the chilly humidity of the cave momentarily. Only a few months had passed since then, but she felt as if that Lily had been another person — a child who had left and would never return. A tear coursed down her cheek for the frightened, naïve little girl she once was.

Manny stirred in his sleep, reminding her of the present and the blessing of escape and the rain. With that thought, she spread the skirt beneath her, and covering her head with the blanket, drifted off herself.

She was dreaming of napping under a shade tree near the creek back home when she awoke to Manny's call. She sat up, unsure of where she was and rubbed her eyes.

"I hated to wake you up, but you've been sleepin' a long time, Lily," said Manny. Lily turned her head towards the cave opening. The rain had stopped, but the trees were still dripping. "Richard stopped by with some more vittles and some medicine for your stomach. He told us to be ready after sundown."

"Ready for what?" she asked, a mixture of fear and hope evident in her voice. She reached for her dress and found it almost dry. The press and warmth of her body had done its work.

"Ready to run again — for the shore. He's takin' us across the Jordan, Lily. We's gonna be in the Promised Land come mornin'!"

* * *

After his evening chores, Richard started preparing for his trip with the two runaways and the ruse that would, hopefully, aid their escape. He'd found a sheet of old sailcloth in the back of the woodshed and gathered his fishing pole and bucket and was about to head out to dig for some bait when there was a knock on his door.

Heart pounding for fear of he knew not what, he opened the door to find Tom staring back at him.

"Richard, I got some news for ya," he began.

Richard pulled him inside with a quick glance to be sure no one else was around. "Yeah? What is it?"

"I overheard Miz Fearn tellin' Massa Fearn that some southerner knocked on the door earlier askin' if they'd seen two young runaways, a light-colored woman and a man."

"What she say?"

"She told him she aint seen nobody new and to go on his way. Said he was all muddy and looked a fright."

"Anything else?"

"She said he showed her a paper he had printed up offerin' a reward and asked where to find Wright Rae and she told him he was over in Madison, 'cross the river."

Richard sighed. If Rae and the various patrollers that worked the river got word of a reward, the odds of successfully getting the pair to safety would plummet.

"Thanks for lettin' me know, Tom. Tell Fearn I'm goin' catfish huntin' on the river after sundown and will be sure to bring him some in time for breakfast. And then you gotta pray I catch some fish and deliver my cargo to Eagle's Hollow without drawin' any attention."

"I sure will, Richard. Good luck. I'd better get back to fetchin' firewood 'fore somebody wonders where I is."

Tom left and Richard lingered for a moment at the door. The sky was darkening in the east. He still had to dig some bait, stow all his gear into his skiff and then move it to a more sheltered spot before he could go fetch Lily and Manny. Then he had to lead them through the dark woods to the boat. The sky was still overcast, and the new moon would give little light. Harris had promised that someone would give the signal about an hour past sundown, so he needed to hurry. He grabbed a shovel, and an old tin can and headed out to find some worms.

Chapter Nineteen

By the time the sun had passed its apex, and the afternoon wore on, Thomas' frenetic energy had waned. He had spent what seemed like hours in the woods and, using the sun as his guide, had eventually headed north where he knew the river and farmland lay. His shoes were caked with mud and his pants covered with burrs and other clinging flora.

Once in the flatlands, he had knocked on several doors of respectable-looking homes, some even rivaling the plantation houses in the south, but his bedraggled looks prompted little respect or a listening ear. Despite offering to pay for a meal and showing them his money, they had done no more than grant him a suspicious look, a cold biscuit and a gulp of water.

Finally, at the door of a modest farmhouse, his offer of cash granted him some relief. The woman who answered the door had promised him a bowl of stew and a lift back to Carrollton from her husband for a dollar after supper. Seeing more of his money slip away galled Thomas, but he knew he didn't have the strength to walk the reported five miles back to where his trunk and a night's sleep at a boarding house awaited him.

Now, heading east once more with the silent farmer guiding the plodding horses, he weighed his options. It was obvious he couldn't find the runaways on his own. Every delay reduced his chances of finding them. He suspected there were abolitionists in the area who would thwart his efforts. The best bet, as far as he knew, was to put up the posters and hope someone's itchy palms would motivate them to act. Greed was apparently all that could get these people to help a stranger, but would the $150 reward be enough?

He couldn't risk more and if he missed his steamer home, he couldn't even afford that.

By the time the farmer dropped him off at the edge of the Kentucky River, he'd made up his mind to beg or buy passage on the next boat heading to Madison, where he could, hopefully, put up some posters, advertise in a daily newspaper, and catch up with the Chastains and their packet back home.

* * *

Manny crouched near the cave entrance and watched the light fade in the forest. He was restless again but forced himself to stay motionless. A few times he'd heard twigs snap and other noises that made his heart race, but he had said nothing to Lily. He told himself it was just deer or other critters, but deep down he knew his owners would not give up easily. Then he grinned at the thought that he was a thief, stealing himself and Lily away from their clutches. He was so close to finally making it across to freedom.

Lily was further in, changing into her now dry clothes and Yvonne's slippers and packing up what little they had in her sack. Manny had nothing but the clothes on his back and no shoes, but little cared. He had roamed this stretch of land most of his life and did not fear rock, root, or thorns as the bottom of his feet were thick with callouses. His muscles cramped and he sat down in a relatively dry spot and waited.

He'd nearly drifted off asleep again when a bird call signaled Richard's approach.

"Lily!" he hissed behind him. "He's here. Come on, let's go!"

Instantly, it seemed, she was at his elbow. Grasping her bag in one hand, she slipped her slender hand into his and followed him into the dimming twilight.

Hiding about 40 yards away in an agreed upon spot was Richard. He quickly covered Lily and her blue dress in a drab green horse blanket and told her to hold it tightly around her. He made Manny stuff the lumpy white cotton bag she carried inside his shirt before they headed north. Richard's serious demeanor and no-nonsense commands sobered the teens and when he started moving stealthily through the undergrowth, they followed without a sound.

Manny took the rear and Lily followed Richard, clasping the rough blanket to her throat, and reaching out for obstacles with her free hand. When she stumbled, Manny would reach out and steady her from behind and Richard would pause his steps to wait on her. The color faded from the trees and soon there were only black shapes in the gloom and branches and fallen limbs that seemed to trip her up every few steps. Manny called a halt.

"We've got to slow down some, Richard, or change tactics," Lily can't keep up."

Richard stopped and turned to look down at Lily.

"Can you ride pig-a-back?"

There was a slight pause. "I don't know, I've never tried."

"Well, let's try. Manny, you help her up on my back and tuck in that blanket, then we's gonna speed up. We don't want to miss the signal 'cross the water.'"

Manny helped Lily climb atop Richard's back and then redraped the blanket over her. "Hold tight to him and the blanket," he hissed as Richard straightened up and plunged forward into the gloom.

"Keep up!" he hollered back to Manny as he picked up the pace. Manny could hear Lily's whispered prayers ahead of him as the ground swiftly slipped away below him.

* * *

Still mumbling the Lord's Prayer as she bounced along on Richard's broad back, Lily's petitions were brought to an abrupt halt when she heard an unsettling metallic clanging ahead in the darkness. Richard evidently heard it too and stopped his forward motion, causing Manny to nearly crash into them from behind.

"What's that?" whispered Manny, almost in her ear as he leaned forward.

Richard's hand reached up to tug at Lily's arm as he released his grip on her and allowed her to slide off his back. He turned around, forefinger held firmly to his closed lips, signaling quiet. "That, my friends, is freedom callin'," he said in a voice so low Lily could barely understand. "That's the signal from the Promised Land that our Moses is ready for us to cross over."

The realization that there truly was someone waiting for them on the other side to help caused Lily to cover her mouth with both hands as tears started stinging her eyes. Manny stood rooted in his tracks, looking to Richard for instructions.

Quickly and quietly, while they were still under the cover of the woods, Richard told them of his catfish story cover and what was expected of them before, during, and after the crossing. He finished his instructions with "Just follow me, don't say nothin', and do what I say when I say to do it. Keep that blanket around you, Lily. Watch your step. Let's go."

Ten minutes later she lay curled up next to Manny in the stern of Richard's little boat, covered with the horse blanket, a piece of sailcloth, a cane pole, a can of worms, and a fish net. There was no room to move. Twice more they had heard the clanking sound from the north, goading Richard to hurry them along. Now, her ear pressed to the boat's bottom, she heard scraping sounds as Richard pushed the boat into the current, followed by splashes and drops of water on her feet as he hopped into the boat.

Soon her ears were filled with the sound of rushing water and the sensation of weightlessness as Richard paddled from shore. Her heart pounded in her ears. Manny also must have felt the tension, because his arm around her waist tightened. She had to remind herself to breathe. Lily forced herself to focus on Richard's rhythmic strokes as he dipped his oar in, first one side, and then the next, dripping heavy drops onto the sailcloth when he switched. The regularity of the sounds comforted Lily for a few moments, but then frightened her when they stopped and she heard Richard's voice, sudden and shrill in the still air.

"Hey, is that you, Gus?" he called.

Lily held her breath. Why was Richard drawing attention to himself in the middle of the river? She felt sick to her stomach and clenched her teeth to keep from gagging.

"Sure is. That you, Richard?" came the answer from not far off.

"Yep. I'm headin' over to my favorite catfish catchin' spot. I figure with all that rain, I should get a boatload tonight."

"Fried catfish. That sure sounds good," called the voice. "I'm huntin' bigger fish. I heard there was a southerner with cash huntin' for some runaways today."

Lily felt Manny's arm tighten even harder around her and she closed her eyes and tried not to breathe as Richard hollered back. "Yeah. Tom said he stopped by Fearn's askin'." There was a moment's hesitation, then Richard added. "Well, Gus, if I sees any runaways, I'll send 'em your way and if you sees any catfish, you can send 'em my way."

Lily heard a distant laugh as the boat bobbed under them. Her legs were beginning to cramp, and she longed to change position. "It's a deal. Happy huntin'," came the voice.

"You, too, Gus," called back Richard. Lily let out a deep sigh and felt Manny relax when the paddling commenced.

* * *

As Richard neared the Indiana shore, he could just make out the tall sycamore where the Rev. Chapman Harris should be concealed. Once the man struck the metal plate hidden in the tree, he wouldn't linger long if the expected boat didn't appear. Richard knew it wasn't out of fear that the massive deep-chested blacksmith would slip away, but because being able to continue his activity as a conductor was so crucial to the network of escape. Several other free blacks had been forced to flee over the years when they had come under suspicion. He was respected by many, both blacks and whites, but only a handful of people knew of his risky clandestine activities.

At Richard's final stroke, a sound came from the shore.

"Whoo whoo … whoo whoo."

Lily jerked in alarm at the unexpected sound and Richard let out a quick hush of warning. Relieved, he cupped his hands around his mouth and echoed the call.

"Stay still," hissed Richard, as he stepped overboard suddenly with a splash that seemed to echo loudly in the river valley. He began tugging the boat on shore away from the current as suddenly a deep voice came out of the darkness.

"Anybody see you? I heard talkin'," Harris said, stepping out from behind the tree.

"Just old Gus. I told him I was catfishin'. I think he bought it, but I'd better be back on the water quick in case he comes lookin' for me. He's huntin' for these two."

"You done good, Richard. Now let's get these young 'uns outa that boat and on their way. I got folks expectin' them up at Ryker's Ridge."

In a flash, Richard took away the fishing gear and sailcloth and the two men helped Manny out of the boat. He faltered as he took his first step on shore, which was not unusual. Richard knew from experience that lying in that cramped position usually caused his cargo's legs to fall asleep. Lily also struggled. She staggered forward and fell face down with a cry. She lay where she had landed, spitting bile from her mouth onto the muddy ground. Richard and the other men stood like statues behind her, listening for any signs of detection.

Suddenly Harris leaned over, smoothed the girl's hair, and scooped her up like an infant from where she lay. He looked toward Richard. The whites of his eyes peered out of the gloom, and he jerked his head in a signal to go. "Richard, you'd best get on with your catfishin'," hissed the big man, "I'll take it from here."

Richard paused only long enough to watch the trio head up into the hills, then walked back and forth in the spot where they'd stepped ashore to confuse any trackers and hopped back in the boat. He had fish to catch.

* * *

Manny stumbled for what seemed the hundredth time. In the near darkness, tree roots and undergrowth made every step an unknown venture. Following the hulking Harris, striding effortlessly up the steep ravine tasked even his energy reserves. Manny was amazed at the preacher's strength and stamina. On top of all that, he was carrying Lily, who had now scrambled onto his back. He wondered how many times the man had made the trek up this seemingly endless incline. Their guide seemed to be following a well-known path that was indistinguishable even to Manny's watchful eyes. Surely, he'd halt for a rest soon.

After a long while they advanced into a deep gully. Ahead, Manny could hear splashing noises and soon found his bare feet stepping through icy water in a rivulet. Just as one foot stepped over onto the dry bank, his other one slipped and he fell, striking his knee on a sharp stone. The pain was intense, and he knew instinctively that he was bleeding. Startled, he lay still, legs akimbo, waiting for a response from Harris, but could only hear footfalls receding in the darkness.

"Mr. Harris" he called in a hoarse whisper. The footsteps halted. A few seconds of nighttime noises filled the gap. Manny didn't move, but whispered louder, "I'm hurt."

After another moment he heard Harris retracing his steps. Manny's eyes, blinking back tears from the pain, strained ahead and finally spied the man advancing, Lily's head peering atop his, eyes wide open.

"Please put me down, Mr. Harris," he heard Lily murmur.

"What's the trouble, son?" Manny saw the man's face come into focus as he bent over.

"I slipped and hit my knee."

"Can you get up? Can you walk?"

"I think so. Give me your hand."

An enormous hand reached out, and Manny grasped it and pulled himself up with a stifled yelp. Standing upright he found his bones were sound, but his knee had twisted, and he could feel a trickle of warm blood dripping down his shin.

"My knee's cut and bleeding. I'm sorry, Mr. Harris. Any hound dog worth his keep will pick up that scent."

"Now don't you fret, son. It can't be helped." He put his hand into a pocket and pulled out a handkerchief, startlingly white in the dimness. "Here, wrap this rag tight around the cut and we'll see if you can go on. I haven't heard any sounds of pursuit yet, but you can never be too sure."

Manny did as he was told.

"I think we can go on now, Mr. Harris, but I may limp a little."

Harris, leaned over again and pointed to his back to signal Lily to climb back up.

"No sir. I can make out now for a while at least. You go ahead with Manny in case he needs help. I'll follow and I'll pray."

"Bless you, girl," chuckled the preacher. "That's right. We aint alone out here. The Lord'll surround us with his angels and make our paths straight. Let's keep moving. We've still got lots of hill to climb yet."

Part Five

Southeastern, Indiana

Ripley County, Indiana
Chapter Twenty

*L*ydia wiped an errant tear from her face and paused before opening the back door and carrying in her buckets of water. Her throat tightened at the memory of Will's forlorn and stunned face when she stole that last glance at him. What had she done? Why had she refused and strung him along? She knew the practicality of the reasons she had given him, yet she couldn't understand or begin to articulate the new deep-down knowledge that the decision had been the right one and she would never truly be happy as Mrs. Will Perry. Just what would bring her true happiness was a puzzle she couldn't solve.

She pushed open the door with her shoulder and walked into the work-room, filled with its familiar smells of fresh-cut timber. The late afternoon light coming through the window aided her steps as she maneuvered around the work bench and wood piles. Before she reached the door to the house, it opened, and Frank's smiling face greeted her and reached for a bucket.

"Hey, Lydia. Guess what?" he asked, effortlessly taking the heavy pail from her.

"You got first in the spelling bee at school again?" she guessed, sure of her answer.

"No. Well, yes, but that's not what happened."

Lydia looked quickly around the room as she took off her wrap. Seth was missing and Jane was rummaging through a box underneath the bed. Suddenly chilled, she sank down in her mother's rocker near the fire.

"Well, what then?" she asked Frank, who quickly sat on the edge of a chair at the nearby table, his eager face lit by the fire's glow.

"Now Frank, we don't know for sure," came Jane's calming voice.

"Oh, yes we do," he corrected, an unusual note of authority in his voice.

Lydia's brow knitted in concentration. "Well? What is it?" she spluttered.

"The Martins just got a letter from Maggie, and they're to expect three packages to arrive any day now." Frank couldn't keep the grin from his face as he teased his sister.

"Packages?" repeated Lydia, her face fixed in thought. Suddenly it dawned on her. "O, packages! Three? Mama, we'd better get busy!"

Jane smiled as she walked towards them, arms full of yarn and some unspun fluff. "Nothing escapes you two, does it? Yes, it looks like our work has begun. All we know right now is they are large, which Frank takes to mean adults, so we can start with warm stockings, which everybody needs. My bones tell me a killing frost is coming soon. Let's get busy," she said, laying the fibers on the table.

"Will you teach me?" Frank asked eagerly, stroking the soft wool.

Lydia laughed aloud. "Why would you want to learn to knit?"

"Because I want to do something to help. Why can't I learn?"

"I think it's an excellent idea," said Jane, easing into a chair beside Frank. "Men need to know how to take care of themselves. You may not always have a woman around to do things for you," she said, thinking of his future. "You can start at the beginning by learning to spin," she said, handing him the wooden spindle with a grin.

* * *

That evening Seth lingered long in the barn, taking unnecessary time to curry Ruby's coal-colored neck and sides. She nickered with pleasure, especially when he ran the comb over her hind quarters, leaning into his arm as he worked through her coat. His mind was full of questions about what the coming of the runaways would mean to the tightknit community.

He thought of what a loss it would be to his family if someone stole Ruby or Annie, whose labor and milk provided so well for their family. Slave labor was even more costly to replace, and he found himself momentarily feeling sorry for the farmers that suffered that loss. Then he shook his head to clear it. Human beings were not horses or cows. He cared for his animals far better than many slave owners cared for their so-called property and was determined to do his part. These vacillating feelings frustrated him, and all the while he was pushing back worries of what would happen if they were caught and prosecuted or sued for damages.

Visions of prison and the farm and all he had worked for being put on the auction block pressed against him like bothersome gnats swarming around his head. He paused his circular brushing and leaned his head against Ruby's hip, closing his eyes against the assaulting images. "Stop," he muttered. Then shaking his head and standing up straight he opened his eyes and shouted, "Stop!" Ruby nickered in surprise. After the silence returned, he spoke aloud at the rafters.

"God, I'm afraid. I trust you, but I don't understand you. Why did you take our little girl from us? Why give us a baby when we're still grieving and all I can think about is if Jane can get through another birth? Why bring these needy people into our lives now when the risks seem so high, and winter is coming on? Why us? Why here? Why now?"

The only answer was the sound of Ruby nuzzling his elbow and Annie's rhythmic chewing coming from the next stall. He put up the comb and walked out of the stall, grabbing the bucket as he walked over to milk Annie. After he settled himself on the stool and had a steady stream going into the pail, his eyes fixed on the toes of his boots. He blinked and saw chubby little feet step on them, and a childish voice demand a dance.

Alice had trusted him completely and loved nothing more than dancing around the floor with him or being tossed high into the rafters, squeaking with delight. His throat tightened at the memories and longing.

"Be like Alice," a voice said in his head. "Trust me even when it's scary and you're afraid. I am with you. I will watch over your family." The voice was calm and steady. "You are here right now, right where I want you to be, and you can do this work I have prepared for you."

Tears began to roll down his cheeks, and he had to sit up and wipe them away, lest they fall into the rich creamy milk. "Yes, Lord," he whispered. "I believe. Forgive my unbelief. Use me. Use my family, my house, my barn, my animals, my gifts. Anything. What does it all matter if we don't have you? You give and you take away and you do it all for your own plans and purposes. Make me your instrument. Make me your servant. Use me for your glory."

Annie started to move away, but he steadied her and finished emptying her udder. Lighter of heart after his battle, he hurried through the rest of the chores and headed back to the house.

* * *

True to Jane's prediction, wintry weather wrapped around the countryside with cold winds that covered the ground with a frosty rime. Even Frank gave in and donned socks and shoes as he set out for school. Seth hurried out after breakfast with Bessie to hunt down the pigs that belonged to them and Cinda that were last seen rooting around an oak grove near the Hillman's cabin. It was high time to get them penned and fattened to butcher. The thought of ham and bacon seemed to motivate Bessie too, as she took off with abandon.

Inside the cabin near the fire, Lydia was industriously turning the wool Frank had spun the night before into a second sock. The fibers didn't match well, but she reminded herself it was for warmth, not fashion. Jane was churning butter with one hand while she rocked, her other hand lying on the small mound that had begun to crowd her lap. The gentle creak of the rocker, the snap of the fire, the splash of the churn, the click of Lydia's knitting needles, blended with the distant ticking of Seth's pocket watch and filled the room. Lydia sighed aloud in a moment of contentment she hadn't felt in months.

"Oh!" Jane muttered suddenly.

Lydia looked up to see her mother's hand pressed against her abdomen.

"Is everything alright mother?" she asked in alarm, pausing in her work. Jane smiled at her, all the while keeping the up and down motion of the churn constant. "Oh, yes. I believe our newcomer has just given me a kick. It's the first time I've felt it."

"Does it hurt?" asked Lydia, thinking of her own aspirations of motherhood. "Not at all. It never hurts, it just feels funny to have your body do things you have no control over. It brings to mind that Psalm that says, 'For thou hast possessed my reins; thou hast covered me in my mother's womb.'* Isn't it amazing, Lydia, to think that God knows this child already and has planned out his or her life? Our baby may very well live into the next century. What will the world be like then, I wonder?"

"I certainly can't imagine slavery will still be a part of it," answered Lydia, thinking of the feet that would fill her stocking.

"You're right, Lydia," said Jane, leaning over to peek into the churn. "Surely people will see the truth behind the lies someday. I just hope it can end peacefully, but I admit I wonder how that can ever happen. The whole business has taken such a stronghold on so many people. They actually believe that black people are inferior and better off as slaves."

Lydia thought guiltily of some of the passages she had read in the book Will had loaned her and of the offhand comments he had made a time or two when they were alone. She knew he was just repeating what he had heard his father say, but did he really believe it himself?

She gazed out the window remembering some of the tales he had told to make her laugh that featured a black person's misfortune and reddened at the thought. She shook her head to rid herself of the memory and then glanced at

Jane. She was relieved to find her mother busy with the butter paddles, readying the lump for the mold. Lydia laid down her work and came over to help.

"Let's make some buttermilk biscuits for supper tonight, Mama. Wouldn't Papa and Frank love that?"

"Why yes, they would," said Jane smiling as she worked, "and I think there's enough to make extra. We can take them over to Rebekah to serve her guests. Won't light biscuits be a treat for those folks after their long trip?"

Mama was always thinking of others. Lydia swallowed a lump in her throat and nodded.

*Psalm 139: 13-14

* * *

When school was over for the day, the school master, Stephen Kelly, asked Frank to bring in firewood for the next day. It was not an unusual request. He was the oldest boy in the school, which consisted of about a dozen area children. After he filled up the wood box in the entry way and went to his desk to gather his slate and books, he turned to go and found Mr. Kelly blocking his way out.

"Frank, I need to talk to you a moment." He looked expectantly at the man he admired so much. "I'm afraid I will need my books back that I leant you." Frank subconsciously tightened his arm around the three books that had been almost his constant companions over the past three school terms.

"But why, Mr. Kelly?" he blurted out despite his upbringing to never question an adult.

"Because, Frank, you have successfully completed every lesson in them. I've been tempted to hold you back, but your examinations prove you have learned all they, and I, have to teach you. I need the books for Paul Jacobson. He's ready for them."

Frank waited for more explanations, but the schoolmaster was silent and looked down at him sorrowfully. "But…" he began but found there was nothing more to say.

"You're a bright boy, Frank. In a few years you could be teaching this school yourself if you could study some more to pass the examinations. I'm sorry. I hope you can find a way to keep on learning. Take care of yourself and your family. And tell your father I'll be needing a few more desks in here by the winter term. Perhaps you can help build them."

With that he stepped forward with his arms open. Frank thought he wanted a hug at first, but then realized he was waiting for the books. Frank laid them in his hands and managed to say, "Thank you, Mr. Kelly. Tell Paul I'd be glad to help him study if he wants to drop by some time." Then he grabbed his jacket and practically ran home, taking a detour past the spring, where he drank long and hard and splashed the redness from his eyes before he headed home.

* * *

Long after his father had blown out the candle below that night, Frank lay restless on his straw tick bed. He'd spent the time after school helping his father build a pen for the pigs out of fallen limbs and seal it up with clay daub. A scattering of corn and vegetable culls had kept them happily nearby, with help from occasional warning yaps from Bessie. When the work was finished, they'd gone in for supper, followed by more spinning and knitting lessons.

Normally the coming of winter didn't faze his natural optimism, with the anticipation of butchering time, Thanksgiving, Christmas, and hunting in the snow. But nothing was the same this year. Not only was Alice gone, and with her the childlike wonder they shared as he taught her about the world and answered her endless questions. He was changed.

The sudden death of his sister and the impact it had on Lydia and the rest of the family had wakened him to the instability of life. He was excited at the thought of helping the church with the runaways, but a new chapter of his life was beginning, and change was never something he craved. His own childhood had ended, so to speak, when he walked home from school today. He hadn't thought about the significance of it or spoken of it to anyone. Now the thought pressed in on him and he fitfully rubbed at his eyes to keep from crying.

The thought of being cooped up in the cabin with nothing to do but farm chores and helping build desks galled him. There was so much to learn about the world, but his hands were tied up with the tight purse strings of his parents.

"God," he whispered softly, "I'm no good as a carpenter. You made me different. Please find a way for me to learn and use what I'm good at to help people. I hate feeling like this. Help me be happy in doing whatever I have to do, and I will trust the future to you. Amen." With a sigh he turned over and soon fell asleep.

Chapter Twenty-one

*B*efore the sun rose, a furtive knocking at the back door set Bessie baying and woke the family all at once. Jane, who always slept furthest from the wall, threw off the covers first. She hurriedly lit a candle, hands shaking from the cold and a touch of fear. Bessie was yapping at her heels so she couldn't tell if the rapping had ceased. Before she could reach for the door, Seth was beside her.

"I'll go," he said, taking the candle from her. His eyes locked onto hers and brought her comfort.

"Who could it be? I hope Ma isn't sick," she whispered, her mind instantly going to her 59-year-old mother.

Seth disappeared with the dog into the workroom. Jane stood by the door and listened to distant voices as first Frank and then Lydia joined her, both wrapped in blankets. Suddenly the door opened, and they stepped back to let in Matthew Martin, who seemed a bit out of breath.

"Pardon me, folks," he said, snatching off his hat and running a hand over his balding head. They could barely see him in the gray light that was beginning to distinguish the windows from the walls. Seth busied himself at the hearth, setting the candle to some kindling to start a fire. Bessie had ceased the cacophony the moment she recognized Matthew's familiar scent and was sniffing at his boots. The others waited silently for him to continue.

"I've come because an hour or so ago we got our visitors," he began.

"Are they men or women?" Lydia broke in, excitement filling her voice.

Jane tapped her daughter's toe in a silent reminder not to interrupt.

"Well, we weren't sure at first because two of them were wearing skirts, but they are all young men, two brothers and a cousin, from what the man who brought them said." He paused for a moment and his eyes went to the fire, that was now crackling and consuming the corncobs Seth had placed under some logs.

"Come sit down here by the fire Matthew and warm up a bit. Then you can tell us why you're here," said Seth.

"I'll get some coffee started," put in Jane.

"Thanks," said Matthew gratefully sinking into the proffered rocker. Jane started filling the coffee pot while Seth poked at the fire. Lydia and Frank sat down silently at the table, looking expectedly at their neighbor.

"I can't linger. The conductor, that's what they call the person who leads them from place to place, said he can't stay long, and I don't like to leave Rebekah alone with all of them at once. One of them stepped in a hole a few miles back and hurt his ankle. They practically had to carry him to our house to arrive before the sun rose."

"I'll be glad to come tend to him," Jane said without hesitation.

"Well, we hated to ask you, Jane, but Rebekah says no one's better than you at fixing something that's hurt." He rose from his seat. "I've really got to get back so that fellow can head back south before he's seen and people start askin' questions. He's a black fellow himself."

"You get going," said Jane. "I'll dress and gather what I need and be along just as soon as I can."

"Thank you, Jane. All of you. Rebekah says you've been knitting and sewing, and even brought over biscuits yesterday. We saved them and they'll be a treat for breakfast. I suppose those young men are famished. See you soon." With that he went through the back door and out into the dawn.

* * *

The Martin cabin sat near the foot path that ran alongside the creek. Though it was still early morning when Jane and Frank neared, they took a detour through the woods that led to the barn rather than approach the front door. Frank had insisted on coming to escort her and be a "lookout" for anyone that might be curious about the early morning visit.

Jane was glad of his company and his help in carrying all the things she had gathered to take. On the way he had told her of his schoolteacher's farewell and her chest had hurt at the news, though she stayed silent and let Frank speak. He already had plans to borrow books from Pastor Ned and her mother, who had a few volumes saved from her days as a teacher.

She spied the barn ahead and slowed her steps. The sound of hay being forked and tossed told them Matthew was feeding his stock. Frank went ahead and entered, stopping just inside the door and Jane followed.

"Mr. Martin?" hissed Frank.

Matthew's head peered at them over a stall at the end of the barn. "Oh, it's you Frank, and Jane too! Welcome. Go right on in, Jane. Frank, I could use your help out here, if you don't mind. With three more mouths to feed, I've got to dig up some of those taters we buried out by the woodpile. 'Bekah said she'd make some soup with the last bit of cured ham we've got saved. We'll probably be butcherin' our hog next week. Did your pa ever catch your stoats?"

Jane took the things Frank was carrying and left him talking animal husbandry with Matthew. He was like an uncle to the boy. Not bothering to knock, she managed to turn the latch at the back door and stepped into the lean-to of the cabin. Footsteps approached before she reached for the inner door and Rebekah's tired face greeted her when the door opened.

"My, what an armload you have. You should never have carried all that from your place. Matthew could have stayed longer and waited for you."

"No, no," said Jane, laying her things in a chair. "Frank came with me. I left him in the barn to help Matthew."

"Well, that's a relief. There's so much to do that I can't think what to do first. The man that brought them left just as soon as Matthew returned, and now I feel the responsibility for these men weighing on me."

"Matthew said one of them was injured. Maybe we should start there."

"Yes, of course. They were all exhausted. We sent the other two up in the loft and they went right to sleep after eating some biscuits and eggs. The other man is in our bed, though I doubt he's asleep. His ankle is all swollen and I'm sure it pains him, but he hasn't complained."

Rebekah took up the lamp and walked to the bed in the corner. Jane followed closely behind. A still form covered by a quilt lay silently facing the wall, with just the top of a curly head showing. There was no sign of awareness that the women were nearby.

"What's his name?" asked Jane softly.

"Bert, I think."

Jane leaned over the bed. "Bert? Are you awake?"

The quilt was pulled down a few inches and two wide eyes stared out.

"Yes'm" he almost croaked out.

"My name's Jane. Would you let me look at your foot? I've brought some things that may help it heal."

Bert nodded and turned over on his back, then reached out and pulled the covers off his legs. Jane carefully removed a holey sock, revealing a misshapen foot. Her hands gently prodded the swelling feeling for signs of breakage. She asked Burt to wiggle his toes and rotate his foot. He complied, but gasps escaped his lips, despite biting into them to quiet his cries.

"Just a bad sprain then," said Jane, suddenly all business. "Rebekah let's get some cold water to soak those bandages I brought in, and I'll prepare a poultice." She turned back to her patient while Rebekah went to do her bidding. "Now Bert, I want you to relax and stay off that foot as much as possible. We're going to make you all better in no time, you'll see."

* * *

An hour later the women were resting from their labors in front of the fire. Matthew and Frank were still busy outdoors. Jane's feet were propped on a stool at the insistence of her friend, and she was enjoying a slice of toasted bread spread with fresh butter. Rebekah's hands were restless in her lap. She picked up a stocking from a nearby table and began examining it closely.

"This is fine work, Jane. That tight knitting will keep their feet nice and warm this winter."

"That's Lydia's work, not mine," Jane said, pleased to hear her friend's praise. Frank helped too — by spinning the wool. He's become quite good at it. Lydia is an excellent seamstress and knitter. She surpasses my skills and wants to sew clothing for all the runaways that may come our way if we can get the cloth."

"My Maggie is a better cook than a seamstress," Rebekah put in, still stroking the stocking. "Oh, I nearly forgot! The man that came from Neil's Creek brought me a letter from her. It's still here in my pocket. I haven't had time to read it."

"Well go ahead and read it; don't mind me," said Jane, leaning back into the padded chair. Her eyelids were suddenly heavy in the quiet and warmth.

"No, I want you to hear it as well," said Rebekah, unfolding the sheet of paper. "It's dated November nineteenth. 'Dear Ma and Pa, I hope this letter finds you well and that the packages I sent arrived as promised. Mr. Phillips was so kind to post them for me. He has offered to do similar errands for us in the future. Trade here in Lancaster is keeping all of us busy.'"

"I thought she lived in Neil's Creek," interrupted Jane, confused.

"Neil's Creek is the church and surrounding community. The nearest town is Lancaster."

"Oh, sorry for stopping you, Rebekah."

175

"'In fact,'" her friend read on, 'I am expecting two more bundles by post soon and after some time will mail them on to you, when circumstances allow. I have happy news to share and think you will be glad. I am expecting a baby, due around midsummer.'"

Rebekah nearly stood up in her chair, clutching the letter. "Oh, Jane! A grandbaby at last! Wait till I tell Matthew!" She whisked off her spectacles and brushed away tears.

"What wonderful news! God is good," responded Jane, giving her own swelling bump a loving pat.

"I must go stay with her and help her out when the time comes," said Rebekah, then added, "That might complicate her work in 'trade' however, couldn't it?"

"Yes, I suppose so, but it will work out somehow. Does she say anything else?"

Rebekah's eyes searched the letter, then began reading again. "'Charles is busy with the farm and helping teach at the little college the church started here last year. It is growing in numbers and has students of all colors and both sexes — quite radical to some folk's minds, but we feel it is in obedience to the Great Commission. Please write as soon as you may and let us know how everyone in the household is doing. Love, Maggie.'"

Both women were silent for several seconds, lost in their own thoughts. Jane could hear soft snoring coming from the sleeping men. Rebekah's face held a fixed smile and Jane's mind was racing at the news that a college was just a day's drive away. She couldn't wait to tell Seth.

* * *

The Cowpers and their neighbors spent the next few weeks in a flurry of tasks from dawn until dusk. Frank proudly brought home a huge tom turkey for a Thanksgiving feast that included Rev. Ned and Cinda. The last of the bird was made into a huge pot of soup they ate three days straight. When it was gone and the pot cleaned, their Thanksgiving guests came back to help with butchering the hogs. The process from gunshot to sausages, smoked ham, salted pork, and bacon took many hands and hours of work

During that time Lydia had somehow managed to sew three shirts for the men at Martin's and Frank was halfway through a book the pastor had loaned him containing the coastal travel journals of botanist John Bartram. During that time Lydia had barely spared a thought for Will and what he might be doing. To avoid chance encounters, she'd asked Frank to fetch the water and he'd been more than willing to oblige, but if he'd seen Will at the spring, he'd never mentioned it.

Today the weather was warm for mid-December. Frank was busy felling trees and Lydia went to fetch water for the evening. The sun was dappling the fallen leaves on the familiar path to the creek through the bare branches of the trees. Lydia blithely swung the water pails and hummed "God Rest Ye, Merry Gentlemen" as she made her way. She was glad for a chance to get out of the cabin with its lingering smells of blood and lard.

Running into Will was the last thing on her mind, but then she heard a voice joining the carol's tune and stopped short.

"Is that you, Will?" she called out, hoping her imagination had just tricked her.

"Who else?" he asked, peeking out from behind a giant elm tree. "I told Ma I was gathering hickory nuts this time." He smiled at her, then stepped out and walked to meet her. She still hadn't taken a step, her pulse quickening. "It's been a long time, Lydia. Frank said you all were busy butchering, but I kept hoping you'd come back to see me." He reached out a hand to gently tug her braided hair, but she took a step back.

"Sorry, Will," she said in a rush. "I didn't come to see you. I came to fetch water."

He forced her to look in his eyes. "Are you sure? You said you needed a few weeks. Well, it's been more than a month now and I've got to know what you've decided. Can I start building us that cabin I talked about?"

His familiar smile and twinkling eyes were appealing. Lydia closed her eyes and looked away. "I told you I need time. I'm needed at home, and I don't know when I'll feel ready. I care about you Will, but if you must have an answer right now, it must be no." She could hardly believe her own words. She turned and continued walking down the path. She heard footsteps behind her and then felt a hand on her shoulder jerk her around.

Will's usual smile was gone, replaced by a mouth set in anger with knitted brows over eyes that burned into hers. "Well, you sure led me on a pretty dance all summer and fall, didn't you?" He squeezed her upper arm hard. "To think I wasted months mooning over a girl who encouraged me only to toss me aside like a dog with an old bone."

"I didn't mean to hurt you, Will. It's just that things have changed at home." Truthfully, she realized that she was the one who had changed.

"Well, I haven't changed," he said, almost as if he'd heard her thoughts. "But I'm getting out of Flat Rock for now, maybe for good."

This surprised her. "Why? How?" she asked.

"My Pa's brother in Kentucky, my Uncle Hal, is opening a mercantile down in a place called Stamping Ground. He's asked if I can come help him set everything up and teach him how to make orders and run the books and such. Pa said

I could if I wanted since winter is setting in. I wasn't going to, but now I guess I'll go. You don't care for me and maybe a change will be good for me."

"I do care, Will. Really, I do," she began, but he brushed her aside and started off in the direction of his home.

He turned back to find her rooted to the spot, a tear running down her cheek. "Yeah, we'll see how much you care when I'm gone for months, maybe years. Maybe I'll quit carin' about you first." And with that parting shot, he went over a ridge and out of sight. Lydia stood frozen in place. Despite feeling sure about her decision, an empty hole seemed to open inside her.

Jefferson County, Indiana
Chapter Twenty-two

Manny and Lily sat on the floor in the garret wrapped tightly in blankets as still as proverbial church mice. Below them muffled voices began singing and a smile broke out on Lily's face at the familiar tune. In one sense they *were* church mice, hidden away for weeks now in the attic of Ryker's Ridge church, living off the generous "crumbs" of its members.

By day they could safely do no more than talk quietly and take turns looking outside through a chink in the wall they plugged up with wadded newspaper between peeks. In the middle of the night, they could get up and move about, although Manny could only walk directly under the ridgepole of the roof without hitting his head and his restless spirit was in misery in the tight space. Their only light came from a small window in the roof that allowed them a view of the sky during daylight hours and just a touch of moon and starlight on clear nights.

Once a day the pastor or other church member came to empty their waste bucket and bring them food and water. Lily's upset stomach had settled, but her abdomen swelled. Mr. Harris' wife, Patsey, had confirmed her worst fears when she'd examined her — she was expecting a baby in early spring. The woman said the pregnancy would greatly complicate their flight north and arrangements would have to be made for her confinement period.

Images of a round-faced baby with Henri's features haunted Lily's dreams. Whatever would she do with a baby? She was overwhelmed with fears of the future every time the thought of childbirth and motherhood came to mind, so she forced herself to forget. Manny never mentioned it, but he knew, and the worried expression on his face when he thought she wasn't looking brought reality back to her, unbidden.

Down below the singing had stopped. Then the familiar voice of the pastor rose and fell, unintelligible for the most part. He had told them that although most of the church knew of their presence in the attic, they must never chance making any sound during services. After several minutes of sitting still under the blanket, Manny was soon asleep, lulled by the muffled voice and exhaustion from a night of pacing. Lily reached over and covered his bare feet.

Several times over the past few days he'd shared his frustration of their situation with Lily, declaring he was going to sneak out some night and take off on his own. Then Lily would remind him of the dangers, of her own vulnerability, and tell him to trust that the godly people sheltering them would move them when it was safe.

"Surely Master Thomas and Master Chastain have given up by now and gone back home, but they might have paid people to hunt for us. We've got to wait until they give up. We've got to believe that God, who got us this far, is going to see us through," she'd pleaded. At times, even though he was several years older than her, Lily felt a maternal tug towards Manny, who had no memory of his mother or really anyone who had shown him kindness.

After what seemed hours to Lily, legs cramping from sitting still, the noises below diminished until she heard silence, and then the familiar sound of a gentle knocking on the floor.

"Tap tap tap … tap … tap". The pastor had told them it was Morse Code for the number three, representing the Trinity, and that if they heard anyone knock in any other way, they were to be silent and ignore it. Manny woke up instantly and began crawling over to the trap door to open it.

* * *

Later that night, just before midnight, the familiar knock that signaled a helper was below awakened Lily before Manny, doing his nightly pacing, was aware. He paused when she suddenly sat upright and strained to listen. Outside he could hear nothing but creaking tree limbs and rustling leaves. Barely any light pierced the darkness as the glimpse of November sky overhead was clouded.

The tap, tap, tapping, came again and Manny walked over to the trap door and opened it. His heart was racing as he peered below. A shadow seemed to fill the open space and a deep voice said, "It's time to go, young 'uns. Hurry up, now."

After the morning service, the pastor had told them to be ready for Mr. Harris to come and move them along at last. Lily had stuffed all their belongings, which now included several articles of clothing for both of them, in her pillowcase. Manny took it from her and handed it down below. Harris's big hand reached up and Lily took it and began descending the ladder to the dark room below. Manny quickly followed and the big man closed the trap door, hurried down, and then put the ladder back in its place.

They stood still waiting for further instruction, Manny bouncing on the balls of his feet and Lily hugging herself. "We've got a ways to walk," said Harris. "I hope you're up to it. Be quiet and just follow me. We can't keep Anderson waiting long."

Without another word he slipped out the door and headed straight for a grove of trees just behind the church, turning his head left and right at frequent intervals. Manny hurried behind Lily who practically had to run to keep up with the strides of the big man. At first fearful that it would be slow going, he soon realized that they were following a path of some sort, which skirted around obstacles before they loomed into sight.

Manny's pacing had long relieved the stiffness in his healed knee, and he was itching to run. He silently cursed every crackle of twigs and leaves under their feet, but hearing no word of warning from their guide, soon realized that the wind created enough noise to mask any sound of their travel.

He had no idea where they were headed, except that it was in a northwesterly direction from the river. He knew next to nothing about what lay north of Madison, except that it was said to be chiefly flat farmland. How they were supposed to move unseen through that type of territory was beyond him. They trekked on for what he guessed was a couple of miles through the woody hills, then Harris stopped at the edge of a clearing.

He turned to look at them. Lily's breathing was labored from keeping up the pace set by Harris. Before Manny could suggest it, the big man took the pillowcase from her and handed it to Manny and then scooped her up and took off through a corn field, running down the rows of stubble left behind after the harvest. Delighted to give in to his yearnings, Manny sprinted close on his heels as they made a dash for the next cover of trees.

* * *

About two miles away, William Anderson sat silently in the driver's seat of the wagon he had "borrowed" from the livery near his home in the Georgetown section of Madison. He was concealed from any travelers on the road on a farm lane of a fellow abolitionist. The wind whipped the fallen leaves onto the backs of the horses, and they skittishly stomped their feet.

While still in Madison, under the cover of darkness, he had hitched the horses to the wagon, shoeing them with the special carpet covers that had been fashioned for such clandestine activities. This greatly reduced the din of horseshoes on the pavement and allowed him to slip out of town and up the steep hills north of the river bottom to move escapees on to their next destination.

He had learned his methods from George de Baptiste, who had been a leader in the free black community until forced out of town. Though determined to continue his conducting, the activity was becoming increasingly dangerous, and Anderson could still feel the terror he and his neighbors had felt just months ago when a mob from northern Kentucky had swarmed over the Georgetown neighborhood last year looking for fugitives. They had torn up property seeking runaways, threatened everyone with jail and worse, and nearly drowned poor Griffith Booth in the river while torturing him for information.

After that, Booth and several others moved north, forcing those left to rely more on Harris and others who lived outside the city for help in piloting people north. Anderson wondered how long they could continue. Rumor said stricter laws for those harboring or helping runaways was being demanded by proslavery factions in Congress with Kentucky electors being some of the strongest proponents. He knew it could mean large fines and possibly prison for white folks, but for blacks like him, a return to slavery or hanging would be a foregone conclusion.

Shaking his head to chase away the fear, he bowed his head and prayed for the two fleeing his way. Harris was running late. He'd agreed to linger in this spot for one hour only. He checked his watch. He'd give the preacher ten more minutes. To pass the time he began humming "O God, Our Help in Ages Past," a hymn that never ceased to bolster his courage.

On the fourth verse he stopped at the call of an owl rising above the wind. When it was repeated, he scrambled down and hurried to the back of the wagon to ready it for its human cargo. On cue, just as he was lifting the canvas cover, two figures dashed from the woods to his side and crawled underneath, one in a skirt and one in pants. He laid gunny sacks over them filled with apples and potatoes, taking care to give them room to breathe, then secured the canvas top over them. He waved a hand to the unseen Harris, climbed back into the wagon and took up the reins.

Just as the horses lurched forward, he turned his head and spoke loudly to the lumpy pile in the wagon bed. "Whatever happens, don't utter a sound. And hang on! We've got to make tracks if we're gonna make our connections tonight."

* * *

Maggie Walton had tried to sleep, but the expectation of her visitors had caused her to toss and turn. A restless night was not unusual. Though still in the early stages, her pregnancy frequently kept her awake with indigestion. At other times her mind wouldn't let her sleep as she planned and anticipated the arrival of her firstborn. Beside her Charles seemed undisturbed by her restlessness.

After another ten minutes she left the warmth of the bed and wrapped herself in a shawl. The monotony of knitting usually helped clear her mind. She was about to settle in a chair by the still glowing embers in the hearth, when the distinct clip clop of an approaching horse could be heard above the wind through the thick cabin walls.

"Wake up, Charles," she called to him as she hurried to unlatch the door, "They're here."

Charles sprang into action and was pulling on his clothes by the time John Tibbets walked in, followed closely by two silent figures. Martha quickly shut the door.

"I can't stay, folks," said Tibbets. "Charles and Maggie, this is Manny and Lily. I'll see you folks at church." With that he let himself out and before anyone spoke or moved, Maggie heard his horse pulling his buggy back down the lane.

Maggie lit a candle and set it on the table. "Won't you sit down?" she said, indicating the two chairs nearest the fire. The pair sat down without comment. Maggie studied their shadowed faces in the glow of the flame. The boy looked to be a few years younger than Charles, medium-built with a high forehead and eyes that darted around the room before coming to rest on hers. The girl's pale complexion and hazel eyes startled her. She had met several light-skinned slaves, but this girl's visage showed no noticeable signs of her race. She was thin and Maggie, already alerted to her condition, was instantly concerned for her health.

"I want to welcome the two of you to Neil's Creek. There are many of us in this area from our church who help people like you. We believe slavery is wrong and against God's will. We will provide a place for you to stay until decisions can me made about the next stop on your journey."

She glanced at Charles who looked up from where he was feeding the fire to smile at her. She smiled back knowing he was happy for her to take the role of nurturer and teacher to those who sheltered in their home. When she glanced back, the girl met her eye and smiled shyly.

"We thank you for your hospitality," she said, nudging the boy with an elbow.

"Yes'm, thank you," said the boy.

Sensing their nervousness, Maggie encouraged them to take off their wraps and relax. While they did so she set the kettle on for tea and prepared some bread and butter that she casually set before them with tins of water. "Now, eat up and tell me all about yourselves. The better we know your stories, the better we can help you," she began.

* * *

Lily paused behind the cabin to watch the sun rise over the distant tree line. She was just returning from gathering the eggs but couldn't resist stopping to watch. The distant clouds turned rosy and golden as if painted by an unseen hand behind the lacy leafless tree limbs. She breathed a satisfied sigh and spoke aloud. "Thank you, God, for Maggie and Charles and Manny and all your blessings." Then she took one last glimpse and walked through the door with her basket.

She and Manny had been at Neil's Creek for almost a month and Christmas was near. She had shared with the couple how Christmas had always been a special time of anticipation because that meant a special meal and Mizz Willson gave her new things to wear. Manny had shared similar memories over the supper table of getting the day off from some of his chores, a tasty treat, and new clothes.

"Five today, Maggie," Lily said handing the basket to her hostess and smiling broadly.

"Wonderful! Maybe we won't have to eat one of them for Christmas dinner after all. I hope Charles can shoot us a turkey. One old hen wouldn't stretch far with six mouths to feed!" She immediately began washing the grime off the eggs.

Lily, getting out a bowl for them, looked over at her puzzled. "Six? Are you expecting more runaways?"

"Not that I've heard. No, I was thinking about our babies. You and I are both eating for two now and we need extra. You're still too thin, I'm thinking."

Lily looked at Maggie's abdomen, which had just recently started swelling, then glanced down at her own and wished she hadn't. According to Maggie, in just three months the baby would be ready to be born and her belly could double in size. Lily couldn't even imagine it. She had tried to forget the fact of her condition, but a few weeks ago the babe inside her had started moving around, reminding her of his or her presence several times a day. Maggie loved putting her hand on her to feel what she called kicks and the rhythmic thumps she said were hiccups.

"Oh, yes. I forgot," mumbled Lily. The baby was the reason she couldn't stay with the Waltons much longer and she hated the thought of leaving. She was happier than she ever remembered being when she wasn't thinking about the future. Maggie's baby wouldn't come until August and those months between the expected births was the reason she couldn't stay. Lily blinked and a tear escaped her eye.

"Now don't you worry," said Maggie handing her four of the eggs to crack for breakfast. "We're going to find a real nice place for you to stay. You'll see."

That afternoon Charles and Manny both came home smiling from the school where Charles was helping him, and several others, learn to read. Manny reported he had learned to read several new words and Charles surprised Maggie with a letter from her mother. She shouted for joy and took a hairpin out of her reddish hair knot to open it.

"Let's all sit down, and I'll read it aloud. Ma's letters are always so full of news," she said.

Her audience in place, she began to read. Lily listened patiently at the unfamiliar names. The men staying with her parents in a place called Flat Rock were doing well and would be staying several more weeks — maybe until spring. A man named Bert had hurt his ankle and it was healing well, and someone named Jane was expecting a baby in March. When Maggie read that part, she stopped and laid down the letter. Lily and the rest looked at her questioningly.

She looked at Lily, then at Charles and smiled. "God provides a way, doesn't he?" Charles returned her smile and nodded. Maggie looked back at Lily with a serious expression and put her hand on her shoulder. Lily was confused and held her breath, knowing something life-changing was about to be revealed.

Ripley County, Indiana
Chapter Twenty-three

*I*t was Saturday, December 29, and Jane was vigorously sweeping up the dirt Frank had tracked in when he last filled the wood box. "Mother, you've simply got to sit down and put up your feet," said Lydia from behind her. Jane turned to see her standing there, hands on her hips in that no-nonsense posture that reminded Jane so much of her mother. She opened her mouth to protest, but her daughter's brown eyes snapped back at her in defiance, and she handed her the broom. As she eased herself into the rocker, Lydia hurried over and pushed a stool under her feet and added a cushion for height.

"Be sure and look for cobwebs in the corners," she called to Lydia sweeping briskly behind her.

"Yes, Mother. Of course," answered Lydia with that exasperated tone Jane knew too well. She sighed and looked down at her feet, barely visible over the growing bump in her lap. Her eyes grew wide at the sight of what lay on the cushion. Her ankles were practically indistinguishable from her fat feet. Her hands and face were unnaturally swollen too. She knew it wasn't uncommon during pregnancy and had experienced it before, but the severity of it alarmed and frustrated her.

Then there was the matter of her size. Though she should have at least eight more weeks to go now that the new year was approaching, she was almost as large as she was when Alice came. The women at church, even her mother, predicted twins and the very thought of the possible complications that brought to childbirth frightened her. She never voiced her fears, even to Seth, who seemed preoccupied and kept himself and Frank busy in the workshop.

Lydia came into view, sweeping the floor around Jane's feet. The last few days she had been unusually quiet and seemed to be fighting some internal battle. When the men at the Martins were settled and Rebekah sent word that they didn't need anything more, Lydia's uneasy spirit had returned and she'd become testy and short with Frank in particular, who seemed to be going through his own inner struggle. She closed her eyes and prayed each of them would find their place and purpose soon. She was just about to doze off, Lydia having found a quieter occupation, when a strong kick to her ribs informed her that even her unborn was unsettled.

* * *

In the workshop, Frank was carefully measuring the wood his father had just planed. He was double checking his calculations on where it should be cut for the school desk's pieces, avoiding the actual work. It had been his idea to make the tops slanted for an easier writing surface and to add a carved groove to hold slate pencils. Although he enjoyed the designing and mathematical aspects, he was still inept at the actual hands-on work of carpentry. What Seth could do in five minutes, it took Frank twenty, and then the results would often be flawed.

He looked over at Seth, expertly chiseling the edges to prepare the joint for the seat's back and front and could no longer keep silent. He felt like a tea kettle about to whistle. "Pa, I have to say it." Seth looked up from the intricate work as if just realizing someone else was in the room.

"Say what, son?"

"I'm just not cut out to be a carpenter like you. I've tried to learn and do what you tell me, but it's just not in me. I'm sorry. It must be a big disappointment for you. I don't know what I'll do to earn a living. I guess I can always farm and hunt, but I'm just not a craftsman," he confessed, afraid to look his father in the eye.

Seth laid down his chisel and took a step toward him. Frank looked up. He was now eye level with his pa's chin whiskers.

"I know that son, I've known it for quite some time." Frank looked at the ground. "I know it and I'm not disappointed in you," Seth added quickly, placing his hand on Frank's shoulder. Frank again met his eye.

"God made you a craftsman too, but a craftsman of words and ideas. You've got the makings of something great in you — a teacher, preacher, writer, or even a lawyer. But you'll need more schooling than you can get here. Your ma and I have been praying a way can be found to make that possible. In the meanwhile, you just do the best you can with whatever needs to be done and keep on reading everything you can get your hands on."

Seth then plucked up his chisel and turned back to his work. Beside him Frank felt a huge burden lifting from his shoulders. He took a deep breath, then placed a board in the vise, tightened it and confidently picked up the saw.

* * *

After Sunday services the next morning, the family lingered at Grandma Cinda's cabin to hear some news from Matthew and Rebekah. After the rest of the congregation left, Seth helped put away the benches, as usual. But inside he was battling anxious thoughts of what news might be coming. Had the Martin's visitors been found out? Would Matthew be arrested? He shook the thoughts away as he placed the last bench in the storage shed and headed back to the house.

Pastor Ned, Cinda, Rebekah, Matthew, Lydia, and Jane were gathered around the table, talking about their Christmas celebrations in the only chairs available. Seth joined Frank, warming his backside at the nearby fire. Suddenly the room went silent, and all eyes went to the preacher

Ned cleared his throat. "Folks, the Martins got a letter from their Maggie yesterday and as it concerns the work of the church and you, he said glancing first at Jane and then Seth, we've asked you to stay and hear what she had to say. It's a bit cryptic, but I think we've figured out what she's proposing. Would you please read the letter aloud Rebekah?"

Seth and the others looked at her and she pulled a sheet of paper from an envelope, hands shaking slightly, and began to read. "Dear folks, I hope you have a blessed Christmas and I trust all of those under your roof are thriving. Charles brought home a fat tom turkey this morning that I'm getting ready to pluck and dress for tomorrow's Christmas dinner. I have a parcel I'm getting ready to send your way. It needs to go soon. If I delay too long, I may have to send two packages. I'm thinking it would make a perfect gift for the Cowper family. Talk to Jane and see if she'd be willing to accept it. I believe she and her family will find it a blessing. I'll be expecting a reply from you around my birthday. Happy New Year to all. May 1850 be a year of many blessings. Love, Maggie."

Seth and the rest remained still, each absorbing the letter's content. Matthew broke the silence. "Bekah and I believe we understand what Maggie's trying to say," he began.

"Wait," said Lydia, holding up her hand to silence him. "May I see the letter, Rebekah?" she asked, holding out her hand. The older woman handed it across the table to her and her eyes quickly scanned the familiar script of her old friend. A grin broke out on her face, and she looked at her mother and then at the Martins. "I think she has a runaway who's expecting a baby soon and she thinks, since our baby will be here soon too, that our house would be the best place to hide it."

Seth, overwhelmed at the thought of two, maybe three babies in their house, plus a runaway to hide, wasn't following Lydia's logic. His face showed his confusion and apprehension as the Martins, Cinda, and Ned began talking excitedly, confirming that her guess matched theirs. Frank sprang forward to join in the conversation. Jane, a soft smile on her lips met his eye and nodded.

"Seth, the rest of you," said Jane in a firm voice to get their attention and hush them. "I can see Maggie's point. A baby can't be silenced. A baby can't easily be hidden. But if folks are expecting to hear a baby's cries or perhaps two babies' cries," she smiled, patting her abdomen, "it wouldn't arouse suspicion. This poor woman and her child need us, and unless you have an objection," she looked again at Seth, "we would be honored to shelter them."

Southeastern Indiana

Chapter Twenty-four

Manny sat silently on the ledge of his sleeping loft on the morning of January 15th and watched while Maggie prepared Lily for her trip north. The sun had not yet risen, and bitterly cold air hit the back of his neck from a gap in the chinking beside him. Lily looked miserable as Maggie helped her slip on an extra pair of woolen stockings. Her face, now wider than it had been, was pale in the light of the lamp and even from his lofty perch, Manny could tell she was fighting back tears.

He couldn't help feeling a sense of guilt that he was permitted to stay on while she had to leave. The Waltons and their kin and church members scattered around the community had begun to feel like family in the weeks they'd been there. To his knowledge, no one was seeking them, at least for now, and he was able to walk side-by-side to the schoolhouse most days with Charles, cutting across country and staying off the roads. Now he and Maggie would be staying at her in-laws and out of sight until Charles returned from delivering Lily to Flat Rock, wherever that was.

"There now," said Maggie, stepping back from Lily. "Let's try on my bonnet and be sure your hair is tucked in." Maggie's hair was reddish brown whereas Lily's was honey-toned. Lily obediently stood still and lifted her head so that the poke bonnet could be placed, and its yellow ribbon tied under her chin. Maggie pushed tale-tell tendrils of hair behind the brim and then asked Lily to turn around so she could check the back. "It's perfect. I never much cared for that hat because I can't see to the side, but it will suit our ruse ideally. Tell Ma I want her to keep it. It may come in handy again."

The door creaked open, and Charles came in from hitching up the wagon, his breath steaming. "It's a cold one, but there's not much wind and I think we'll have some sun, at least to start with," he said, grabbing up Lily's packed pillow-case, now bulgier than ever. "Are you ready?"

Manny saw Lily nod, then lean over and tug the back of Yvonne's slipper on more tightly. With her swollen feet and two pair of stockings, he was sure they were barely fitting her.

"Oh, I'm going to miss you so much," said Maggie, enveloping Lily in a hug that started the tears flowing for both. "Tell Ma and Jane and Lydia and everyone hello from me, both of you, and keep warm and safe. I'll see you tomorrow evening at your father's, Charles. Lily, put this blanket over your lap to keep warm and hide your bump. Keep your head down if you pass anyone on the road, and try to remember you are me, Maggie, if anyone tries to speak to you, but I hope that won't happen."

Charles paused a moment to pray for their journey and in the loft, Manny mumbled his first prayer to the unseen god Lily and these folk so earnestly believed in.

* * *

Even though the bonnet was maddening because it severely restricted her vision, Lily was glad of it as the plodding horses put miles between the familiar and the unknown. She didn't even try to hold back the tears that dripped into a pool of dampness in the chin ribbon. Charles didn't try to make small talk, and for that she was grateful.

The tears she'd shed in leaving Maggie had been replaced by a wave of home-sickness for the cozy little farmhouse where she'd grown up in Jessamine County. It surprised her, but she sincerely missed Miss Willson. The stoic woman had been part of her life from birth and the only mother figure she could really remember. She had held Lily as property, but she had taught her to cook and sew and take care of the house and farm. Best of all, she had read scripture to her and passed on her faith in a higher power. Even if she had done it as merely as "Christian duty," Lily was grateful, none the less.

Genuine grief for the woman, sorrow over the loss of her childhood inno-cence, and worries for George and Joe and the girls sold at the auction over-whelmed her. Then she remembered Manny and the thought of never seeing him again engulfed her. She realized she had never thanked him for all he had done to help her. She had been so self-absorbed this morning, she'd barely even said goodbye to him. It was like waking up from months of walking in a stupor to a drenching in icy reality. Sobs shook her and a wail burst forth she couldn't repress.

Charles quickly reined in the horses. "Lily, are you alright? What's wrong?"

She reached in her dress pocket for a hankie and wiped her face and blew her nose before answering. "I'll be fine, Charles. I'm just grieving my losses, that's all. You can keep driving."

Charles whistled to the horses and the buggy began rolling through the ruts once more. Head down, Lily tried to focus on the brown backs of the horses. Then she felt a hand patting her shoulder. She turned and glanced at Charles' face, nodding at her and smiling.

"Yes, Lily. You're leaving all that you've known behind you and what's ahead must look a bit frightening. But whatever the future holds, remember that you are your own person now. Nobody will ever own you again, God willing. You have a faith in God that I know the Cowpers will help you grow in. They are loving, godly people and I have every confidence you will be treated well for as long and you and your baby stay under their protection."

Lily nodded, wiped away the remaining tears, and sighed deeply.

* * *

Will's feet straddled the stuffed carpet bag on the floorboard of the buggy. He silently stared at it as his father droned on beside him, oblivious to his inner turmoil. The day Lydia had thwarted his plans he had written his uncle to accept his request for assistance in setting up his store. Plans were quickly made to catch a boat headed for the Kentucky River in Madison and then meet his uncle in Frankfort to travel overland from there east to Stamping Ground.

They were to spend tonight in Versailles and his pa had promised to buy him his first beer in a real tavern. Up until now he'd been excited about that and the chance to travel. He had hardly given Lydia or leaving his parents a passing thought. But now reality hit him as the miles rolled by and his sober silence in the wake of his father's chatter was the result.

The buggy made a turn and the constant jolting and swaying ceased to give way to smooth movement. He felt an elbow dig into his ribs.

"Will? Are you awake?"

He shook the thoughts from his mind. "Yes, Pa?"

"I was telling you we'd really make good time now that we've hit the Michigan Road. Just feel how smooth it is!"

Will looked up and noted how Andy's head was high and his feet seemed to fly over the constructed surface. He smiled, enjoying the sight, but then remembered that his horse was another thing he'd be leaving behind and the joy quickly left. He looked back at his feet.

His father was silent for a few moments, then announced that another buggy was headed their way. Will glanced up with only the slightest interest. Two people were in the vehicle approaching from the south. He hoped his father would just drive right past.

"I wonder who that is? The buggy doesn't look familiar," his father said beside him.

Before Will could speak, he saw him pull back on the reins and slow the horses. The other buggy did the same and soon they were side-by-side.

"Well, it's Charles and Maggie Walton," said his pa. "I'll bet you're heading up for a visit with Maggie's ma and pa. I hear their mighty excited about a grandbaby coming."

"That's right, Mr. Perry," Will heard Charles say. "How's your family?"

"They are just fine, Mr. Walton. I'm taking Will here to Madison to catch a boat into Kentucky. He's going to live with my brother in Scott County for a spell to help him set up a store." Will felt another nudge from his father's elbow. "Say hello, Will."

He looked up obediently and saw a somewhat familiar face and the figure of Maggie Martin leaning over arranging blankets around her feet. "Howdy Mr. Walton. Howdy Maggie." Charles nodded and Maggie lifted a hand and waved as she continued tucking in blankets.

Charles cleared his throat. "I'm afraid we can't stay and chat. We've been on the road since daybreak and Maggie's feeling the cold. Good luck to you, Will. Nice to see you again Mr. Perry." Without another word the man eased the reins, chirruped to his horses, and rolled past.

* * *

The next morning the Cowper family was lingering at the table over a big breakfast of pancakes and cured ham. Jane was noticing Frank surreptitiously scraping the remains of syrup off his plate while Seth listened to Lydia's idea for how to rearrange the sleeping quarters for the newcomer. Suddenly a memory came unbidden to Jane, and she laughed aloud causing her family to look at her questioningly.

"I'm sorry for interrupting everyone, but Frank scraping up every drop of his syrup made me remember that time Alice licked all our plates. Do you remember?" she said, her shoulders shaking in silent giggles.

"Yes!" said Seth, a big grin spreading over his face. You went to clear the table after pancakes and all the plates were clean. You asked Alice what happened, and she said, 'I don't know, Ma. I didn't lick them.'"

"And her lips and nose and forehead were covered with maple syrup," added Frank.

"And her hair and hands were all sticky too," Lydia chimed in.

They all chuckled remembering Allie and her boisterous charm, then they quieted almost simultaneously, the ache of her loss hitting anew.

"I never thought I'd say this," said Lydia, "but I'm tired of quiet. And I miss having a sister," she said, her voice quavering slightly.

"Well, Lydia, with this one making an appearance soon," Jane said, patting her belly, "and another babe and mother expected any time now, I'd say the silence will soon end."

"Ahoooo! Ahoooo!" As if on cue, Bessie, who was sitting near the front door, began an excited baying and sniffing at the latch and wagging her tail. Beside Jane, Lydia stacked the dishes and set them aside, then peered out the window near the door. "It's Rebekah and Maggie! I'd know that poke bonnet of hers anywhere," she reported. Jane rose and rushed around straightening up the cabin.

"I'll bet they have news of our 'package'," said Frank, joining her at the window where the newly risen sun was coloring the view. The women were looking down at the path, taking care with their steps in the dim light.

Soon they heard an unusual cadence of tapping at the door. Seth swung it wide to let the pair in. "Friends! What a treat to see you two," said Jane, walking forward to greet them. Rebekah stepped aside to reveal a girl in Maggie's cap whose hazel eyes were wide with fright. She looked down, eyeing Bessie with trepidation. Jane arrested her steps as she and the others were stunned into silence, their faces frozen, mouths rounded.

Rebekah broke the silence, "Folks, I'd like you to meet your guest. This is Lily. Lily, meet the Cowpers." She began pointing at each one in turn. "This is Seth and his wife Jane, and Lydia and Frank."

The girl nodded shyly.

"Ahooo!" split the air, causing Lily to jump.

"Oh, and this is Bessie," added Jane, laughing, giving the hound dog a scratch, "Welcome Lily. Come in and make yourself at home.

The End

Historical Note

The decades before the Civil War, especially in the states that straddled the dividing lines of slave and free, were particularly contentious. The national issue of slavery pitted neighbor against neighbor and split family and friends along ideological lines that are not unlike contemporary America. Slavery may have officially been abolished 160 years ago by the passing of the 13th Amendment, but its repercussions still can be heard and felt daily in this age of artificial intelligence, drone warfare, and instant communication.

A Wishful Eye focuses in on a tiny portion of the United States in the last half of 1849: north central Kentucky and southeastern Indiana. It was inspired by the stories passed down in my family about my maternal grandfather's grandparents: Daniel and Sarah "Sally" (Judd) Adams. Sarah Adams (followed shortly by Daniel) was one of ten founding members of the Union Church, organized as a Free Will Baptist congregation in a settlement called Flat Rock in Ripley County, Indiana, in 1843. Their church covenant stated, "We cannot receive slaveholders into the church nor those who believe that slavery is right."

Family stories abounded for generations about ancestors hiding slaves in cellars and barns and then official evidence of Underground Railroad activity was found in the written journals of John Tibbetts, an Underground Railroad conductor from Jefferson County. I owe much of the information I used to write *A Wishful Eye* to the historic research which was done in the region in the late 1990s by Diane Perrine Coon for the Indiana Department of Natural Resources' Underground Railroad project in the late 1990s.

About the Author

D.L. McIntyre is the penname of Debra "Deb" (Monroe) McIntyre. A native of Versailles, Indiana, she currently resides in Georgetown, Kentucky, with her husband of 43 years, Cleon, and dog, Ginger. They have three grown children and three grandsons.

McIntyre spent approximately 15 years as a small-town newspaper journalist before returning to college where she wrote for the public relations department.

She graduated from Berea College, Berea, Ky., in 2011 with a degree in educations studies and is an education specialist with the Kentucky Department of Corrections, teaching GED classes.

She serves as a small group leader and worship team member at her church. In her spare time, she enjoys reading, watching television, playing word games, caring for her grandsons, and wandering in the woods to refuel her spirit.

A free ebook edition is available with the purchase of this book.

To claim your free ebook edition:

1. Visit MorganJamesBOGO.com
2. Sign your name CLEARLY in the space
3. Complete the form and submit a photo of the entire copyright page
4. You or your friend can download the ebook to your preferred device

Morgan James BOGO™

A **FREE** ebook edition is available for you or a friend with the purchase of this print book.

CLEARLY SIGN YOUR NAME ABOVE

Instructions to claim your free ebook edition:
1. Visit MorganJamesBOGO.com
2. Sign your name CLEARLY in the space above
3. Complete the form and submit a photo of this entire page
4. You or your friend can download the ebook to your preferred device

Print & Digital Together Forever.

Snap a photo

Free ebook

Read anywhere